ELITE
MEMORIES

MEMORY TRANSFERS BOOK 2

DAVID J. GIBSON

ISBN: 979-8-9988560-0-6 (Paperback)

ISBN: 979-8-9988560-1-3 (Digital)

Print Edition: **Library of Congress Control Number:** 2025910429

City of Publication: Carbondale, Illinois, USA

CONTENTS

To my parents, Ken and Stella Gibson, who always let me go my own way.

Whatever goes on two legs is an enemy. Whatever goes upon four legs, or has wings, is a friend.

George Orwell, *Animal Farm*

CHAPTER ONE

A ROUTINE PROCEDURE

Year 2150

Inside the Boston Center

Damon had wanted to enjoy the party. After all, the Guards and Underlings theme had been his idea.

His costume was simple. He had stitched a large orange 'U' onto the front and back of an old gray tunic, put on a pair of well-worn, brown trousers, and not washed his hair for three days. These days his skin had a sickly, pale pallor, anyway. Not feeling well, he lay on a couch in Jak's apartment nursing a virgin orange daiquiri. It had been tough to give up drinking the last few weeks.

"Great costume," exclaimed Petr. His Elite friend entered the apartment. "You look just like a starving Underling!"

"Yeah, it's not too hard for me to look starving these days," said Damon. "Your costume is neat, too. I like the fake boils you've put on your face. You look sick."

Jak was dressed in black body armor, the uniform of an Elite guard. He was buffing a shiny black helmet with his sleeve.

"It's a real guard's helmet. Cost me a fortune from a black marketer."

"Cool, I like the orange flash on the side. What does it mean?"

"Yeah, I think it means I'm an Elite guard, a captain or something. Definitely not a farm-raised, low-ranking Underling guard."

"You're the man, Captain," said Petr. "You can boss us all around!"

Everyone at the party was familiar. There weren't many other young 'first body' Elites like him in the Center. Environmental pollution had reduced the fertility of the Elite and Underling populations alike.

It was early evening, but most of his friends were already wasted on a combination of drink and drugs. Jak's luxury apartment was on the upper floor of a housing block in the Boston Elite Center. Since his parents were well off, it was larger than most. The setting sun streamed in through the large windows and cast a rosy hue over everything. In the middle of the room, techno-music blasted from the life-size hologram of a popular band. A few barely sober friends were dancing, swaying in and out of the hologram. Damon's attempt to dance with a pretty young girl ended with him staggering into the bathroom, where he threw up. Unperturbed, she moved on to dance with someone else.

Damon envied his healthy friends. They had energy and were doing something with their lives. He had tried to see his father a few days ago but was told to make an appointment. Sick, and a college drop-out with no job. His depression and lack of self-worth was getting worse.

He closed his eyes, hoping to sleep away the party.

Raised voices in the far corner caught his attention. He peered over through half-closed eyes. A tall, gorgeous girl with legs up to her shoulders was wagging her finger in the face of a short, nervous looking guy called Leon. "They shouldn't get more food or other rights. Why should they? We need them to farm food and work in the factories and mines."

Leon said, "But, but." His words tumbled out. "The environment outside of the Centers is awful. They need more food and health care to work."

"Hey, Damon, tell Pudge-face here the truth about our Elite rights," the girl yelled across the room.

The girl was Shannon, the daughter of a wealthy Elite couple who hobnobbed with his father and other senior Elites. *Why haven't I dated her yet?* The stammering guy she was assailing was Leon, a total loser. Damon couldn't even tell what his costume was supposed to be.

Raising his voice to cut across the music, Damon said, "Right, Pudge-face—I mean Leon, they're all totally replaceable. Only farm-raised Underlings need extra food to be healthy and fit enough for special uses."

Pivoting to a more promising topic, he added, "Oh, and Shannon, I love your fashionable guard's costume. Come tie me up."

She smirked at Leon, then turned giving Damon a come-hither grin.

"Let's get outta here," said Jak. He stood up, straight and commanding, in the middle of the room. "We have these great costumes. I bet we can pass for real guards and Underlings."

"I dunno. I'm not feeling too good. Besides, where would we go?" replied Damon.

Petr roused from a stupor. "There's a way out of the Center that comes out outside of the wall where there's a whole bunch of Underling shacks."

Damon turned to Jak, "Alright, I'll come along as far as I can."

Shannon rushed over, ignoring the hapless Leon. "Captain, escort us out!" She grabbed Damon's arm and pulled him to his feet. He held onto her shoulder, allowing her to guide him after Petr and Jak, and the four of them left the apartment.

Damon didn't recognize the area of the Center where Petr led them. After about a half hour traipsing noisily through corridors and across paths from one building to another, Petr turned and faced the three of them. "Hush, we are by the exit. Assume your roles as sick Underlings or tough guards."

Damon didn't have to pretend to be sick; he was already nauseous and lightheaded. Chronic fatigue added to his malaise. The drugs the doctors gave him were clearly not curing him—each dose only seemed to make him worse. "I'm coming," he said, leaning heavily on Jak's arm.

"Get off me, you stinking Underling," Jak hissed, playing the part of a guard.

Damon staggered along unassisted. "Okay, okay."

They were outside in a deserted area of the gardens. During the day, entitled Elites wandered around breathing filtered air under the sky dome that protected everyone in the Center. Like rich nineteenth-century Parisians promenading around the Luxembourg Gardens, they admired ornamental flowers and ignored the Underling gardeners toiling to keep the beds watered, fertilized, and free of weeds. But at night, the stone statues created a ghostly air.

Finally, the group reached the east wall of the Center. Petr pushed aside a thick cover of shrubs to reveal a door. The wall towered forty or fifty feet into the night sky. The steel and concrete barrier stopped unwelcome Underlings from getting in, but also stopped Elites from getting out.

"Come on." Petr leaned down and stared into a retinal scanner on the door. The door swung slowly open quietly revealing another thick wall of shrubs.

"How the heck?" said Damon.

"I used to work in security, remember?" replied Petr.

Yeah, of course, you had an actual job, didn't you, Petr. Until they fired your arse for smuggling food to Underlings. But how do you know how to escape the Center like this?

"Jak, go through first," Petr directed. "Lead Damon and I as Underling prisoners. Shannon as a junior guard, take up the rear."

As directed, they followed Jak through the door and pushed through the shrubs. A rough, dirt track ran in both directions along the base of the wall. Trees arched over the track, which tunneled below. Damon doubled over in a fit of coughing at the odor of rotten eggs that permeated the outside air.

Shannon followed Damon out through the door. "Shouldn't we all be wearing masks out here?"

Petr emerged from the shrubs pushing into Damon. "Shut up, you two. Of course not. Only you and Jak wear a mask. Damon and I are trying to look authentic Underlings. Come on, keep moving."

The four of them walked slowly, single file, following Jak as he turned to the right on the trail. Under the trees it was as gloomy as a cave. A cold drizzle made Damon uncomfortable and miserable in the thin, rag clothes of his costume, and he struggled to keep up. When he stumbled over tree roots and rocks, Petr nudged him, and Shannon poked him in the back with her gun.

"Hey, careful. Is that a real gun?"

"I dunno. I got it from a friend. It looks real, don't it? I don't think it's loaded."

The trail widened out and ramshackle huts came into view. Their roofs were supported against the Center wall.

"Well, what do you know," muttered Shannon. "Real Underling houses. Look how these people live."

"Houses, my god. These poor people live in lean-to sheds made from plywood and cardboard," Petr replied.

"No, they don't all live like this," said Damon. "My father used to take me on inspection tours. Out in the country they live in small cottages and apartments in communes, towns, and on farms. They have jobs and enough food."

"Hmph, rather them than me," said Petr.

"Can it, you three," Jak growled. "Eyes front, else I'll have to start roughing you up."

Faces appeared in the open doorways and windows, staring silently at the 'two guards and their prisoners' walking past. A few emaciated children clung to the legs of adults. There was apparently no electricity, or water or other utilities. Inside the huts, Damon could see open fires being used for cooking. Wisps of smoke curled out from holes in each roof.

"Damn," muttered Jak as they approached a large, steel-banded gate in the wall. Flanked by two imposing towers, it was wide enough to allow two-way vehicle access. Two guards wearing masks stood silently in front of the closed gate. It was obviously a well-used entrance during the day, allowing Underling tradesmen to bring goods into the Center.

We are screwed now. Damon didn't dare speak out loud.

When they reached the gate, one of the guards stepped forward. His weapon hung down at his side, but his gloved hand on it suggested it might come up at any moment. Acknowledging Jak's assumed senior status he saluted. "Captain, state your business."

"Stand easy, Lieutenant. I'm taking these two back down to their hovels by the river. They've been working for me back up the hill. I don't trust them to go back alone."

"Okay, proceed."

Jak led the group past the gate and turned down a narrow track into the woods out of sight of the wall and the Underling houses. "Christ, I about shit myself back there."

"Well," said Petr. "We are Elites. These two guards on the gate were junior ranked Underlings. What could they do to us?"

Shannon giggled and rolled her eyes at Petr. "Yeah, no problem. We just flash our ID bracelet and walk in the gate."

Feeling lightheaded, once they were out of sight of the guards, Damon sat down on a log. "You're both right. Screw the two guards. We're Elites. We can do what we want. Anyway, I'm done in, guys. Get me home before I faint."

Jak said firmly, "Let's circle round back to the door in the wall we came in and return to my apartment."

A sudden rustling in the bushes announced the appearance of a half-dozen Underlings. They quickly surrounded the group. One of them stepped forward, squaring up to Jak. He was dressed like most Underlings with a gray-brown tunic and pants. The orange U on the front of his tunic was the only bright spot. His dark shoulder length hair was unkempt and flowed down to a ragged beard streaked with gray.

Waving a long knife at Jak's face, he sneered showing a mouthful of yellow teeth, "We 'ave you an' your Underling guard outnumbered, Captain." He spat out the last word with disdain, suggesting to Damon some familiarity with challenging the guards. "How's 'bout you let our two Underling friends go?"

Damon and Petr froze, not knowing what to do. The last thing Damon wanted was to go with these Underlings. They'd only have to check his ID bracelet and know he was an Elite masquerading as an Underling. What if they figured who his father was?

Jak stayed in character. In an authoritative voice, he barked, "Don't even think about it. We have weapons that will take you all down in seconds. Sergeant, cover this Underling, and don't hesitate if he moves toward me or our Underling prisoners."

Damon hoped the bluff worked. It wasn't clear Shannon's weapon was real, let alone loaded and synced to her mind. *Shit, her helmet isn't even real and can't transmit commands to her weapon.*

The standoff was certain to go bad. Damon jumped when the two guards from the gate came bursting through the trees. The lieutenant fired his weapon raking the five Underlings who fell to the ground in a heap. "Don't worry," he said to them. "I set it on stun, they'll come round soon enough with nothing more than a headache."

"Thanks, Lieutenant," said Jak. His voice quavered, earlier bravado clearly gone.

"Think yourself lucky, Jak Snyder," the guard said sarcastically. The use of his full name startled them all. "After you left the gate, our scanners showed us who the four of you are. Come with us."

The guards escorted Damon and his friends back up the hill to the gate and into the Center. They were made to wait in a small drafty room inside the gatehouse. Security monitors on one wall surveyed the area outside the wall. Still only dressed in his costume of rags, Damon started to shiver.

After an interminable wait, the on-duty captain of the guard, an Elite, came in. Tall, he towered over them. "I don't know what game you young first-body idiots were playing, but masquerading as Underlings and guards is dangerous. The Underlings would have killed you if my guards hadn't arrived when they did. My junior guards don't take kindly to your games, either."

Petr sidled over to the guard. "Um, excuse me, Captain. Can we have a quiet word, privately?"

"Why?"

"Well, I just want to share something beneficial."

Petr walked past the guard Captain who followed him slowly out of the room. A couple of minutes later, they came back. The guard addressed the four of them, including Petr. "Get out of here and go back to your fancy apartments. I don't want to see you again."

Dismissed and embarrassed, the four of them trudged back.

"What the hell was that all about?" asked Jak. "Did you know the captain?"

Petr smirked. "No, not personally. I just reminded him of a few debts he wouldn't want made public."

Jak raised his eyebrows. "Okay, fine. Thanks, I guess."

Damon was just grateful for Petr's intervention and wasn't about to question what he had done. Besides, he felt even worse after all the activity and nervous excitement. He threw up, and Shannon helped him to his apartment.

A sharp pain in his head woke Damon the next morning. He groaned as he tried to sit up, recalling the events of the night before. The party had been a mistake. Shannon had left sometime in the night, disappointed with his poor "performance." He was too sick these days to have fun, let alone satisfy a woman.

Life sucks.

The bones of his hips creaked as he swung his legs to the side, touching his feet to the floor. He swayed as he stood up.

"Good morning, Damon," Nav, the home system, said. "Happy birthday."

"Shut up," he replied. After a big sigh from scarred lungs, he added, "Open the curtains."

They slid open silently. Shutting his eyelids didn't stop the light from stabbing his eyeballs with a vengeance. Another groan later, and he was on his way to the window.

"You have a scheduled prerecorded message from your late mother for eight a.m. today. It is now eight a.m.," said Nav.

"No!" he said. Even machines get flummoxed sometimes. Nav hated to be told not to do something it was set up to do. But he couldn't hear that message yet.

Mom, talking from beyond the grave again. Probably telling him, as she did every birthday, how much she loved him and how proud she was of him, even without knowing what he would become. She had last seen a happy eight-year-old playing with toy jet cars before taking her own life.

Ha.

"Don't talk to me unless I address you by name, Nav," he added. It was not beyond that system to try to fulfill its mission in some sneaky way. It was obsessive-compulsive.

"Very good."

Later he would listen to Mom. Later, in better health. Things would seem possible then.

His view from the eighty-first floor was one of the best in the Center. The Charles River shone bright and blue. It must have been cleaned—two days ago it was a foul dark green mess. To think, only one hundred years ago, before the claudtrom—the closing of the doors, as it was known—this was a derelict district of Boston; now it was prime real estate in the Center.

Things change all the time. People too. Although not his damn father—the tyrant always looks the bloody same.

His pace picked up a little and he snapped his fingers to attract Nav's attention on his way to the kitchen. "Nav, news."

A holoscreen materialized over the counter as he walked in.

Nav said, "Holo-concert by pop icon Neona Nova attracts record crowd in London."

"Oh, please. Not more of that techno-crap music," he muttered.

"Shanghai Center restricting overseas rice shipments in trade dispute."

Who cares.

"Buenos Aires Center launches giant plasma rocket with fifty Elite astronauts and one thousand Underling workers, to establish first Lunar Center."

As if. It will blow up like the last one.

"Nav off. Double espresso, now."

The machine nearby on the counter started brewing right away. Had he been told he shouldn't have stimulants before the procedure? Maybe. Nav was probably dying to say something; he'd already uploaded all the prep instructions. But it couldn't talk, unless he prompted it, and Damon was already sipping his Ethiopian delight. As a matter of fact, where was his water pipe? He wanted a smoke. *Might as well keep abusing myself for a few more days.*

For his twenty-second birthday the only present Damon wanted was a brand new body.

He was too sick to entertain his preferred options, like getting a tattoo on his butt (he'd already done that for his twentieth) or paying a hooker to get laid for the first time (sixteen). Instead, by necessity, he chose a memory transfer. With his new healthy body, parties would be fun again. Of course, his father had forbidden him to register for a new body: "*Not now, you're not sick enough.*"

Ha. No problem that the transfer of two thousand credits to Petr's account couldn't solve. With a fake ID bracelet from Petr, his father would never know until after the procedure. It was better to ask for forgiveness than permission.

After using the fake ID to register weeks ago, he'd chosen for his birthday today to visit the Underling farm and choose his new body. The "farm" was a large nondescript four-story, windowless building outside against the far eastern outer wall of the Center. It was not under the Center's protective dome. There was a single entrance for Elites, in the Center wall. Underling workers and new two-year old children, destined to be memory recipients, entered through a door fronting the outside. The children would never leave until selected in their late teens for memory transfer or to report to guard training. Razor-wire topped the walls and security cameras captured anything moving within fifty feet.

A small sign, "Office of Underling Memory Recipients," announced the farm as Damon approached. He paused at the security door and spoke into the security camera. "Anatoly Zuur, I have an appointment."

A click, the door opened. He stepped inside and was greeted by an anxious-looking Underling staff member. "Good morning, sir. Let me scan your ID bracelet, please, so I can bring up your application details. Please look into the retinal scanner for DNA confirmation."

Damon placed his right wrist with the ID bracelet he'd gotten from Petr against the scanner while the staff member read the information displayed on a holoscreen. He peered into the retinal scanner hoping the contact lenses embedded with Anatoly's DNA worked.

"Thank you, Mr. Zuur. Everything checks out."

So far, so good. Whoever Anatoly Zuur was, he must have been sick enough to warrant a memory transfer.

Damon leaned forward across the desk where the staff member had retreated. He looked at the name tag pinned on the breast of the man's crumpled and ill-fitting blue uniform. "Listen, AJ, no one must know about my memory transfer. There will be an ugly scene if anyone finds out. Understood?"

The borrowed ID may have worked, but there was still the possibility someone would recognize Damon and alert his father.

The staff member was now visibly sweating, despite the air conditioning.

"Yes, of course, whatever you say Mr. Zuur. Every--everything is kept confidential. We-we-I mean-I've selected three Underlings for you to choose from. You know, based upon the requirements in your application. Given your, um, status, I've selected our best three for you. The two you don't select will be assigned as security guards, which as you can imagine have a high standard of physical fitness."

"Yeah, that sounds fine." *I hope you're not an example. You're an untidy mess. Can we get on with it?*

The staff member murmured instructions into a microphone taped to his throat, then addressed Damon. "Follow me to the viewing room."

With little enthusiasm, Damon followed the staff member. He would much rather be cured and keep his own body than get some second-rate Underling substitute. *Needs must.*

They entered a small room with a couple of chairs in front of a viewing area. Across the front was a large one-way window. Following directions, Damon sat down and looked through to a large room. Three young adolescent men sat quietly in chairs around a small table. The room was brightly lit and had no additional furniture.

"I'll leave you now, sir," said the staff member. "You can see their specs on the holoscreen. They will be given directions to display a number of physical skills. Speak into the microphone on the desk if you want them to do anything specific. Tap their number to make your selection on the holoscreen and return to the entrance to check out."

"Got it," said Damon and the staff member left the room.

Almost immediately after the staff member left, the three Underlings stood up and started jumping around, going through a series of squats, push-ups, and other activities that resembled an exercise routine.

The three young men were physically similar. Fit, muscular, and obviously very healthy. *Any one of these will be an improvement over my sick body.* They were naked, and the shortest of the three was well endowed, which would surely help Damon score a few more girls. He could try again with Shannon. But no, the other two were good enough in that department, and Damon didn't want to be short. He tapped the screen and the short man left the room.

One of the two taller men stumbled while doing lunges. Damon made up his mind and tapped the holoscreen again to reject him. The remaining man walked over with a slight smile on his face, almond eyes staring at the glass window.

Hoping the screen was indeed one-way glass, Damon returned his gaze. What must he be thinking now that he knows he's selected for removal of his memories? Perhaps, like a Roman gladiator, he believed in glory following death. The man's body had the perfect proportions of an Olympic athlete, his toned muscles highlighted by a slight sheen of sweat. Damon was shocked to see the man getting an erection. Damon hastily punched the holoscreen and confirmed his selection. The lights in the room went off and he lost sight of his new body. Jumping up, he ran from the building back to his apartment.

⸺◆⸺

In the week that followed, Damon spent his days and nights dreaming about what he first wanted to do with his new body. On the morning of the procedure, Nav annoyingly woke him early, providing a bland breakfast of juice and cereal, along with his morning meds. *At least I won't need these after today.* Despite his protests, Nav wouldn't give him coffee. *I'll disable the little shit when I get back later today.* At nine-thirty, he left for the appointment. *My day of destiny.*

After a short, two-stop ride on PulseRail, he arrived at the Medical Center. He took the ascendatron to the memory transfer unit on the third floor. When the elevator doors opened, he stepped out slowly.

The reception area was a brightly lit room with about thirty chairs arranged in three rows. An obsequious man dressed in a plaid suit was hosting a game show projected from a large holoscreen attached high on one wall. Canned laughter from an unseen audience responded to his every comment.

Across the far side of the room sitting behind a desk, was a cute young nurse. "Good morning, sir. Do you have an appointment today?"

"Yes. I'm Anatoly Zuur and I'm here for a memory transfer."

The nurse calmly checked her monitor. "Indeed, you are. We have you scheduled at ten a.m. You are in your original body, correct? Not that of an Underling?"

"Yes. This will be my first memory transfer."

Her eyes swept over him, and a slight twitch of pretty lips said more eloquently than any words would. Then she spoke, "You need it."

She removed his ID bracelet. "It will be updated and attached to your new body after the procedure is complete." Then she placed a plastic wristband with his name and birth date around his right wrist: "Anatoly Zuur. DOB March 21, 2128."

She was glancing at his date of birth. *Yes, I'm a ruin at twenty-two, my beauty. But wait until I came out of that surgery room all spruced up.*

Sucking in her cheeks, she proceeded to look through his info, asking him more questions. Her painted nails tapped on the keyboard. He found it annoying to stand there answering questions without getting to ask any. *Is this your first body? Or are you on your fourth one?* But he answered dutifully to every one.

"Very good," she said. *Finally.* "Who will pick you up after the procedure?"

"Someone will come," he told her with confident vagueness.

She gave him the dour look of someone who knows better than to trust young liars. *She must be older than she looks.*

But he wasn't lying. He had sent a message on a timer to his father—the only relative he had left. He would get it once the procedure was over, and hopefully show up. Though, more likely, he would send an assistant. Hopefully not his awful new wife.

Now it was his lips that twitched with amusement, imagining the nurse's face when the great Taurus Najor—her boss, really—appeared in a rage to demand of everyone HOW his only son had gone through the procedure without his knowledge.

Thankfully, Damon would be on drugs and would not mind all the shouting.

"Please take a seat in the waiting area. It won't be long." Her tone was dismissive. Maybe she was sick of him, or she believed someone would come.

"Don't I get a wheelchair?" He asked. He had the right to one. Walking, even down that bright, hopeful corridor, tended to leave him out of breath. He was all skin and bones with next to no muscle mass. A flicker of pity crossed the nurse's eyes and she summoned a wheelchair by pressing a few buttons.

Yes, he was a pitiful thing. Still, as he sat on the chair and waited for the orderly, he winked at her. "I'll come and thank you when I'm done."

Definitely old; she shook her head in disapproval as he was pushed away. Perhaps she knew he had done this to himself. What's a body for, if not to party, anyway?

An orderly pushed him over to the waiting area and left him next to a gray-haired old woman also in a wheelchair. Hunched over, she burrowed into a pink shawl wrapped around her shoulders. *Do I look that sick?*

I hope the old lady doesn't try to start a conversation with me. I just want to get this memory transfer done and get out of here in my new body.

"Hello, young man," said the woman right on cue. "I'm Cynthia. Are you here for a memory transfer? You look too young."

"I'm twenty-two years old, but have been sick for a couple of years," he grunted, trying to be polite.

The woman gave him a sorrowful smile.

Two years ago, he had been reasonably healthy. Like many other Elite youth, he had led a life of self-centered decadence. He attended college, but paid little attention to the lessons, more concerned with where he would party later that night. But that had all changed as he had got sicker from spending too much time hunting outside the center without wearing a mask. His father had pretty much disowned him, lacking the patience for a sick and lazy son.

"The doctors have given up on me. It seems that a memory transfer is the last chance I have before the disease takes my life."

Worried this old lady may be the last person he spoke to, he asked, "How is the procedure? Will it hurt? Will the Underling body be as healthy as he looks?"

She looked at him kindly. "Don't worry, it's a quick painless procedure. I've been through it twice before. The Underling body you'll get will be well nourished after being farm-raised since he was donated by his parents as a two-year-old."

Comforted by her comments, Damon closed his eyes and tried to relax.

When his name was called fifteen minutes later, an officious male nurse checked his wristband and pushed him through the double doors by the receptionist's desk into a brightly lit corridor. He was taken into a small room furnished with a large reclining chair, two smaller fold-out chairs, and an open medical cabinet filled with scary-looking tools.

"Strip off your clothes and put on this blue gown. The ties go at the back." With that, the nurse left the room.

Damon was familiar with this routine. His medical condition had necessitated numerous hospital visits over the last few years. He didn't like the gowns; at six-three, they were too short and left his butt cold and exposed.

Before he was ready, an older, female nurse came in. "I'm Nurse Gladys, and I'll be supervising your care today. Please finish putting your gown on. You can't do the procedure naked. I need to take your vitals and set you up with an intravenous saline drip I'll put into your left arm. It shouldn't be too uncomfortable."

Yes, it will hurt. It always hurts when they say that it won't.

The nurse raised her eyebrows at his weight. "Hmm, you are grossly underweight, almost too light for the procedure."

"Please, it will be fine. I won't be needing this diseased body anymore."

The next part surprised him. "Now sit down as I need to shave your head so you can put on the memory-transfer cap."

She pulled out a pair of electric clippers and shaved his head. His long dark locks, including his beard and man bun, formed a pile on the floor.

Always a fan of wearing his dark hair fashionably long, he wasn't happy with the loss. He consoled himself that after the procedure his mind would be in a new, healthy body. He could grow his hair any way he liked. The procedure couldn't come soon enough.

After getting prepped, he was told to lie on a gurney. The saline drip in the IV hung from an elevated stand she pulled alongside the gurney.

"Would you like a warm blanket?" inquired one of the other nurses assigned to move his gurney.

The nurses pushed him from the prep room, and a few yards down the corridor they pushed him through a set of double doors into the memory-transfer room.

Nurse Gladys checked his wrist band again. "This is pod two of three. Each can accommodate up to a dozen patients at a time along with their new body."

The old lady from the waiting room had been wheeled in and lay on a gurney waiting quietly for her procedure to start. She glanced over at him and smiled. "The blue gown matches your handsome blue eyes."

"Oh, um, thanks. I'm told I got them from my mother." He wondered whether she was flirting.

He counted eight other patients, all much older than him, making the room almost full and uncomfortably claustrophobic.

It's like being in an old-people's home. He became more impatient for the procedure to get done.

There was an empty gurney next to him.

"The gurney is for the Underling who will receive your memories. He is straight from the farm and is being prepped as we speak. He will be brought in already unconscious after your memories have been captured by the cerebral mapper and uploaded into the memory-transfer unit," explained Nurse Gladys. "I'll leave you now in the capable care of the memory-transfer technicians. I'll check in with you after the procedure is complete."

She squeezed his hand. "Don't worry, it will be over soon," she said as she left the room.

Between Damon and the gurney for the Underling stood the memory-transfer module.

"Lie still, sir. This will just take a few minutes," said one of the white-coated, masked technicians. She then gently inserted twenty needle-like electrodes into the skin across his shaved scalp, covering them and keeping them in place with a mesh skull cap. The electroencephalographic electrodes were not too uncomfortable, causing a prickling sensation rather than any pain.

"These electrodes will pick up the electrical activity of your brain and your memories transferring them wirelessly to the cerebral mapper." The technician spoke rotely, probably a routine speech she had given hundreds of times.

Raising his gaze, Damon found the cerebral mapper above his head. The large box-like processing unit, the nuts and bolts, so to speak, was responsible for digitally capturing, mapping, and processing the neural oscillations representing memories. The mapper would capture his mind and initiate a wireless transfer to the coordinates corresponding to the Underling's brain. With the recipient next to him, there was little chance of the signal going to the wrong place.

A keyboard and a holoscreen attached to the cerebral mapper displayed scrolling green computer code, graphs, and tables of data. Watching these data, the technician could control the memory transfer. A technician wearing hologoggles was already tapping on the keyboard.

One of the technicians injected anesthetic into his intravenous drip. "Count backward from ten, please."

The room turned dark as he went under before getting to "five."

Chapter Two

A LOST MEMORY

Shanya Tourni, PhD came down to the memory transfer unit to conduct a routine check. She needed a break from the drudgery of administrative duties that increasingly took up her time as the Center's Director and chief scientist.

Pod One was quiet with a couple of nurses clearing up after a routine set of memory transfers. The beds were being stripped down, cleaned, and readied for another session. A sharp smell of disinfectant filled the air.

Pod Two was a different matter. A pair of bodies lay on adjacent beds and a technician stood beside them.

The technician looked up as she came in. "We lost the memories of a patient," she said. "Anatoly Zuur."

As director, Tourni had responsibility for the smooth running of the memory transfer unit. An Elite, she was in her fourth Underling body following several successful memory transfers. Her expertise in the science of the memory transfer had made her valuable to keep around. She had helped develop the process currently in use and knew every detail.

She walked over to the bed and looked down at the man still strapped down and wearing the mesh skull cap. Wincing at the sight of his emaciated body, she pulled her lab coat tight around her beige shirt as if to protect herself from disease.

She looked up and into the eyes of the technician. "We've got a problem."

"What do you mean?" the technician said. "We always lose some patients during the memory transfer process. Recently, more than one per session."

"That's not the problem. I recognize this man, he is Damon Najor, the son of Taurus Najor, the Center leader. We cannot lose his memories."

"No, he can't be." The technician examined the plastic wristband, then pulled back an eyelid, and used a hand-scanner to check his retina and found contact lenses. "Look, the wristband confirmed him as Anatoly Zuur. I didn't think to look any closer. For a change, all transfers were going well today."

Tourni shook her head. "Remove the contact lenses and scan his retina again."

The technician did as she was told, gasping as she showed the scanner to Tourni. "How on earth?"

Tourni closed her eyes and took a deep breath. This was not going to end well. "Why was Damon Najor using a borrowed ID to get a memory transfer?" she asked the technician.

"I don't know. I mean, it looks like he was dying, so he must have used the ID to book himself in like anyone else. He's old enough and didn't need parental approval."

"But what about checking that he is who he says he is?"

Realizing this technician was only the last of several people who were likely fooled, Tourni, rubbed her temples with her fingers. Smoothing back her long dark hair, she adjusted the silver clasp, to stave off the coming migraine.

"Who is Anatoly Zuur and what's his political coding?"

The technician ran a query to the Center database. "Um, he has political coding M - moderate Elite."

Tourni looked into the technician's eyes. "Damon had another man's ID that was clearly being circulated and sold on the black market. Damon Najor has a political code X — reserved for members of Najor's inner circle. His memories should never, ever, be lost. Correct the memory transfer record."

Tourni sat down on a chair by the side of the bed with Damon's body. Resting her chin on her chest, she closed her eyes and took some deep breaths. She needed to look into memory transfer security protocols. How many times had a borrowed ID been used?

The technician was crying. "But, I followed protocols based upon his ID. Both he and the Underling are alive, unconscious, but with no cerebral memories or activity. We are searching for his mind signal."

"I'm guessing his father doesn't know?"

Before the ashen-faced technician had a chance to answer, a tall bull of a man crashed through the double swing doors and strode angrily into the memory-transfer room. Standing over six feet, six inches, with long silver-gray hair swept back from his angular face, he cut an imposing figure that befit his community status. His blue eyes held a piercing stare boring into the soul.

An entourage of nervous assistants and security agents followed in his wake. The normally quiet room became crowded and the air charged with angst.

"Where's my son!"

"Over here, on this gurney." The nervous technician pointed, recognizing Taurus Najor, the Center's leader.

Striding across the room, Najor bent over his son Damon, strapped down on the gurney. Dr. Tourni looked at the boy on the bed, seeing him for a moment as his father might. Thin, sallow, translucent skin. Prominent blue veins were exposed on his neck and arms. The young man had obviously been suffering ill health for some time.

Taurus Najor looked from his son, pinched brows flexing, and Dr. Tourni turned her attention to the Underling who was supposed to have received Damon's memories.

The Underling was, per protocol, about the same age as Damon. But he was muscular and lean, with a healthy glow to his olive-colored skin. He looked like someone who had spent a lot of time outside. He was also unconscious, strapped down, and enmeshed in a spider web of medical tubes and IVs. Both Damon and the Underling wore the mesh skull cap with electrodes covering their skull.

"Sir, here's your son," said Tourni, drawing Najor's gaze back to Damon. "I had no idea he was—"

"What happened to him?" Najor roared.

The white-coated medical technician hovering over Damon turned warily toward Najor and replied through her medical mask, "His mind doesn't seem to have transferred, sir."

"Explain," barked Najor.

Dr. Tourni belatedly noted the absence of a mask. She lamented the breach of the sterile environment.

The technician nodded to the unconscious Underling next to Damon. "As per protocol, we wiped the mind of the recipient Underling, and then—."

Najor abruptly turned to Tourni. "Find him, dammit— before it is too late."

Tourni shuddered. This day was going quickly from bad to worse.

"But, sir, when this has happened before, we've not been able to retrieve the donor's mind signal."

The memory-transfer process was popular among old Elites, and those like Damon who became ill. Tourni knew Najor had gone through the procedure at least four times before—she had lost count. Metaphysically, he was over 150 years old. The memory transfer process was an important way to maintain Elite numbers since their birth rate was close to zero due to inbreeding.

Tourni tried to recall Damon's specific circumstances and drew up the young man's true medical file on the nearby console. Najor and his wife had not had children until his wife was in her fourth body. Damon was one of the few children born to an Elite in the last few decades. Oh. He became sick in his late teens.

She watched Najor rub his son's hand in an anxious comforting gesture.

"Dammit, there's no reason for my son's memories to be lost. The Underling must have been diseased to be unable to receive Damon's memories."

"No, sir. He's farm-raised since he was selected by the Office of Underling Memory Recipients and taken from his parents when he was two years old. He received a nutritious diet and superior health care throughout his life. He—."

"Did you wipe the Underling's mind properly?"

Najor cut her off.

"Um. Of course, sir," replied the increasingly anxious technician, herself an Underling.

"If you didn't," carried on Najor, "then the Underling's mind would resist the incoming signal deflecting my son's mind elsewhere. Where did it go?"

Tourni jumped in. "We are looking. But as I said, we've never been able to track deflected or misdirected mind signals. The strength decreases exponentially with distance from the cerebral mapper, and we don't have instruments set up elsewhere to detect or capture stray signals. As a misdirected signal weakens, it will just decay to zero and be lost forever."

"Enough." Najor slashed his hand across the space between them and Tourni took a judicious step back. "I know how the process works."

Tourni followed Najor's gaze around the room. All the other beds were empty. Nurses had come in and were stripping the beds down, cleaning and preparing for the next transfer session. A sharp, clean antiseptic smell permeated the room.

"What happened to the other memory transfers that were going on at the same time?"

Tourni turned to the technician, raising her eyebrows. "Well?"

"Those memory transfers were successful. The Elites in their new bodies have been taken to recovery and their old bodies are in the morgue awaiting cremation."

Najor looked completely distraught, even as his angry voice reverberated off the walls as he stormed out of the room. "Your career is over. I'm transferring you to the lithium mines." His gaze pinned her to the wall before he passed the threshold. "Tourni, find my son and report to me immediately."

Tourni entered the main administration building of the Elite Center and made her way up to Taurus Najor's office. She had a feeling of what awaited her inside. She had spent the last three hours with her head memory transfer technician, trying to work out what happened to Damon's memory transfer.

Damon's father, Taurus Najor, had a high opinion of himself, evident from his office's grandeur. Expensive carpets and antiques adorned the room. Oil paintings covered the walls. The man himself was wearing a bespoke, pin-striped navy blue, tailored suit, and had slicked back his hair with oil.

Dressed plainly in brown slacks and a beige blouse under her white lab coat, Tourni perched uncomfortably on the edge of a hard, wooden chair facing Najor seated on the other side of his large oak desk. He glowered down at her, accentuating the power differential between them.

"Your technician botched my son's memory transfer, killing him."

Unlike the Underling technician whom Najor believed had messed up Damon's memory transfer, as an Elite, Tourni had more freedom to talk freely. She relied on that freedom to speak freely now. "I checked the records. The technician did not 'botch' the procedure. The risk to Damon was known, and he accepted the risk, as do other Elites, before the procedure." Her eyes narrowed in resentment of Najor's insinuations that her technician had made a mistake.

"Then what happened?"

Before she had a chance to answer, Najor slammed his fists down on the desk. "If it wasn't your technician's fault, then someone from the outside must have hacked the computer code."

"Again, no. We have no evidence of outside interference."

"No one told me he was scheduled for a memory transfer." His voice bore a small amount of bewilderment. "Ever since his last arrest and the onset of his illness, I've not been able to get the boy to talk to me. His message was timed to arrive after the procedure."

It was clear to Tourni, Najor was grieving. But if Damon had done this without Najor's knowledge, it seemed their relationship had been difficult.

She said simply, "The problem was the borrowed ID he used to sign up for the procedure."

Najor's eyes widened. "What *borrowed* ID?"

"It belonged to a dead man, Anatoly Zuur, a moderate Elite."

Najor ran his fingers back through his hair. Then with a sigh, he placed his forehead into the palm of his hand. "A borrowed ID belonging to a dead moderate. Un-bloody-believable." His head snapped up. "This is your fault. You have no control over the program."

Tourni stared at him in anger and disbelief. Damon's memory loss was due to using the borrowed ID. No other factor. Why wouldn't Najor lay the blame where it might truly belong? On himself and his apparently bad relationship with his own son. She refused to have her team maligned by his misplaced anger.

"We are doing what we need to do—what we agreed to do," she said firmly. Trying to defuse the situation, she said. "The new policy is leading to an increase in the number of lost memories."

"Right, yeah, unplanned losses. That's what we have to tell everyone."

"What else should we say?"

Najor looked down, avoiding her gaze. "Nothing. We say it's a technology problem that's being worked on, nothing more."

Tourni shook her head. Selling an increase in memory losses due to a technology problem was a lie. Memory losses had not been a significant problem when she first developed the process with mice and chimpanzees. Everything was tightly controlled, with the memory transfer unit directly hooked up to the recipient animal. They did start to have some losses when she developed and tested the wireless system on criminals and the insane. But she got memory losses down to one percent after developing the electroencephalographic mind capture process before introducing the program to the Elite population in 2050.

"And where would we be now?" continued Tourni. "Without memory transfers the Elite population would be gone. DNA manipulations we tried to deal with inbreeding problems among Elites failed."

"And, my claudtrom in 2045 was the solution."

Retreating into Centers around the world, and leaving the Underlings outside, had been the best solution at the time. Underlings served Elites, providing the commodities and food they needed.

No, the man doesn't understand basic science. Claudtrom caused the inbreeding problem among Elites. Memory transfer solved it, allowing Elites—or at least their minds—to never die. Elite memories in Underling bodies allows de facto cross-breeding, but doesn't make up for the low fertility rates since pollution still ravaged both populations.

"But, more to the point..." Najor interrupted her momentary reverie. "What are the other Centers saying about their memory losses?"

"They're not saying much. An increase in memory losses to only five percent has not been enough to worry anyone."

Najor stood and paced behind his desk. She followed his gaze back and forth between her and an image of his son displayed on the wall. The image showed the young man when he had still been healthy.

He snapped at her. "You're my chief scientist, not some weak-minded Underling. Deal with any negative publicity about memory losses. And, find my son."

"We had no need to look for lost memories when there was only a one percent failure rate. But now we need to, in order to find people inadvertently lost like your son," she said calmly as she got up to leave.

As she was leaving, she caught Najor muttering, "Get on with it, woman."

She resisted the urge to go back into the room and give him a piece of her mind. Chief Scientist or not. But she discarded the idea. He was the Center leader and could do with her as he liked. He had been leader since the 2043 elections propelled him into power—the last leadership elections he allowed.

She had work to do.

Tourni didn't return to her office, as it was already late and any technicians she might have consulted on a plan had themselves already gone home. Tired and frustrated, she headed toward home, to the apartment she shared with her father.

On the way home, she started past the Lucid Lounge, one of the communal relaxation facilities scattered around the Center.

A break. She could be more clear-headed after a break. Scanning her ID, she was greeted by a virtual host—a strikingly beautiful, tall androgynous individual with short dark hair and copper-bronze skin. "Good evening Director Tourni, how can I help you today?"

Dedicated to Najor's leadership and her work, Tourni was unmarried and childless. She relished visiting the lounge.

"Good evening. I would like to schedule an appointment with one of your hosts."

"Of course. If you'll go through to room 5, I'll send in a host matching your profile."

Although tired, she didn't fail to notice how the room, in reality a personal holospace, matched her desired Greco-Roman classical expectations. The walls and ceiling were a honey-colored stone and the blue and white mosaic on the floor showed scenes of dolphins and other sea life. Vines trailed up columns to a wood-gabled ceiling. In the background, she heard waves breaking against a distant shore.

In the anteroom space, she changed quickly into a cream-white cotton toga with calfskin sandals. Then she sat on a low bench and waited.

A tall, slim, athletic, AI-generated man stepped out from behind one of the columns. He was barefoot and wore only a simple perizoma—a loincloth—that accentuated his toned skin. "Chief Scientist Director Tourni, welcome. I am Nikos. Please, have some refreshment." He handed her a glass of red wine, a Cabernet Sauvignon. "Your favorite."

She took the glass and closed her eyes. Tilting up the glass, she savored the mixed earthy notes of oak and black currant. Downing the contents in one swift motion, she looked up into the pools of the AI's deep brown eyes. "Thank you, Nikos. Call me Shanya."

He sat down beside her on the bench and took the empty glass from her hand. "Please, lie back."

She loosened the clasp that secured her toga. "Let's begin. I'm in a hurry tonight."

Feeling physically, if not mentally relaxed, after her virtual hookup, Tourni continued her journey home to the apartment where her father was waiting.

Her father, Constantine Tourni, was a widowed businessman of Greek descent. He had been fortunate enough to be conducting business inside the walls of the Center during the claudtrom, which granted him Elite status. Unlike her, he hadn't even voted for leader Najor, who joined forces with other powerful leaders around the globe, disbanding country status in favor of the new Centers. The leaders had enforced martial law by claiming a crisis. They had then eliminated elections and established the two categories of citizen.

Fortune favors the bold, though, and her father was an industrious, hardworking merchant whose company brought numerous essential goods into the Center. Many of the hard-to-find goods Elites wanted were procured on the black market and sold surreptitiously to Elites. He was a 'spiv', working on the gray edge of legality.

She kissed her father on his left cheek where he sat in a thickly cushioned chair before his computer where he did much of his business.

"Father, you've been smoking again," she scolded when she breathed in the unmistakable smell of stale nicotine on his breath.

His current body was now sixty-three years old, still stocky, but with a full head of thick and wavy gray hair. He was in surprisingly good health considering his unhealthy habits of smoking and drinking. His vitality attracted a posse of younger widows. It wouldn't be long before he was requesting another memory transfer and a new body. It would be hard to find a suitable farm-raised Underling for her father. He always insisted on young boys of Mediterranean descent with the muscular and sculptured physique of a Greek demigod.

"My daughter," he replied. "It was just a little sweet-scented Vamma Del Sol cigarillo on the way home from my office. The ventilation system on the PulseRail is broken again, and the air stinks of everyone's sweat. I'm helping everyone."

He stood and they went through into the living area of the apartment, expensively furnished to match her father's Mediterranean tastes. The furniture was made from imported stone pine with wrought iron accents and framing. The walls were painted in warm terracotta earth tones and adorned with artwork depicting coastal scenes by artists including Joaquín Sorolla. There was even a reproduction in oil of the famous Picasso *Mediterranean Landscape*. Richly colored rugs covered the hardwood floor.

Her father poured them both a shot of chilled ouzo, which he imported from Mediterranean distilleries.

"Nav, play artist Sotiria Bellou." Rebetiko—urban Greek music—filled the apartment. The two of them settled into cushioned dark leather couches across from a low, white-marbled table.

"What's with the snippy attitude this evening?"

"Sorry, Father, but there's a massive problem at work and my boss is blaming me," she said, sipping from her glass. The soothing anise aroma of the ouzo eased her building migraine. "The memories of Najor's son were lost today after he used someone's ID."

She looked up at her father suddenly. "Does your business ever trade in ID bracelets? Do you manufacture contact lenses with DNA data corresponding to stolen IDs?"

"My dear. Why ask that of me? No, I don't deal directly in stolen IDs. It's too risky. But some of my associates do. There's a need for them in some quarters. You know, powerful Underlings who want a memory transfer."

"My God, Father! Underlings should never be getting memory transfers. And, you know what? One of your 'associates' sold an ID to the son of the Center leader—of all people. Najor is furious. You know how vindictive he can be."

"Don't worry, my daughter. You have the video recordings I gave you? You're safe. He can't touch you."

"Yes, yes, I do. But I need to track down where the ID came from."

"Who did it belong to?"

"Anatoly Zuur—who was already dead!"

"Hmm. I don't recognize the name. Okay, well, I can put out feelers among friends. Besides, I'm sure it's a temporary problem, and you'll find the kid's memories soon enough."

"No, we won't." She shook her head. "Memory losses have recently gone up from the usual one percent to five percent. Officially, Najor's blaming the technology I invented. I've been working with other Center leaders on the project. Now, after all these years of being loyal, he's throwing me under the bus. This problem is bigger than the loss of his son."

"I get it," said Constantine. "If other Elites get wind of it, they will stop using the memory transfer program, especially moderates, and our population will crash, since newborn children are rarer than a bottle of Canava Santorini ouzo."

He sipped from his glass, looking contemplative for a moment. Then he smiled at her. "As your dear, late mother used to say," he said, quoting her mother in their native Greek. She smiled as he then translated one of her favorite aphorisms. "*When trouble comes it's your family who supports you.*"

Both sipped their drinks, and Tourni smiled across at her father. "I know what I have to do. I've already checked the equipment, and it's fine. I need to find someone to comb through every memory transfer in the last few months and pinpoint geographically where the memories may have gone. Perhaps signals don't always degrade to zero and we can retrieve the lost memories and find Damon."

"Is that possible?"

"I don't know. We've never needed to track lost memories before. And even then, I doubt if we can retrieve human memories from what at best will be a very weak signal. Developing the technology to do such a memory retrieval could take years."

"But you must try, no?"

"Yes, Najor's going to be on my back until we find out what happened to his son. I'll put together a team to experiment using Underlings, to see how far we can let memory signals degrade before they can't be retrieved."

"And the lost memory signals. Can you find them?"

"We can look."

⸺◆⸺

CHAPTER THREE

AGITATED CATTLE

Outside the Boston Center

Jacob Giles had not forgotten the horror of seeing a man gored to death by an aggressive cow. It had been a sickening sight. He had been visiting a farm in Kansas, inspecting cattle destined for the abattoir he ran. Only later, he learned the animal had been infected with mad cow disease.

One minute, a Texas longhorn stood quietly as his assistant examined her coat for mange. The next minute, the cow turned her head into him. One of the cow's horns had pierced through the man's thick jacket, and on through his belly. As the cow slashed its head from side to side, the man's intestines spilled onto the ground and his blood painted the soil. His agonized screams carried across the pasture, subsiding only when he died.

Today, Giles leaned on the wooden rail fence bordering the pasture, coughed up a glob of bloody phlegm, and spat on the ground, worried he was seeing symptoms of the disease again. Sucking an old briar pipe that had long gone out, his sun-weathered face creased in concern as he scanned the pasture with the steady gaze of someone who knew every inch of the land and the creatures on it.

Damn, am I seeing symptoms of disease again?

The cattle were not acting normal.

He muttered under his breath to one of his young farmhands leaning on the fence next to him. "Doug, I'm seeing more and more of these critters acting strange."

"Look how that group are huddled in a circle with their heads facing inwards. They're like a bunch of yaks in the tundra defending themselves from wolves," said Doug. "They're grunting and lowing, and shaking their heads from side to side."

Their wide, curved horns locked together momentarily before the animals pulled apart. Some of them scraped and pawed at the ground as though trying to write in the mud with their hooves. A couple jumped up on their hind legs, emphasizing whatever emotion was possessing them.

"That's strange behavior," said Doug. "They look bothered. Are they trying to tell us something?"

"It don't make any sense to me. But, no, they're cattle. They're not trying to tell us anything. They are probably sick from eating contaminated grass. The grass in several pastures is infected and dying."

"Yeah, the bottom pasture is looking pretty bad. There are patches where the grass is as brown as silage."

Giles said, "Perhaps they just got bad feed and have gas. Hopefully, they don't have mad cow disease. Infected cattle have to be destroyed, and the meat can't be eaten. Unless they are infected, they will all be steaks for the Elites soon enough."

This pasture was a three-acre muddy field of churned-up black-and-brown soil at the Northern District Beef Processing Facility. There was little to no grass left—only gnarled tufts of bluestem and fescue. About fifty cattle waited in this finishing pen to be ushered through rusty metal chutes into the adjoining abattoir. The bright overhead sun cast strong shadows on the ground beneath the cattle and the air shimmered with a warm glow as the sun's rays caught dust from the cattle's hooves. Swallows circled overhead, catching a meal of insects. Knowing the cattle would soon be butchered in the abattoir did not diminish the tranquility of the scene.

"Wait, now what are they doing?" cried Doug.

Giles followed his farmhand's gaze. At least a half dozen of the cattle had broken from the circle and were now walking, then trotting, toward Giles and Doug, gathering speed as they got closer.

"They're just inquisitive about people. Typical cattle behavior," replied Giles, although his voice quavered with uncertainty.

Their hooves billowed up dust as they ran faster and their progress became a stampede. The guttural moan of their lowing grew louder the closer they got.

At the fence, the cattle skidded to a halt. They pawed the ground, making messy marks in the mud. Two reared up as though they were trying to get to the men on the other side of the fence. Warm gusts of damp, earthy air from their hot breath enveloped Giles and Doug as the cattle inched closer. Reaching over the top of the fence, they shook their heads from side to side, which showered the two men with spittle. Still pawing the rails of the fence, the angry cattle bellowed thunderously.

Doug staggered back from the fence, clawing at the ground as he rolled across the grass into a thorny briar patch. His hands were bleeding when he jumped up.

"Dang, I've torn the orange U off the front of my shirt. I'll have to fix it before any Elite guards catch me."

"Whoa!" Giles sat up on the damp ground. He struggled up onto one knee and coughed up more bloody phlegm. "What the hell's up with these critters?"

Attempting to recover his composure as he stood, Giles fumbled to pick up his pipe, which had fallen to the grass. He leaned onto Doug and clasped his left shoulder. "Get the good cattle through the chutes, now!"

Staying back from the fence and still supporting Giles, Doug yelled at a couple of the other farmhands. The pair quickly ushered the calmer cattle through the chutes into the abattoir. They walked back cautiously to the group by the fence.

His coughing fit over, Giles pointed to the cattle with his pipe. "These ones have to be destroyed. The meat has to be incinerated. Get their brain tissue tested for mad cow."

Armed with electric cattle prods, the farmhands guided the remaining cattle toward another set of chutes that led directly to the incinerator. With a series of whistles, Giles expertly directed his dog to run around behind the cattle, keeping them in a tight group and moving them toward the chutes. The black and white border collie nipped at their heels. The sharp, buzzing sparks of the cattle prods persuaded the cattle to comply with the directions of the farmhands until they were all through the chutes into the abattoir.

A few minutes later, still rattled, Giles leaned his elbows onto the fence again and fiddled with his pipe. He packed the bowl with fresh tobacco, getting it lit after several failed attempts. Wisps of sweet-smelling smoke enveloped him as he calmed down.

Turning to Doug, he said, "I don't know what that was all about. In all my years, I've never seen anything like it before, even from diseased cattle..."

"Hey, look, Boss, someone's coming." Doug pointed to a cloud of dust over the road leading to the abattoir.

A two-seater EV-ATV pulled up at the top of the pasture. Compared to the farm vehicles Giles had, the EV-ATV was sleek and modern with a powerful, long-range electric motor. Two guards got out and walked down toward Giles and Doug.

"Damn it," muttered Giles. "The guards are always watching us."

The two guards were dressed in black with Kevlar body armor, protective helmets and eye shields, and each carried a powerful-looking mind-activated automatic weapon. They stopped in front of Giles and Doug who had turned away from the fence as they approached.

Giles' dog crouched down behind his legs, growling.

"How can I help you, officers?" said Giles. "Hush, Shep."

One of the guards had crimson flashes on his helmet and appeared to be the superior officer. He spoke curtly. "Our surveillance drones indicated a commotion. What's going on?"

"Oh, nothing much, gentlemen. We just had a few boisterous cattle that didn't want to go through the chutes into the abattoir. But we got it sorted now."

"Is that why the boy's hands are bleeding and the U on his shirt torn? You know I can arrest him for improper display of his Underling status?"

"But, but, I fell into a briar patch when the cattle frightened me," said Doug, his voice quavering.

The other guard, the one without flashes on his helmet, came over to Doug and shoved him in the chest with the butt of his gun. "Fell over did you, boy?"

Doug staggered backwards and tripped over a branch on the ground. He landed in another briar patch. The sharp thorns caught his clothing, tearing it more, as he struggled to free himself. The guard straddled Doug and kicked a steel-toed boot into his back. He leered down at him. "Sergeant Hoffman, let's take him in."

Not wishing to inflame the situation, Giles spoke softly. "It's okay, officers. As I said, the cattle are sorted. I'll make sure Doug gets his jacket sewn up this evening."

The sergeant glared at Giles, then scowled down at Doug. Without a word, he turned abruptly and walked quickly back to the ATV. After giving Doug one more kick in the back, the junior officer trailed behind. The guards left as fast as they had arrived, the hoverjets blowing up a cloud of dust.

Doug grimaced and slowly got up, pulling spines off his clothes.

Giles saw Doug was shaking. "Get the label on your jacket fixed up tonight, and keep your head down for a few days. Hopefully, the junior officer will forget about you and won't come sniffing around to make more trouble."

Doug spat a wad of the smokeless tobacco to the ground. Several years younger than Giles, he had only been in this job for a few months. Blond and skinny as a rail, Doug had the endurance of a long-distance runner, and put in long hours without tiring. Giles didn't know too much about him, but had been impressed with his work ethic so far. He hoped this run-in with the guards wouldn't bother him too much.

Giles looked from side to side. "Damn guards," he muttered. "We have to fight against the system."

Doug looked at Giles curiously.

Giles spat on the ground, then ground his spittle into the mud with the sole of his work boot. He wandered off towards the next pasture where more cattle were waiting.

Perhaps young Doug might make a good recruit. He can take over from me when I get too old.

"Come on, Doug, get back to work. And, where's that damn dog of mine? Shep, get over here."

The effects of environmental degradation and climate change had been obvious to Giles for the entire twenty years he'd worked at the beef production facility. The cattle had been coming in from the outlying farms thinner than usual and often malnourished. With his staff, he tried to fatten them up. Due to his efforts, they'd had a large degree of success, but he was keenly aware of a decline in meat quality.

Giles was in his office in the abattoir planning the arrival of herds of 50 to 100 cattle. They came in on trucks from all around the region. Some were from cattle farms nearby and he knew many of the truckers. Others came in from farms as far away as 800 miles, spending up to twelve hours on the road. Giles didn't know these truckers as well, since they came by less often. Regardless, Giles maintained an extensive network of cattle truckers, which allowed him to gather a lot of useful information on Elite activities over a wide area.

Deke Smith had just arrived with a herd of 50 Texas Longhorns from a farm 300 miles to the south. As a truck driver, Deke traveled all over the region from farm to farm, and to the beef processing facility. He was one of Giles' most trusted messengers.

Hearing a knock at the door, he turned away from his holoscreen. "Come in. Hey, Deke. Got those cattle unloaded?"

Immediately, Giles' dog leaped up, barking and dry humping Deke's left leg.

"Shep, get down and shut it. You've seen Deke before."

"Hi, boss. Yep, all settled into the south pasture."

As usual, Deke was dressed smartly in pressed denim jeans and a crisp plaid, long-sleeved pearl snap shirt. He liked to affect the traditional good cowboy image from his polished alligator skin cowboy boots to the white Stetson on his head. He obtained all these fashionable clothes from his contacts in the black market.

Giles didn't say anything, although the outfit was all a bit over the top for a truck driver, and the orange U Deke was required to place on the front and back of his shirt made it all look a bit ridiculous.

"Grab some coffee from the pot. Kick the dog off the chair and take a seat. And take off your damn hat."

Deke didn't take off his Stetson, but he poured a cup of coffee and sat down on the wooden chair in front of Giles' desk.

"What do you have for me?"

"I've got this month's coal train schedule for the Midwest." He pushed a battered tablet across the desk.

"Okay, let's see what opportunities present themselves for some mischief."

Giles squinted at the screen through the cheap reading glasses he was forced to wear these days. He was interested in the shipments of coal from the mines to the power plants that ran the industrial factories. Without coal, the power plants couldn't produce electricity to fuel the polluting industrial plants, and less carbon dioxide would be released into the atmosphere.

"Look here. Perfect. This coal train will be passing over the viaduct that crosses the Kaskaskia River on the twenty-third at around six in the morning. Too bad if the viaduct fails as the train is crossing, heh?"

This looked like a good opportunity. In his younger days Giles took an active part in these activities. These days he had to be satisfied with covertly coordinating acts of eco-sabotage.

"I want you to visit Mariah Martinez, leader of the Peoria group, and let her know what needs to be done. Take young Doug with you. He needs to get more experience in the world."

A week passed before Giles was again sitting in his office with Deke, who had brought in another cattle shipment.

"I tell you, boss, that woman, Mariah, is fantastic," said Deke. "Her group did an amazing job taking out the bridge. Boom! Everything exploded. The train and all the coal is now in the canyon and will never get burned."

"Yeah, she did a good job," said Giles. "It looks like you scuffed up your expensive jeans."

Deke brushed some dust from his jeans. "Yeah, boss. I'll have to get a new pair. Doug did great, by the way. He was nervous, but is committed to the cause. Anyway, I'd better get on the road. I've a load of sheep to pick up tomorrow down Canton way that need to go to the livestock auction."

Later that day after Deke had left, Giles gazed across the field at a herd of some 50 cattle fattened up over the last few weeks on a high protein feed. He was perplexed. As usual, these were Texas longhorns, favored for their highly marbled and tender beef. Their coats were a glistening mahogany brown befitting their 'finished' state. Their beef was considered the 'best of the best' and Giles was justifiably proud. However, the beef and other animal production facilities, like this one managed by Giles, were run by Underlings exclusively supplying Elites.

Most of the cattle meekly stood around grazing on a few sparse tufts of grass. Others drank from stone water troughs, and some others were taking a last meal (little did they know) of protein supplement from open food sacks hanging on metal poles. But as he had seen before, a few cattle weren't standing quietly or eating. Three or four of them paced back and forth, clearly bothered about something. Some scratched the ground with their front hooves, as though drawing figures in the mud. Others faced off with each other, shaking their heads back and forth, weirdly appearing as if they were arguing.

Seeing this unusual activity again perturbed Giles. The cattle in these finishing pens were usually calm from eating so much. More than that, he was suspicious of something, but he couldn't put a finger on why he felt that way. It was the second or third time he'd noticed this sort of behavior. He'd have to ask friends who managed other cattle facilities if they were seeing similar behavior. Fortunately, this time the cattle didn't charge toward him.

Not one to dwell too much, Giles snapped out of his pondering and yelled at Doug, "Move them through the chutes, it's getting late."

"Yes, boss." With yips and yells, he and the other farmhands ushered the herd forward. The cattle that had been behaving strangely moved through the chutes with the rest of the group, although, to Giles, they appeared frightened compared with the rest of the herd. Forty-five minutes later, all the cattle were through the chutes. They went into the arms of the robots and machines in the abattoir where they would be slaughtered, butchered, and packaged.

Before he stepped away from the fence, Giles thought he heard buzzing and looked around for the source of the sound. Raising his hands to shade his eyes, he thought maybe something flew overhead. Hopefully not a buzzard, he thought. They were enough of a pest at the discharge points where the unused parts of the cattle came out of the abattoir. When he didn't see anything, he shook his head and walked back to his office.

———————◆O◆———————

CHAPTER FOUR

BECOMING A DOG

D amon woke with a jolt.

He lay on the ground on his stomach. His tongue was hanging out and he was panting.

Huh?

Above him was a cloudy sky, crisscrossed by dark smoky plumes. If he was outside, why wasn't he wearing a mask? He pressed up to sit, feeling damp grass beneath him.

WTF?

Last he recalled, he'd been laying on a gurney as the technician injected sedative. "Count backward from ten" she had said.

Something was wrong.

Gingerly, he stood up. On four legs. Why was he standing on four legs instead of two? Why was he viewing the world from only two or three feet off the ground? Why were his hands covered in fur, with claws gripping the soil?

A long furry black structure behind him caught his eye. He spun around to try and grab it with his muzzle, but it eluded him. He spun around again, and again, but it was always out of reach.

Stupid idiot, that's my tail.

My tail? I've got a tail?

"Shep, get over here!" A man's voice sounded somewhere behind him.

Who's Shep?

Turning toward the voice too quickly, he stumbled on unsteady paws, dropping his nose against the ground. Righting himself, he moved warily toward the man.

He licked the hand the man held down by his right side. The salty tang of the skin on the back of his hand was reassuring. He shook his head to clear his mind—something wasn't right. The man leaned against a split-rail fence smoking a pipe despite an obvious hacking cough tearing up his lungs.

"Hey, I know you. You're Jacob Giles, my master!" he barked.

"Hush now, boy. You'll spook the cattle."

The last of a herd of cattle were moving through chutes into a large concrete building—he knew the place—an abattoir. He recognized the animals as cattle with a familiar rotten egg odor. The building reeked of sickness, and metal, with a sharp tang of iron hanging heavy in the air. The bloody smell of death.

But that wasn't really the problem. Despite these sights and smells, it was all familiar. How could cattle, an old man, and an abattoir be familiar to him?

What was going on?

He followed Giles—something inside telling him the man was his master. Why did he recognize this old Underling? They slowly made their way along a muddy track to a small cottage next to the abattoir. Inside he was greeted by a woman—Giles' wife, Elizabeth.

Lucky Giles. Most Underlings lived in hovels outside the walls of the Center or drab apartment blocks around industrial plants and farms.

Electricity was rationed to three hours a day and no one had air conditioning.

But this house was an ancient single-bedroom cottage built with local wood and stone. Inside, Damon found the minimum of homemade wooden furniture. A few thin quilts were hung on the walls. Damon wasn't used to such spartan living arrangements.

It was a cold evening. Giles settled down to wait for supper as Damon patrolled around the house sniffing the chair legs and cracks between the wooden beams in the white-washed walls. He checked the bedroom, the living area and kitchen at the far end. A yeasty aroma of baking bread came from a wood-burning range. There was an array of familiar scents, nothing untoward—the pungent, acrid odor of ammonia from mice urine in the walls. Just to be sure, he rubbed his anal glands against the furniture to scent mark. Any dog coming into the house would know immediately this was not their territory.

How could this be HIS territory?

Elizabeth snapped. "Shep, stop doing that, you're stinking up the house."

She dropped the knife she was using and followed him around the cottage wiping down the furniture with a bleach-soaked cloth. "Jacob, doesn't it bother you when he does that?"

His head in clouds of tobacco smoke, Jacob didn't answer.

Finally satisfied with his check of the cottage, Damon settled down and dozed on a thick rug by the log fire in the hearth. The heat from the flames, burning logs of seasoned oak from the local forest, nicely warmed his fur. Growing up as an Elite in the Center with central heating, Damon had never seen a real fireplace before.

He huffed out a sigh. The sensory overload was disconcerting—a heightened sense of smell, enhanced hearing, new vision, and enriched tactile dimensions.

He had a yearning for raw meat. And smells! There were layers of scents he had never known before. Lying by the fire, he could smell the wood burning, the musky smell of the dry wood next to the fire, and every herb Elizabeth was using in cooking. The odors of wood, food, and humans permeated the house. More than that, he picked out his master and the tobacco smoke from his pipe on his breath, along with cheese and onion he had eaten for lunch. The acrid odor of the abattoir infused Giles' jacket and clothes. Everything carried a detailed story.

He was a dog called Shep.

His hands were covered in black fur—-they were paws. So were his feet. His arms and legs, his whole body, was covered in fur. He had a tail that wagged uncontrollably whenever Giles looked at him. His tongue lolled out of his mouth and he started panting when the fire became too warm. He edged away from the hearth.

Was this a sedative-induced dream?

Horrifying images of running on four legs, chasing cats, and barking and growling, passed through his mind and his head jolted up with a yelp. His memory transfer must have gone horribly wrong. Instead of transferring his memories into the fit body of the unconscious Underling next to him in the hospital room, his memories had been apparently transferred into this dog. How was this possible? How was he now outside the Center?

Elizabeth put down an earthen bowl of dry brown pellets and food scraps in front of him. She carried the calming scent of the kitchen mixed with lavender soap. "There you go, Shep."

Before he had a chance to think more about his concerns, he jumped up and wolfed down the meat-flavored pellets in about thirty seconds flat. He left the potato and carrot peelings and looked up at Elizabeth, panting and wanting more. His tail wagged like a spinning windmill.

"That's all you get, boy. One bowl of food or you'll throw up."

The duality of two minds in the same body confused him. He slumped back down as she took the bowl away. He had barely tasted the food; it went down like downing a shot of bourbon. At least his belly didn't feel as hungry as before. Although Shep had enjoyed the food, Damon was less than enthusiastic. He was used to a diet of cooked, hot food including a variety of fresh meat and fish, steamed vegetables, rice, and pasta. Which he usually washed down with vintage wines imported from across the globe. Where was the coffee?

Who was this couple that owned the dog Shep? Jacob Giles seemed to be some sort of local official who lived with his wife Elizabeth. She was a large woman and fit Damon's image of a farmer's wife. She dressed in a homemade, blue plaid cotton dress that came down to her ankles. Her dark hair was long with streaks of gray and tied back in a bun at the back of her head. The sleeves of her dress were short, to her elbows, revealing scabbed sores on her forearms. Sores showed on the back of her neck below her hairline. The sores must have bothered her. Now and then, she rubbed a greasy-looking lotion on them.

Between Giles's hacking cough and her sores, they didn't seem to be very healthy. Were all Underlings sick, or was it just them? It was probably due to the pollution he'd been shielded from inside the covered dome of the Center.

He settled back down again. Giles and Elizabeth ate their supper at a wooden table in the kitchen. They chatted about their day. While he dozed on and off, unsettled thoughts raced through Damon's mind. It was pathetic how these people lived. It was primitive. Did they really have to cook and clean? Where was their Nav?

Listening to the couple, he learned more about their life that Shep didn't understand. Damon learned he was in the house of the overseer of the Northern District Beef Production Facility near to the Boston Elite Center where Damon had lived all his life with family, friends, and other Elites.

But, how had he gotten here, in this house, with this old Underling couple? He had been preparing for his memory transfer—a routine procedure. With an aging and sick population of Elites in the Center, a large number of memory transfers were carried out every day. He had read online that a small number of them didn't work. In these cases, the lab technician who'd explained the procedure to him said the Elite and the intended Underling recipient became unconscious, mindless vegetables and were euthanized. He had scoffed, assumed he would not be one of the "lost memories."

But now? Well, he wasn't a mindless vegetable. He was a dog! Did the technicians transfer his memories into a dog as part of a new experimental procedure? Surely, his father wouldn't have sanctioned it. Fine on Underlings or prisoners, but not on an Elite like him. Was Giles in on a plan to get a smarter dog?

Agitated, he leaped up and started barking and running. After a few minutes, he paused and chewed on a chair leg.

"For goodness sake! Will you never learn to stop chewing the furniture, you mongrel!" Elizabeth yelled and swatted his backside with a broom.

"Giles, what's up with your dog tonight?"

"Hey, help me! I'm Damon Najor. I'm trapped inside the mind of your stupid dog. Take me back to the Center. Now!" he yelled at Giles and Elizabeth. But all that came out were loud annoying barks.

He jumped up, putting his front paws onto Giles' leg where he sat at the table. "It's your fault, old man," he barked. "Take me back home!" His barks turned to whines.

Frustrated and anxious, he ran in circles again around the living area and rubbed his muzzle against Giles' legs.

"Jacob, take your dog outside and tie him up." Elizabeth sounded exasperated. "Really, Jacob, sometimes you are unaware of your surroundings."

Giles got up slowly from the table where he was eating his supper. "Come on, boy, outside." He tied an old rope leash around Shep's neck.

Tied up outside, Damon huddled miserably on the flagstones of the courtyard, trying to find cover from the evening rain.

The duality of two minds occupying one body was disconcerting.

He jumped up, barking again, when a man came in through the gate of the courtyard and approached the door.

"Hush, Shep," said Giles opening the door. "Evening, Doug, thanks for coming round so late."

"No problem, Boss. Hey, get down Shep."

Damon fought to control the innate behavior of Shep straining against the rope that tied him up as he sniffed Doug's crotch and dry humped one of his legs.

Doug shook off Shep and went inside the cottage. Damon was left outside shivering in the rain. He tried to settle down but his mind was a mess of confused emotions.

He was going to have to learn to stop Shep's dog instincts catching him by surprise and overwhelming his human intellect. Shep was semi-sentient, but seemed unaware of Damon's presence in his mind. It was clear when Shep wanted to do something physically, like relieve himself or eat food, or, ugh, lick the floor, but Damon had to allow for that. It was like an expanded subconsciousness.

He needed to keep his own sentience under wraps. After all, although he had tried to talk to them, Giles or Elizabeth might get suspicious if their dog started acting too odd. Damon wasn't sure how Giles would react when he found out his dog was now partly human.

Beyond that, Damon was furious. Did the Underling technicians in the memory transfer unit make a dreadful, stupid mistake? That annoying old lady was probably now running around in the body of a young, nubile Underling. When would they realize their mistake? When they did, would they transfer his mind back into the Underling? By now, his father would have been told and must be raising hell. When he got back to the Center, and into his new body, Damon would make sure all of the incompetent memory transfer technicians were sent to a penal colony.

———◆O◆———

As Damon got used to his new life, he became familiar with the daily routine in Giles' house.

Giles was an early-bird who woke up at the crack of dawn. Today, red morning sunlight slanted through the shuttered windows on the east side of the cottage. The sounds of Giles and Elizabeth moving around their bedroom woke Damon with a shock from an unsettling dream—Jak and Petr were parading him around on a leash at some sort of dog show. Then he peed on the floor, the crowd jeered, and his father, who had been watching, stormed out.

Damon could hear and smell Elizabeth bustling around the kitchen preparing coffee with fried eggs, mushrooms and tomatoes for Giles' breakfast.

The smell of breakfast pained Damon as he awaited his bowl of scraps.

The dream he had awakened from was becoming a recurrent nightmare. In addition, sometimes Shep's simple and happy dreams of chasing rabbits intruded into Damon's mind. But in his head, they became twisted into larger figures that chased him down dark tunnels with walls closing in on him. As the figures got closer, he struggled to escape through structures reminiscent of celestial black holes. Who was chasing him? Where was he going, where would he end up?

"Okay, Shep. Come on, let's go." Giles' voice roused him from the nightmare.

No matter what the weather was like, Giles would head out first thing each morning to walk around the pens and check on the cattle.

Today, Damon walked with Giles in one of the pastures examining cattle recently arrived from Kansas. As usual, one of Giles' farm hands was accompanying them. Even Damon with his inexperienced eye could tell they didn't look good.

Giles was upset about the condition of the cattle. "Look, Doug," he said, pointing with his briar pipe. "Those mangy beasts aren't fit for processing. They've got dull coats, dim eyes, and are practically lame. What's their body condition score?"

Doug tapped icons on a hand-held device. A small hologram floated in the air, displaying scores. "They have a three out of ten BCS score, based upon their low body fat and poor muscle tone, Boss."

Giles squinted at the figures. "I swear. It's the damn polluted soil poisoning the grass. More and more of the cattle come to us thin and underweight."

He shook his head. "It's not good enough. Double their protein feed for the next week. Include extra soybean meal for muscle development, and molasses for energy. These cattle need to be much better if we are going to get good steaks out of them. Otherwise, they'll be good for nothing but ground beef."

Doug tapped more icons and dry feed matching Giles' requirements were delivered by a bee-buzzing drone to the feeding toughs scattered across the pasture.

Damon trailed around with Giles, allowing Shep to sniff for rabbits and squirrels. Shep already knew his way around the pastures, but Damon concentrated on listening, so he could learn more practical matters, such as where tools and equipment were stored. He also wondered if there were other animal-human mix-ups like him.

If he could find someone to talk to, he could explain his predicament. He had barked at a family of rabbits, a stray house cat, a group of horses, and even a rat in one of the barns. "Hey! Hello! Can anyone understand me?"

Several of the cattle were showing unusual behavior, but they always ran away if Damon got too close. After checking the cattle, Giles had lunch in the barn with the farm hands before spending the first part of the afternoon in his office in the abattoir. Damon followed him into the office, and slouched to the floor.

The office was small and tidy, but grubby. A single bulb hanging from the ceiling cast a dim light. A single window, obscured by grime, provided a distorted view of the parking lot outside of the abattoir. The aroma of Giles' pipe tobacco and the cheap coffee he drank were a relief compared to the stench of the beef processing area they had passed through. A couple of old shelves held a few dusty books and binders. Damon noted the titles related to cattle production, feed, and diseases. A tawdry-looking girlie calendar was pinned to the back of the door. Presumably, Elizabeth never came here.

Damon wondered what Giles did for his job as supervisor beyond wandering around and telling the other Underling workers to "get on with it." To be fair, he did spend a lot of time in his office, using an old computer. He also coordinated the distribution of the meat to Elite Centers. Damon heard him on the phone many times discussing deliveries to the nearby Center. Most of the meat from the abattoir apparently went to the local Center, but Giles apparently also sent sizable shipments of frozen meat to other Centers.

Today, he closed his office door before going on the computer. From Damon's position laying on the floor of his office, the holoscreen was too high up to see well. He jumped to get a better view.

"What do you want, Shep?" Giles asked. "Do you need to go out again?"

But Damon had caught a glimpse of a message Giles was writing. "...your group must stop the oil shipment from being delivered."

Damon lay back down, concerned about what he'd just seen. Giles wasn't looking at porn after all. It seemed he was writing to environmental groups across the country, coordinating activities of sabotage to disrupt the transportation of coal, oil, and other non-renewable resources. Damon wondered if he'd ever heard of sabotage to the Center supplies. But this did explain Giles' frequent absences for three and four days. Damon suspected he was taking part in these environmental activities.

Giles muttered while typing into his computer. "What do you think about this possibility, Shep? There's a shipment of coal being delivered to the Pittsburgh Power Plant in two weeks. Let's see. It's a convoy of five trucks coming from the Cumberland Mine, fifty-three miles to the south. Usually, their coal is transported by rail, and then by barge for distribution across the country, but the Pittsburgh Power Plant is running low on coal and needs extra supplies. It would be too bad if the coal never reached them." He laughed and looked down at Shep as if he were expecting a response.

Damon gave him Shep's best innocent, doe-eyed look in reply.

"Deke will be here tomorrow with a shipment of cattle. I'll send him and Doug down to the local environmental group with the schedule, and some ideas on how to hijack the shipment. Too bad I can't get away for this one."

Hearing this, Damon looked up at him with baleful eyes, vowing that when he got back home, he'd make sure Giles was hauled in for questioning. This type of behavior by an Underling must not be tolerated. Perhaps his father might show him respect if he reported this environmental network.

Other than his environmental activities, Giles appeared scrupulously honest. Perhaps that was part of his cover up. As far as Damon could tell he didn't keep any of the meat from the abattoir for him and Elizabeth, or sell any of it on the thriving Underling black market the other farmhands talked about. No doubt he understood if he was caught stealing and selling meat he would be demoted to cleaning toilets for the rest of his life.

After more than an hour of work, Giles muttered about a "damn meeting," logged off, and closed down his computer. Taking one last swig of cold coffee from an old chipped mug he kept on his desk, he left his office.

"Gimme some of the coffee," Damon whined.

Giles beckoned Shep to follow. "Hush. Come on, boy."

The early morning sun was obscured by low clouds and drizzle. Shep and Giles walked together in the gray rain over to an old hover-truck parked outside the abattoir. It had once been a sky-blue color but rust covered much of the weathered surface. The paint was chipped and the chrome dulled. Despite rusting paintwork, it was a workhorse and the neodrive engine still ran well. It was Giles' pride and joy. The passenger door creaked as he opened it. "Up, boy."

Damon lay on the bench seat snoozing as they bumped along gravel roads away from the beef processing center. He didn't recognize the agricultural and forest landscape they passed through and had no idea where they were going. As he navigated the roads, Giles listened to annoying country rock on the truck's neodrive, singing along in a flat baritone. There wasn't much more Damon could do but wait in frustration for an opportunity to find a way to get his memories back into a human body.

Damon woke up to the sounds of harsh voices. Giles stomped on the brakes, stopping the truck abruptly. Damon peeked over the hood at a security check point. Guards charged either side of the truck, yelling at Giles. He calmly lowered the driver-side window and the nearest guard scanned his ID bracelet.

"State your purpose for visiting the Center."

"I have an appointment with Torrance Hanley, head of food security."

"Sure you do, and I'm the Queen of Sheba."

"Check your list if you don't believe me."

What luck! They were at one of the gated entrances to the Center and Giles was going inside. After checking his hand-held communications device and without apology, the guard waved Giles over to a parking area just outside the gate. Giles turned off the vehicle and it settled down to the ground as the hover-thrusters disengaged.

This was his chance to escape!

If he could get out of the pickup, he'd make his way to the memory transfer unit and get this mistake with his memory sorted out. He leaped up on the seat and started barking.

The guard came back over yelling, "Live animals belonging to Underlings aren't allowed in the Center. Leave your damn dog in the vehicle."

Giles whipped his head around. "Sit, Shep. Stay!"

Before Damon had a chance to do anything, Shep obeyed his master. Giles opened his driver's side door and got out. The door quickly closed behind him. Damon was trapped. He knew about the strict live animal policy in the Center. All live animals required an ID collar, showing registration to their accompanying Elite owner. Underling-owned dogs like Shep didn't have ID collars.

Disconsolately, he looked at the movement around him. Underlings were going in and out of the Center. Some came in old vehicles like Giles' hovertruck, parking next to them, and carrying goods into the Center. Others walked in, pushing wheeled handcarts loaded with vegetables, fresh bread, and other produce. Most were dressed in old, shabby earth tones, all brown and green, except for the bright orange "U" on the front and back of their jackets or dresses. Drab, rough textiles. As an Elite, Damon was used to seeing and wearing colorful and fashionable clothing. He shouted, trying to get their attention, but the barking was ignored except by guards who came over and yelled at him through the window that Giles had left cracked to give him some fresh air.

Worn out with barking, he eventually settled down and fell asleep. When Giles returned, he jumped into the truck and left in a hurry, muttering. "Damn, Elites. Bullshit questions about cattle production. A total waste of my time."

As they traveled back, it was dark outside and raining hard. Sitting up on the passenger seat, Damon couldn't see the road in front. The rain ran rivulets on the windscreen with a tiny area cleared by the wipers that Giles peered through. Goodness knows how he navigated.

They finally reached the cottage and rushed to the door. Warmth and shelter embraced them when they stepped inside. Giles settled into the large old wing-chair next to the fireplace. He started to pack his briar pipe with fresh tobacco and recounted his day to his wife. Shep settled at Giles' feet, drying off his soaked fur. Damon sighed.

As she did every evening, Elizabeth bustled around in the kitchen area cooking a supper of carrots, onions, and potatoes

"Look," she said. "I bought a bag of Kernza flour from the local market, so there's fresh bread baking in the range. Won't that be lovely?"

Giles didn't answer, and looked annoyed that Elizabeth was interrupting his tale. Damon could smell the mouthwatering, yeasty aroma of the fresh cooking bread filling the air. He had never experienced anything so comforting in the sterile atmosphere of the cafeterias and restaurants in the Center.

Elizabeth brushed tan-colored flour off her blue apron. "How did the visit with Torrance Hanley go?"

"Seeing as I've hardly ever been into the Center before, it was eye-opening, to say the least," he replied. "Those folks live in luxury. I've never seen such opulence. Expensive furniture, large rooms, fancy artwork on the walls, restaurants and cafés with fashionably dressed people milling around eating and drinking."

Damon whuffed. He knew all about it.

"Not my style," Giles added.

"As if you'd ever have the chance, love!" Elizabeth laughed. "What did Hanley want?"

"He asked 'bout the cattle I've been processing recently. Meat yield is down. He didn't need to remind me. Something's going on, but he didn't want to say. He was worried about something."

Whorls of pungent smoke coming from his pipe obscured his face. "Some guards had seen our cattle acting strange and he became annoyed when I told him that I didn't see too much as the cattle were heading into the abattoir."

"What's wrong with the cattle?" Elizabeth asked, chopping a carrot.

"As I told him, I didn't know. The tests for mad cow disease came back negative. I told him I don't know what's going on. That was it. After that he dismissed me, and a guard escorted me out. The guard was an Underling and muttered that there's been problems with some medical program. Although I can't for the life of me think how that's related to our cattle."

Perhaps Giles didn't know what was going on, but Damon was sensing a very disturbing pattern. If his mind had been transferred into a nearby dog instead of the intended Underling, perhaps other Elite minds had been transferred into other animals like the cattle. Any Elite whose mind was transferred into the cattle was now dead, slaughtered in the abattoir. This must have been going on for a while. How many Elites had died a horrible death as their cattle hosts were slaughtered?

He shuddered, thinking back to his last meals in the Center. He had enjoyed a juicy steak. He may have eaten beef from a cow hosting an Elite mind.

Perhaps the memories had been transferred into other animals and were alive, but probably very confused. Perhaps he wasn't alone. He needed to find the others.

He vowed to escape.

———◆◇◆———

Before escaping and returning to the Center, Damon needed to learn to speak. Barking at people wasn't working.

He needed to be able to talk with the memory transfer scientists when he got back into the Center. There was a reckoning coming.

Initially, he had difficulty getting Shep's vocal cords, lips, and tongue to pronounce human speech. Half the time he was arguing with Shep for control of the vocal cords and vocal folds, but the dog was just too simple-minded. And too easily distracted by scents or sounds.

He finally managed a few strangled woofs—a few breathy words, like "hallow" for "hello", but no hard consonants.

He did not try to speak with Giles or Elizabeth. As Underlings, they were not in a position to help him. The experience with Giles in the Center showed him how Underlings were treated as second-class citizens. As a rich Elite kid, Damon had treated Underlings as servants, but he saw now how wrong he had been.

Unfortunately, Elizabeth caught him trying to speak. He had been lying by the fire muttering a few simple phrases.

"You poor thing Shep. You must have a throat infection. Stay still while I give you a dose of this cod liver oil."

She forced open Shep's jaws and poured a large spoonful of disgusting, fishy, oily, and slightly bitter liquid down his throat.

"Ach!" He gasped and tried to back away. Elizabeth was surprisingly strong though, and gripped him between her legs, delivering another dose of the oil.

Damon had endured Shep eating all sorts of gross things, including fresh cattle dung, and the cod liver oil was every bit as bad. Despite this, he vowed to keep practicing human speech, but only when alone.

Without speech, he'd be doomed to remain a dog, and he'd never get his revenge on those responsible. He was going after them.

CHAPTER FIVE

DAMON'S ESCAPE

Although he was beginning to enjoy the rural comfort of the Giles home, Damon longed to return to his former life. He did not have a plan, but hoped to reach the Center and explain his situation to someone he knew—anyone, his friends, guards, perhaps his father. They would take him to the memory transfer unit where his memories would be retrieved from Shep and properly placed into a healthy young Underling. Correcting the mistake would allow him to resume the comfortable life he enjoyed before his body became ill.

He fell asleep that night dreaming of resuming his life as a healthy, rich Elite. Shannon would beg to have him back.

As dawn broke, Giles let him out of the door to do his business. Taking charge of Shep, Damon instead bolted across the yard in front of the house and ran under a wooden rail fence.

He ignored Giles' cries. "Get back here! Shep! Damn you, bloody dog!"

Within moments, Damon reached a dusty gravel track that ran in one direction toward the cattle pastures. In the other direction, it snaked up a hill. He'd been down the track to the cattle pastures before. It would not take him toward the Center. Instead, he turned right and ran up the hill. At the top of the hill, the track curved to the left.

This is it, I'm going the right way, he told himself. Wrong. The track stretched off for miles into the distance among golden fields of tall corn. There was a scattering of small workers' houses along the track but no sign of the Center.

With decreasing hope, he traipsed along the track for a couple of miles, cursing that he hadn't paid attention while in Giles' hovertruck. Other tracks forked off to the left or the right, but with no signs, he randomly chose which ones to take. Narrower tracks twisted down into forests or corn fields, but none of these looked to be going anywhere like the Center. Then it started to rain. A cold, relentless drizzle soaked through his fur. After two hours of water dripping off his snout, he was lost. He'd taken too many random choices at forks in the road without paying attention to any landmarks.

Then, unexpectedly, the track he was following dead-ended into a larger metal road. Embedded LED lights lit up the rainy gloom indicating he had reached an important highway. Giles had driven along a highway like this shortly before they reached the Center.

No road signs told him which way to go, but ahead in the distance to the left, the glow of a city brightened the gray clouds. Reinvigorated, he turned left and trotted toward the light.

The road left the corn fields and pastures, and cut through forest. Before long, the wall and transparent skydome with the outline of large buildings in the Center appeared. He was home again!

Approaching one of the main gates guarding the Center, Damon crouched down behind a bush for cover. The guards wouldn't allow him through the gates. Perhaps, though, he could get in through the door he and his friends had used the night of the party.

Cutting down into the forest below the track, Damon snuck around the wall. The fetid smell coming from the Underling hovels under the wall was repugnant even to Shep. He hoped none of the Underlings' dogs would catch his scent. Creeping through the undergrowth of shrubs, he was surprised how far around the wall he had to go before he reached the small door he remembered. It was just as it had been the night of the party—hidden from sight behind bushes.

He approached the door with just the gentle sound of wind rustling the leaves on the trees. Looking both directions, he approached the track skirting the wall. Seeing the coast was clear, he ran across to the door.

He hadn't paid attention to the construction of the door the night of the party, but it was heavy and robust, made from thick planks of weathered wood held together with rusted metal bands. A single, curved iron grip served as a handle. A retinal pad secured the lock.

Dismayed, he pushed the door with his snout, then leaped up to try and push it open with his front paws. It didn't budge. He leaped up a few times trying to align one of his eyes to the retinal pad but only succeeded in banging his eye sockets. The door remained closed.

Ready to give up, Damon turned to make his way back into the woods. Shep's keen hearing picked up the sound of someone walking along the trail. He dove into a bush.

His friend Petr was creeping toward the door. Stopping by the bushes covering the door, Petr looked up and down the trail a couple of times and then ducked down through the bushes. Now Damon understood how Petr knew about the gate the night of the party. This was how he snuck out of the Center to buy drugs from Underling dealers.

Petr placed his right eye against the scanner and the door creaked open. Sensing his opportunity, Damon rushed toward Petr and the open door.

"Hey Petr, it's me Damon," he barked. "C'mon, we're friends. Let me in."

"Who are you, boy?" said Petr. Damon grumbled, which came out as an unintelligible growl. Petr scratched the back of Shep's neck. "Sorry, you can't come in here, you mutt. Off you go."

Petr shoved Shep back away from the door, dashed through, and slammed the door behind him.

Damon slumped down by the closed door. How was he ever going to get into the Center? Was he ever going to become human again? Was he the only memory failure sharing a body and mind with an animal?

Not knowing what to do next, he trudged back along the track and let Shep take over. With Shep's sense of smell and innate sense of direction, he had a good idea how to get back to their Master's house.

But, it wasn't easy to get back even going in the right direction. Passing through a hamlet of a few small mean-looking houses, he was chased by a pack of local dogs. The mangy-looking crew presumably didn't get a lot of care from their Masters. The dogs he'd seen before had been pets of Elites in the Center. Elite pets were well cared for and expensively groomed. Like Shep, these dogs didn't have an ID collar. These mutts were skinny and disheveled. Wet with the rain, their ribs showed through their fur.

The five of them swarmed around him. Shep's mind allowed him to understand what they were barking about. Likewise, he growled and yipped back at them. Since neither Shep nor these dogs were sentient, their level of cognition was limited, making communication difficult. But, it surprised him to learn the extent to which dogs communicated with each other.

"What you want? Go away. We chase you." These simple phrases were repeated several times by each dog. They didn't take turns to speak and didn't seem to care what he said in response.

Through Shep, Damon barked. "I leave, let me go, no hurt."

Taking their cue, he kept barking these phrases as he ran through the village hoping they would leave him alone. They still encircled him, but they didn't attack, so long as he kept moving along the track to the outskirts of the hamlet.

After he passed the last house, the pack peeled off, leaving him alone.

"Go, no come back," they barked a few more times.

Then, they turned around and trotted back to the hamlet. Damon guessed that once he'd left their territory, he was no longer considered a threat.

The encounter unnerved him, and he had learned that interactions and communication with other animals, at least other dogs, would be difficult and dangerous. He should be careful not to enter the territory of other dogs. In such situations, he would need to rely on Shep and his innate canine abilities.

He continued trudging back home in the rain, deferring to Shep's guidance. At a gloomy section of the track that wound its way through the forest, a large, silver-gray male wolf appeared and blocked his path. Escape was impossible; there was no way he could outrun the wolf or fight him off. Damon allowed Shep to lie down on the ground and tucked in his tail. The move was one of humility, and a desire to avoid conflict.

The wolf padded toward him, head held at dominant height. His eyes gleamed like burning red coals. When he reached Damon, he licked his muzzle, making clear his alpha status. Damon quivered, worried he would lose control of his bladder.

"I'm Romolo Caccini, who are you?" the wolf said in a deep voice with surprisingly clear English.

Damon was shocked. Was the wolf the result of a failed memory transfer like him? Did he have a human mind in his animal host?

Lifting his head slightly off the ground, Damon said, "I'm Damon Taurus, what do you want?" His vocalizations in English were labored and unclear, but he hoped understandable enough.

Widening his eyes and pricking his ears forward, Romolo acted surprised to learn Damon's name but quickly recovered his composure. "Relax. I suspected that you were an animal with Elite memories when I saw your encounter with the pack of mutts in the hamlet back there. You did the right thing to keep going and not engage with them."

"Thanks. I let my host-dog take the lead. I was relieved to get away."

"Come with me." Romolo veered off the track into the forest.

Not sure, but also not willing to be alone if there were others he could connect with for help, Damon trailed well behind up a steep rocky slope. They emerged onto an open glade where the granite substrate was exposed through the sparse vegetation. The glade offered a broad view of the forest landscape below and the trees glistening in the rain. In other circumstances, Damon could have appreciated the beauty of the setting.

Romolo sat down on some rocks ignoring the drizzling rain. "Sit next to me."

Damon obeyed his commands, wondering what the wolf wanted with him.

"I'm out here looking for new animals like you. The memory transfer unit in the Center operates daily, and there's a constant stream of new animals that are recipients of Elite memories, like you and me. The memory losses have increased, with the majority being moderates who have crossed the extreme Elites led by your father, Taurus Najor and his sycophant sidekick, Shanya Tourni. But, I'm perplexed, how come your memory transfer failed? Your father must have wanted it to succeed."

Damon was unsure where this conversation was going but decided answering Romolo's questions might allow him to ask some of his own. He managed to vocalize a few breathy sentences. "I didn't tell my father I was undergoing the memory transfer. We didn't talk much. I used a borrowed ID from a moderate Elite—I imagine that was the problem."

"Unfortunately, that makes sense. Anyway, I tell all new animals like you there is no going back. Don't even think about it. The guards don't let animals into the Center. We think they'll start hunting us down soon. You wouldn't make it through the gates into the Center. You have a new life now."

Damon slouched down on the wet rock. This news was unexpected, was there really nothing they could do?

"Can't the technicians just reverse the process, pull my mind out of this dog, and transfer it into a new human host? This accidental transfer into another animal must have happened before."

"No. The memory transfer can't be reversed. We think memory transfers in animals have been going on for a while. Elites may not even know. Regardless, you are in your dog host forever now. Some have a difficult time accepting this. I saw the guards shoot and kill a bobcat who kept trying to get through the gates into the Center. He didn't believe me and was slowly going mad in his new host."

Damon dropped to a sad hunch.

Romolo went on. "Anyway, when you are ready, go deeper into the forest, and you'll be met by other animals. They will take you to join a growing group of us that are setting up an animal society. Off you go. I've got to stay on the lookout for more of us."

Romolo turned and trotted back toward the trail. Unsure what to make of this encounter, Damon gave Shep leave to get home. He wasn't ready to join other human-animals yet.

The rain drizzled down as he trudged back. He made it back to his master's house just as darkness was falling. Soaking wet, he slumped down outside the door and howled.

Elizabeth came out after a couple of minutes, looking not at all happy, "Oh. There you are. Where have you been all day? Look how wet and dirty you are. I'm not letting you inside like that."

With surprising dexterity, she grabbed Shep by the scruff and tied a thick rope around his neck. She tied the other end of the rope to an old iron ring embedded in a stone wall near the door. The ring clanged against the wall when she let go, like a gong announcing Damon's captivity.

"Let me free, you old witch," he barked. "Get me hot food and fresh coffee."

Elizabeth ignored Damon's barking. "Stay here. I'll bring out some food and water."

A few minutes later, Jacob Giles brought out a bowl of food scraps. "You poor boy. Elizabeth won't let you in tonight. Don't worry, we'll go walk around the cattle pastures tomorrow morning and you can chase rabbits."

Unhappy with his lot, Damon ate the food, grateful to fill his stomach. How he missed a hot meal. His annoying Nav at least had prepared good food.

But, he was home, so to speak, and had a lot to think about. Was he not going to be able to get back into the Center and get back into a human body? Unbelievable. The wolf said there were others like him. Should he go and find them? One thing was certain, he didn't want to spend his life as Giles and Elizabeth's dog. Sheltered under the eave of the cottage, he shivered as the rain continued through the night.

A week later, Damon made another attempt to escape, but this time, he wasn't trying to get back into the Center. Instead, he went looking for other animals like himself. *Are they really like me—a human trapped in an animal body?*

He needed to escape and find others like himself whose mind transfer went awry. *Why do I want to do this?*

Perhaps if he found out enough about the other animals, he could somehow tell the memory transfer scientists or his father more about what was going on. Admittedly, it wasn't like him, the spoiled-brat Elite kid, to be helpful to anyone but himself. He wanted to get back to his life of decadence. He would also do his best to get the technicians responsible for his memory transfer screw-up to be transferred to the lithium mines. Purely selfishly though, he needed to find out more about the outcome of the memory transfer failures. While waiting for his chance to get back into the Center, he could do this best as Shep, working with other animals.

Accompanying his master every day on rounds of the cattle pens, pastures, and the abattoir gave him the chance to make better escape plans. The best opportunity was to run off while Giles was chatting with the farm hands out by the pastures. Giles spent a lot of time gossiping with them, telling crude jokes, and paying no attention to Shep as he ran around the pastures chasing rabbits.

Ten pastures, each about five to ten acres, spread across a large area surrounding the abattoir. A good mile away the pastures ran adjacent to forest. Damon waited for a day when they were down at the bottom pasture by the forest. His plan was simple—disappear into the forest and seek other animals like him.

After a frustrating long week during which Giles spent his time idly chatting up at the top pastures by the abattoir, the opportunity to escape arrived.

The day was overcast and gray with rain drizzling down. The weather didn't bother Giles in his green waterproof waxed jacket and rubber boots. Damon wasn't keen to traipse around and get mud stuck between his claws, even though Shep didn't mind at all. Perhaps there would be more rabbits in the rain.

"Come on, Shep," Giles said. "Let's go check the cattle down in the bottom pasture."

Finally.

They made their way through the muddy fields. The cattle were standing in groups of half a dozen or so, looking forlorn and wet. A few of them were halfheartedly eating feed from troughs. If any of them were disturbed, they weren't showing it.

When they reached the bottom pasture, Giles fiddled with the gate. So Damon ducked under the fence, and dashed off into a nearby grove of trees, crashing out of sight through the shrubs bordering the woodland.

Ignoring Giles' cries to return, Damon bolted down a stream bed deep in the forest. With no ideas how to find other animals, he picked his way downstream, stepping around moss-covered rocks and checking trees for scents.

He wasn't used to the darkness of the forest. Large oak trees mixed among the smaller hickories and elms their canopy overlapped thirty feet in the air, obscuring the sky. Shafts of sunlight filtered down through the canopy, making bright spots where insects danced. A scattering of shade-loving plants like poison ivy, Virginia creeper, and an assortment of sedges huddled between the rocks on the forest floor. He found no trails, and it didn't look like anyone had been in the forest for a long time.

Without warning, a crack sounded louder than the gurgling stream. Looking over in the direction of the sound, he saw a pair of ruby-red eyes shining in the gloom of the forest. He froze, letting his eyes adjust. Less than ten feet in front of him was a large coyote. The coyote must have caught his scent.

A glance to each side and behind revealed three other coyotes.

Their hackles were up, as each growled low and aggressively. The coyotes were all about his size and weight, but he was definitely outnumbered. In a fight, Shep would be no match for one of them, let alone all three.

Were they wild coyotes about to attack, or did they have Elite memories? This could be much worse than his encounter with the pack of dogs in the village. Coyotes are natural predators and might view him as a meal.

Afraid to run and be chased down, he scratched "I'm human, help me" into the sandy bank beneath his paws. He tried to say, "hello," but his breathy, anxious vocalization was only a weak whimper.

After a long standoff, the lead coyote came over and scratched in the sand. "We too are Elites." With a nod of his head, the lead coyote motioned for Damon to follow.

They led him deeper into the woods for about a mile. They went fast, having no trouble with the rocky terrain and steep slopes. Damon struggled to keep up. One of them lingered behind, nudging his rump whenever he slowed down.

At last, they reached a dry, rocky cave that went back several feet into the base of a sandstone cliff. The cave was dark, but he could see other coyotes and bobcats moving around inside—their eyes glowed like hot coals. The number of animals in the den suggested a pack of at least a dozen. They looked wary of Damon, and he sensed they hadn't met a dog before.

Communicating with the animals was difficult at first—much as it was with the wolf Romolo. Coyotes at least are closely related to dogs—at least in the same genus—*Canis latrans* and *Canis lupus*, respectively. They communicated via their canine host, Shep in Damon's case, with yips and barks as he had with the dogs in the village.

"Me friendly, dog," Damon said.

"We friendly, coyotes," one of them said, responding in kind.

"No hurt, want friends," he replied.

"Why we friends you?" came the discouraging response.

Though semi-sentient, Shep lacked the cognitive ability to use complex words such as "Elite," or construct complex sentences. Damon was learning to take over his voice with his mind to allow for human speech in English, his native language.

Damon's human vocalizations and speech were still difficult to understand, but the coyotes had mastered an understandable human voice. At first, he responded by scratching important words into the sand around the stream that ran past their den, mixing it up with Shep's vocalizations and human language whenever possible. Scratching in the sand was difficult and time-consuming, but clearly necessary until he mastered speaking.

The animals were soon responding in English to his scratched questions and choppy vocalizations.

"Who are you?" the largest of the coyotes asked.

"Damon Najor, son of Taurus Najor, leader of the Boston Center," he grunted, scratching 'Damon', 'Najor', and 'Boston' in the sand.

"We are all Elites. We know who your father is," a bobcat replied.

Okay, I get it. They know who I am and don't trust me.

"You are welcome to stay with us while we all work out what we need to do," said another coyote.

"Welcome to stay" was just a nice way of saying "you will stay" as one or two animals were always watching Damon, or blocking his path to the cave entrance so he couldn't run off.

After some difficult days, his human voice vocalizations improved. He was now able to converse quite clearly with the others, though they had been animals longer than him and already learned how to vocalize in English. It was not like he had to learn a new language. He was making good progress in using Shep's vocal cords, voice box, lips, and tongue. Shep likely had no conscious understanding of the concepts Damon was communicating to the animals. He seemed to prefer pacing—which got blocked—or laying in a tight, nervous crouch, eyes darting from animal to animal.

The eldest coyote, Robert Giovanni, told him all the animals in the pack were the result of memory transfer failures. They had all been important, senior Elites. All were very angry about what happened.

Robert approached Damon, laying bored under a shrub gnawing on a rabbit bone. Formerly a lawyer, he explained, "I was one of your father's colleagues although I disagreed with many of his policies. My old body was ailing, and I underwent a routine memory transfer, which went wrong."

"My father mentioned you as a good colleague," Damon said. "I'm sorry the memory transfer failed for you."

"Of course, I knew the odds of failure. We all did. But we were not told it was up to five percent," Robert complained. "There's nothing we can do about our situation now, and we have to find and help others who suffered memory transfer into animals. We plan to search far and wide, and get in touch with other animal groups which may be out there."

"Yeah. I want to help," Damon said, pushing past his first selfish thought of wanting to go home. There were plenty of parties he planned to attend in his new body. He'd been looking forward to showing off the fit body and attracting plenty of young women.

"You can help us," he said. "But I remember you from the Center. You got in trouble with the security forces a few times. We need to know you're not just trying to get back into the Center with the hope of having your memories retrieved into an Underling body."

A male bobcat joined them. Sniffing the air, he circled a few times then settled down. His amber eyes were half-closed as he scanned his surroundings.

Both Robert and Damon regarded him cautiously.

"I'm Eli Ackroyd." The bobcat's voice was smooth, a sign he'd learned how to control his animal's vocal cords, folds, and voice box. "Before my body got too old, I worked with Shayna Tourni running the memory transfer units. I should have requested a memory transfer a year or two ago, before the failure rates went up. I started to notice an increase in failure rates among certain elites and made the mistake of challenging Tourni about it. She became very annoyed, telling me not to 'meddle' in things that didn't concern me. Nevertheless, I'm quite certain it is not possible to separate and pull out human memories from that of a semi-sentient animal without mental trauma to both."

"Yeah, I'm starting to get the message," Damon muttered, feeling inferior to these two forest animals, and annoyed by their unsubtle warnings.

Robert glared at him. "I am leading the animal society outside of the Center."

Yeah. He knows what I was like. Damon was going to have to behave.

"No, I get it," Damon said. "Romolo told me. I'm not planning to go back to the Center."

Robert went on. "You can help us meet more animals, especially those that are not predators like us. As coyotes and bobcats, we inspire fear in other animals when we approach them, but you'll have better luck as a sheepdog."

"My dog host lives with Jacob Giles, the manager of the local abattoir," Damon said. "Cattle were acting strange in the finishing pen, but he had no idea what caused their behavior. He was even called in for a meeting with his supervisor. The guards were suspicious about low meat yields, although he didn't think the two were related."

"Interesting. Okay, spend most of your time with him and let us know any developments by the Elites," Robert said. "Even though Giles is not an Elite, he has a senior position, and because of his job has Elite contacts."

Damon considered the other things he'd heard Giles talking about. Perhaps... "He also coordinates activism among Underling environmental groups."

"Does he now? Interesting. Again, pass on to us anything you find out that might help us."

Damon nodded thoughtfully. Staying a dog may have some advantages. He need not be such a selfish brat from now on. For the first time, his life would have purpose—he could be useful and valued by others—as he helped plan revenge on the idiots that messed up his memory transfer.

You don't mess with the son of the Center Leader and get away with it.

CHAPTER SIX

CHATURA

Chatura Singh was examining drone footage from around the New Delhi Center where he lived. The security forces dispatched drones to survey areas ahead of their patrols to identify potential threats from Underlings. The drone, flying at an altitude of 5,000 feet, provided a stunning view of small, scattered farms. A dusty-looking farmyard sprawled next to a few squalid-looking stone buildings. He knew this was where Underling farmers lived. He zoomed in. The farmyard was about a third of an acre of dusty bare soil. Weathered chest-high sandstone blocks formed a wall around the yard. A stone water trough stood in one corner. A small herd of sheep and goats milled about in the farmyard.

Normally these domestic animals didn't show any remarkable behaviors, but today, instead of grazing on the sparse tufts of grass and other plants in the yard, three or four of the mangy-looking animals paced around, pawing and scratching on the soil. Squinting, he thought the animals were writing on the ground. Crazy. But one animal would scratch out something and others would cram around looking at it before another animal took a turn. He cursed under his breath. The drone footage didn't have sufficient resolution to allow him to read the scratchings. Nevertheless, the remarkable scene suggested the animals were communicating with each other.

Domestic sheep and goats can't write.

But that's what they were doing.

He worked alone in a small, basement office of the New Delhi Center. In his office was a single Formica desk, an old swivel chair, five holoscreen monitors, and several high-powered computers linked into a remote supercomputer system. The room was dark, lit by the flickering glow of the monitors.

An Elite, Chatura was an epidemiologist tracking disease spread among Underlings. Elites didn't particularly care about the Underlings, but they did get bothered when food supplies to their Centers were threatened, or Underlings couldn't work because they were sick and dying. Diseases ran rampant among Underlings because of the global poisons they endured in the air, and their poor nutrition, receiving only the food the Centers would not take. Malnutrition, various cancers, and autoimmune diseases were common.

Most days he ran computer models and filed reports. Mornings were spent writing computer code and setting the models to run. Afternoons were spent writing reports about what the models showed. He would then send off his reports to his supervisor and move on to the next project. Rarely did he hear back from his supervisor, but he presumed that his reports were okay. Twenty-three years old and single, he lived and worked alone from his apartment. But he was content. Socially awkward, the solitary life suited him well.

Disease tracking didn't take too much of his time, so he 'dabbled' in other projects that provided him opportunities to write computer code. Recently, he had been made aware of increases in failed memory transfers from reports circulating in chat rooms among the computer modeling and gaming community.

From what he'd seen on the drone feed, there was more truth than rumors to the reports that feed animals, like cows and goats, were showing strange behavior.

Investigating these phenomena took ingenuity. Using the archived drone video footage from around Centers on the days following memory transfers, he counted the number of 'agitated' animals. For counting purposes, he defined an agitated animal as one showing unusual behavior different from other animals of the same species in the area. These behaviors included obvious things, such as running around in a circle, trying to escape pens, and this last observed behavior of scratching marks or digging into the ground.

He was now fairly certain the animals were writing messages.

Interpreting his models was outside of his experience. He shrugged, passed on the findings to his supervisor, and moved back to playing computer games while waiting for the next epidemiology model to run.

———•◦•———

Two days later, Chatura's game play was interrupted by a soft digital chime and the rhythmic pulsing of his largest holoscreen.

His Nav announced, "You have an urgent holo-conference request from Shanya Tourni. Do you wish to take the call?"

He had never met Tourni before. The senior Elite, however, was Director of the memory transfer project at the Boston Center. That she was requesting to meet with him made him anxious.

He bit his lip and then spoke with forced brightness. "Of course, I'll take the call."

In a three-dimensional image, Shanya Tourni appeared dressed in a white lab coat over dark slacks and a beige shirt. Her dark hair was pulled back into a tight bun.

"Chatura Singh, I'm a neuroscientist, not an epidemiologist, statistician, or modeler like you. Please explain to me in simple terms the findings you passed on to your supervisor."

He gulped. His report had been passed up the chain to Shanya Tourni?

Chatura was nervous talking to such a senior Elite, and he generally had a difficult time communicating verbally with other people, especially women. Tourni's slim Underling body wasn't much older than his, and she projected confidence, suggesting a no-nonsense sort of person.

Without looking Tourni directly in the eye, and while rearranging a set of pens on his desk, he began his explanation of his process. "I, um, downloaded 150 years of anonymized memory transfer records from each Center, separating successful transfers from failures. Plotting transfers against time, I fitted Lowess smoothing curves to the scatterplots to visualize the shape of the relationships—"

"Wait." She held up her hand. "Just tell me what it showed. I don't need you to repeat the details from your report."

"All right, less details. Okay, the logistic curve, that was the first graph, means the rate of unsuccessful memory loss transfers was increasing very fast. Doubling every month over the last three months before stabilizing around five percent. An increase from the usual one percent may not seem like much, but it is statistically significant. The curve was the same at each site across the globe. When the curves were superimposed on top of each other, they overlapped completely with identical regression slopes and coefficients. I used different colors for each site to make them easier to see. It was a global pattern and—"

She cut him off again. "What else?"

He felt himself begin to sweat. "Um, yes, I've been looking at drone footage of animals around the Centers. Er, the electromag drones have ten-centimeter resolution sensors across the visible, infrared, and far-red frequencies, allowing a multitude of images to be examined, and optimizing wavelength ratios for different purposes—"

"Stop," Tourni yelled. "Get to the point."

"Right." He swallowed and drew in a calming breath. "I can track and graph animal numbers."

"Okay," interrupted Tourni. "I get it. What about the animal graph?"

"Ah, yes, that was hard to plot. I had problems finding agitated animals in the drone footage, especially when they flew or ran into forests. Dolphins tended to dive down into the ocean and out of sight. But I used a training data set of twenty percent of the data, and a machine learning algorithm to conduct a Liposki classification, that allowed me to—"

"Okay," said Tourni even less patiently. "Agitated animals? Can you get to the point please, Chatura?"

"Yes, of course. The graph plots the dates of memory losses against the dates of agitated animal observations. Simply put, for every lost memory transfer, there is an agitated animal—an animal acting strange. These behaviors include things such as running around in a circle, trying to escape pens, and scratching marks or digging into the ground. Cattle were pacing in a pen outside an abattoir near the Boston Center, reindeer were racing across the frozen tundra around the Helsinki Center, and dolphins were swimming in circles in the bay outside the Melbourne Center. The parliament of rooks living around the London Center was unsettled, and horses were galloping in crazy circles on pampas near the Buenos Aires Center. The animals were writing messages on the ground."

"Okay, that's enough detail, but animals writing on the ground?" Tourni's dark eyebrows arched upward and soft creases appeared on her forehead.

"Yes, but I couldn't read them. Anyway, there's a lag. The agitated animals didn't start to appear until two weeks after the memory losses started to increase."

"I don't see how that's relevant. Anyway, what animals are you talking about that are getting—what did you call it?—agitated."

"Well, I looked at several and of course, I couldn't see small animals like rats, mice, or snakes, and of course not insects, which are too small to see on the footage—"

"I appreciate that, Chatura," interrupted Tourni. "What sort of animal?"

"Semi-sentient animals. Animals that have an ability to feel and sense their surroundings, and have a conscious awareness. Dogs, horses, cows, sheep, goats, many birds such as crows, that sort of thing. Even dolphins. Small animals and insects are unlikely to be affected."

Tourni sat further forward in her chair. His palms started to sweat, as he felt she was getting closer, towering over him. Damp patches spread in the armpits of his T-shirt.

"You mean for every memory transfer loss, there's a semi-sentient animal reacting to the failed transfer?"

"Yes, there is now. There wasn't at first, but there is now. Of course, as the philosopher David Hume suggested, correlation doesn't mean causation. The relationship between the two may not mean anything."

"If I didn't know you were being serious, I'd think you were joking," she said.

"Err, no," he said, confused.

"Okay, I know this isn't funny. Chatura, report back to me when you know more about what these animals are doing." Her hologram disappeared as she left their meeting.

After his awkward call with Tourni, Chatura's curiosity was piqued again during the review of drone footage. Over the next few days, he found footage with good enough resolution to examine the scratches on the soil made by some of the agitated animals, including cattle in the pen outside the Boston Center, and the rooks arranging twigs on the ground near the London Center. The scratches and twigs formed letters that resembled some English words.

Array Wah - Wow, in his native Hindi. *How could animals be writing in English?*

Chatura was surprised and appalled as it seemed there was only one conclusion—some humans were now animals.

Could he do something to help?

His orders were to report to Tourni. So, though nervous, Chatura called the Boston Center's memory transfer director. He had never initiated a holo-call with a medical director as high up as Tourni. At best, he'd called for a check-up with his own Center's doctors. He ran his hands through his dark hair to smooth it down, and hoped he wouldn't look too disheveled. His hair was kept fairly long, only giving himself a buzz cut every six months. Today he wore one of his treasured black

T-shirts showing a bright image of Qualar, one of his favorite video game characters.

With the twelve-hour time difference between New Delhi and Boston, it was early afternoon for Chatura, and the middle of the night for Tourni. He was surprised when she answered immediately. Her hologram showed her still dressed sensibly for work, a light blue blouse buttoned up to the top under her starched white lab coat. She must have been working late in her office, though she still looked as prim and proper as ever.

"How can I help you, Chatura? Is this to do with the agitated animals?" she said.

"You asked me to report back when I had more information." He fought to keep his responses short, remembering how upset she had been when he rambled. But it was hard.

Tourni looked questioningly at Chatura.

She raised her eyebrows. "What have you found out?"

"Ah, yes." He wiped his hands on his pants. "I, uh, I've been examining high-resolution drone footage of animals around some of the Centers." He found comfort in details, and continued. "At 5,000 feet on clear days, the drone's sensors can distinguish things only a few inches apart." He smiled, hoping she might smile back. "It is amazing. You should take a look at it. I can share my screen and show you some images—"

"I'm sure it's excellent footage," she said. After a pause, Tourni continued. "And I trust your interpretation. Get to the point. What have you found out?"

Chatura almost bit his tongue. He'd rambled again. "Right, sorry. I can see groups of animals writing on the ground with their paws and hooves."

"What were they writing?"

"They were asking for help with words and phrases like 'SOS', 'we are human', 'we are Elites'." He took a breath, fighting the urge to give her a complete run down of every word and phrase he'd been able to identify.

He couldn't gauge Tourni's reaction. Her expression remained tight, seemingly unmoved.

He continued. "There is something weird going on. Is it possible that memories from Elites suffering lost memory transfers have ended up in these animals? Are these animals now sentient, not semi-sentient like they were before, but now fully conscious?"

Tourni's brown eyes had widened the longer he spoke and he worried her next words would be to tell him to get to the point. But he didn't know that he had a point, just questions.

"I don't see how it can be possible," she finally responded. "Animals can't acquire language. And they certainly can't write, except a few primates making a few marks with sticks."

That wasn't really what he'd said; what if the animals had been given human thoughts? But he didn't know how to say that any other way.

Tourni, in any case, didn't seem to be listening. "The Elites in the Centers will be furious if it's even suggested their memories are transferring into animals."

Chatura agreed that was probably a fair conclusion, but he didn't say so, intimidated by her angry glare. Like he was at fault somehow.

She slashed at the air. "And who knows how the Underling families will react if they learn their sons and daughters taken from them as babies and raised in farms have been sacrificed on some animals."

Chatura had thought about this himself. "Underling honor is supposed to come from knowing that your family member is now physically, if not mentally, an Elite. Who wants double food rations, occasional meat, and a higher place on the housing list if your Underling family member's body is a vegetable? I never considered Underling Honor status to be worth it. This would make it even worse."

"Careful, Chatura. Speaking like that is dangerous," said Tourni. "Anyway, don't mention this to anyone."

Who would he tell? Working from home, Chatura barely even called the other data analysts colleagues, much less friends.

Hologram-Tourni rested her forehead in the palm of her right hand. "I've had enough problems keeping the memory transfer program going at the Boston Center. The electrical supply to the facility has been intermittent and Elites have been complaining about their place in line for memory transfers. We've also had problems getting a good supply of healthy Underlings from the farms. So many are undernourished and less healthy than the Elites whose memories they are supposed to receive."

Silence fell between them for a long moment as Chatura tried to think of something to say. Tourni was right; things were really not good.

"I'll take care of it," Tourni said abruptly.

He straightened. "Shall I continue monitoring agitated animals?"

"Yes, please. And let me know again if anything changes. Thanks, Chatura, you're doing a good job."

Her hologram dimmed, and she left the meeting.

"Bye," he said to the dead air.

Chatura was surprised Tourni had said so much about the problems going on. Was she stressed or unconcerned? Awkward socially, he had such a hard time understanding people sometimes. Which was why he preferred staying home.

In a state of nervous shock from the meeting, but pleased with the compliment about his work, Chatura ignored the disease model that had finished running and watched more drone footage of the agitated animals.

———◆◇◆———

Chatura's follow-up reports to Tourni had revealed agitated animals trying to communicate around all ten Centers worldwide.

A possible solution clearly lay in trying to get hold of one or more of the agitated animals and scanning for the memories of Elites. But how could she do that without explaining her theory to the technicians? After three days, she realized she had to convince Najor that this was the approach they needed.

She met with Najor in his office. On his desk were several small holograms of his son Damon when he had been still young and in good health. Her gaze drifted over images of the boy with his friends or his father in the countryside around several Centers in different parts of the world. In one, he was riding an elephant. That had to be near New Delhi. He looked relaxed, wearing a wide grin as he sat upright in the howdah atop the elephant's back, holding the wooden rails for balance. In another, he had posed alongside a lion he had shot. He grasped the animal's mane with one hand, pulling up its head, and gripped the stock of a big game rifle in his other hand. His father crouched on the other side of the dead animal looking proudly at the camera. Tourni wasn't comfortable with such displays of wealth and decadence, and she opposed hunting game animals for pleasure, but she could understand Najor's grief at the loss of his son.

Najor looked up from his desk as she came in and sat down. "Did we have an appointment? What do you want?"

Ignoring his brusque manner, Tourni said, "One of my computer experts has been reviewing drone footage of what we are calling agitated animals around Centers. These animals are scratching out messages on the ground, seeking help."

"Well, there have been reports of cattle acting strange around our Center, but my head of food security dismissed them."

She shook her head. "I believe it is a serious issue. We think the lost memory signals have ended up in the minds of these animals. Since they were semi-sentient, they were able to receive the memory signals, just like a wiped Underling mind."

"That's absurd! Why would we be just seeing this now?"

"We don't know. It's a new development, but it is happening. It must be related to how the memories are being lost from the memory transfer units. With respect, sir, I recommend the memory transfer program is stopped, or at least halted, until we can work out how to stop the agitated animal problem."

Najor looked haggard, unshaven. Even his bespoke Saville Row suit imported from London Center was wrinkled. Despite his obvious grief over the loss of his son, Najor looked visibly annoyed with Tourni's suggestion.

He leaned forward in his chair, the veins in his neck straining, and pointed a finger at her. "The program must not stop. Deliberate memory loss was the idea of my bloody father-in-law Sydney double-barreled Fortesque-Hamilton, the leader of the London Center. God, that man is an annoying little shit. I don't know why I ever agreed to marry his daughter after Damon's mother died. The agitated animals were not part of the new policy. And neither was the loss of my son's memories."

"We did agree to his policy, sir," said Tourni. *I know what you mean about his stuck-up daughter.* She'd met Viola Najor, nee Fortesque-Hamilton, as a young woman.

"Yes, yes, I know," he barked. "But don't share the increased memory loss rate or this animal problem with other Elites." He shooed her out with an impatient wave of his hand.

"But, sir. We're already spreading problems with the memory transfer program. There is dissatisfaction that too many loved ones aren't coming through the procedure."

"You're the medical director, fix the problem." His tone was flat, making it an order.

"Sir, but we agreed the policy was necessary."

"Enough!" Najor jumped up to his feet. "I'll have you arrested on subordination charges."

He leaned forward over his desk until his face was just inches from hers. A pungent smell of onions from his lunch, mixed with stale coffee made it almost impossible to stay close. She held her breath as he yelled.

"I'll instruct the security forces to kill all these damned agitated animals. I'll send out guards around our Center to track down and exterminate them. The other Leaders will be told in our Council meeting tomorrow to do the same around their Centers."

Tourni moved back as far as she could in her chair. "What? What about your son? He may one of the animals you order killed!"

"For God's sake! We need to get rid of any evidence that Elite memories are ending up in animals. The failed memory transfers must be described as exactly that, failures. That's the whole point. It's a technology issue. There are a lot of weak-minded Elites I need to get rid of."

Tourni jumped up and ran out of the meeting, shocked at Najor's plan. She hadn't considered memory losses as death, just ... ceasing. But killing the agitated animals knowing what they knew was cold-blooded. None of this was going to end well. Najor was going too far. She needed to protect herself and her father—screw Najor. That he wasn't even going to let her try something to find his son's memories in the animals... Well, cruel seemed too simple a word.

—◆◦◆—

The next day, Chatura attended the council meeting Najor convened with Elite Center leaders and their staff. As a senior analyst, Chatura's role was to support the New Delhi Center leader, Rajid Khan. He was nervous as he hadn't yet reported to Khan about the seeming link between agitated animals and the failed memory transfers.

The meeting was held in a large conference room in holospace adorned with traditional oak-paneled walls, a polished central table, and a leather-upholstered chair for each Center leader. Supporting staff sat in two circles of wooden chairs behind their respective leaders.

Everybody attended as a dynamic hologram making it look like they were all in the room. Chatura's hologram allowed him to move around in the room. But he was too junior to have speaking privileges. He had been assigned a chair against the wall, two rows behind Kahn.

Najor chaired the meeting. He came into the room late, looking angry and impatient. A harassed-looking staff member behind him received the brunt of his anger, and was asked repeatedly to project one report or another on the holoscreen in the center of the room.

After routine business had been concluded, Najor glared at Tourni and asked for her report. She slowly stood up, eyes darting back and forth from one person to another. She gave a short, terse presentation on memory losses and the agitated animals, recounting many of the observations Chatura had passed to her. It surprised him to see his graphs and data showing increasing numbers of memory losses and agitated animals hovering in holospace for all to see. Now he understood why she had asked him to attend the meeting.

Najor interrupted Tourni. "These agitated animals are a problem that needs to be dealt with swiftly."

When Tourni sat down, her face was dark with fury.

A tall, gruff mountain of a man stood and towered over the people to either side. His name plate read, "Major Gorham Kalinski, Boston Center, head of security." Najor gave a sharp nod, giving him permission to speak.

"My guard patrols have encountered groups of these animals outside our Center. They seem to be organizing and have shown aggressive behavior toward the guards. I've ordered my guards—"

"Wait!" Najor yelled, interrupting Kalinski. "How can animals that hunters are used to taking turn on and threaten trained guards?"

Chatura was seated close to Tourni. Moving his hologram into the same space as hers, he sent her a private message: "*Their human minds, with the natural hunting skills of their animal hosts, allow them to anticipate and outwit our guards.*"

Her eyes widened, as they had in his meeting with her, but Tourni dipped her head and passed on Chatura's thoughts to the group. She added, "A couple of guards undergoing memory transfer were recently lost. Their minds may have been transferred to animals outside the Center. As animals, these guards may be coordinating other animals with human memories."

Several leaders of the other Centers rose in outrage, spluttering about this "crazy news!" and "that can't be possible!" "The Elites were lost!"

"That's ridiculous," exclaimed Bruce Matton, the leader of the Melbourne Center. "There's no way the memory transfers at my Center are losing memories like that, let alone allowing the memories to be transferred into a bunch of kangaroos and dingoes roaming around the local bush."

Tourni countered. "Leader Matton, everyone has agitated animals around their Centers."

Rajid Khan turned around to Chatura, two rows behind him. He mouthed silently. "What? Why didn't you brief me?"

Chatura bowed his head, raising his eyes to Khan, mouthing, "I, err. I um. Sorry." *Shit, didn't he see my reports to Tourni?*

The discussion among Center leaders continued.

"Although it doesn't sound credible, it would explain the unusual behavior of tigers, Giant pandas, muntjacs, and other animals around my Center, " said Bin You, leader of the Shanghai Center.

Sydney Fortesque-Hamilton, leader of the London Center, was more dismissive. "Around my Center, we've been saying that our recent memory losses were the result of technical problems. I have staff looking into it, but I too find it difficult to believe that lost memories are now in a bunch of bloody foxes and badgers."

Tourni gave Fortesque-Hamilton a look of disbelief, then jumped back into the argument showing more confidence than Chatura expected. "The evidence is clear. Many of the lost memories from moderate Elites were transferred into semi-sentient animals around all of the Centers."

Directing her comments to the Center leaders, she reiterated. "You all have agitated animals around your Centers."

Bin You asked, "Can we capture the animals and retrieve their memories back into humans?"

Tourni shook her head, glancing at Najor briefly. "We've tried a few things. The technology we'd need to establish to find that out would take too long."

Fortesque-Hamilton jumped in. "You heard her. It would take too long. The problem now is to get rid of these animals."

Tourni looked impatient. "Correct, as Major Kalinski said, these animals are a threat to our guards and any Elites working outside our Centers."

The Center leaders looked around at each other with anxious, befuddled expressions. Chatura was bothered by their lack of leadership in an uncomfortable silence.

Abruptly, Najor stood, his face flushed red with fury. "Center Leaders and Tourni, into my private office. Now." His hologram froze and grayed out, indicating he had left the conference room holospace but was still online elsewhere.

The other Center leaders' holograms went gray one by one.

"What's going on? What's this about moderate Elites?" murmured Chatura to one of the other staff members still sitting in the holospace.

"I dunno. I bet some of the Center Leaders know more about these memory losses than they want to share."

"What more could there be? If Fortesque-Hamilton wanted to get rid of some Elites, why not just kill them or have them disappear to the mines?"

"Too obvious," said the other staff member. "He wants deniability, putting the blame onto technical problems."

An uncomfortable silence descended on the room. Chatura hadn't thought about the animals being the Elites that Fortesque-Hamilton wanted killed. He darted his eyes around, anxious. The other staff members sat in a tense silence.

Ten long minutes later, Najor, Tourni, and the Center Leaders reappeared back in their chairs. Najor had a grim look on his face, but he
still looked angry. The other Center leaders looked like scolded school
children. Tourni avoided eye contact with other people in the room,
examining her fingernails.

"We will kill all the agitated animals and continue the memory transfer
program." Najor barked the order, the veins in his neck bulging. "If
it becomes public knowledge, Tourni will work with staff at memory
transfer units at other Centers to ensure acceptable levels of loss, and stop
the transfer into animals." He turned to his head of security. "Kalinski,
shoot to kill. Get onto it. Immediately."

The holograms in Najor's conference room flickered as the other
leaders looked away from their cameras. Tourni's face stayed dark, with
clearly suppressed anger.

This is going to make everything worse.

Najor's hologram flashed off, ending the meeting.

Why is he so bothered about the agitated animals?

———————•◦•———————

Chapter Seven

SHOOT TO KILL

R obert was right, Damon didn't inspire as much fear in other animals as the predatory coyotes.

A few days later, he called him over. "Damon, we got word of a group of five horses nearby. You are going to help us talk with them."

"Yeah, sure," he replied. "What do want me to do?"

"Approach them first, get their trust, then a couple of coyotes and I can talk with them," he said.

Damon wasn't too comfortable around Robert, worrying he would tell the others too much about his youthful activities. He also wasn't keen on Robert's leadership style. It reminded him too much of his father's aggressive approach to dealing with people.

Nevertheless, a few hours later, after an uneventful trek through the forest, Robert, two other coyotes, and Damon approached a field of five horses over on the east side of the Boston Center. The field was a typical pasture of grazed-down grasses with a scattering of stubborn thistles ignored by the horses and a few battered woody shrubs.

The coyotes and dog lay down within a thicket of shrubs at the bottom of the field, downwind of the horses so they wouldn't scent them.

Robert addressed one of the two coyotes. "Keely, you scouted the area. What are we looking at?"

"At the top of the field there are five horses we think have received Elite memories. They are American Quarter horses, a popular breed kept for riding. The building is where they are cared for by Underling stable hands. Elites come here when they want to ride the horses."

"Where are the stable hands?" asked Damon.

"There's no one here now as their work is done for the day."

"Okay," said Robert. "Damon, approach the horses with care and see if you can talk to them."

The coyotes stayed back at the far end of the field, hunkered down in a clump of sumac while Damon crept along the edge of the field toward the horses. Seeing him, they backed up into a tight group against the wood rail fence in the top corner of the field. He stopped when he was close and lay down, creating what he hoped would be a nonthreatening posture. He was still coming to terms with being a medium-sized dog. The thousand-pound 15 hand-high horses loomed over him.

Clearly, the horses were nervous about Damon, but they would have been more terrified of the coyotes. The long muscles in their upper legs quivered. The whites of their eyes were more visible than usual, contrasting with the dark color of their irises as their facial muscles tensed.

With considerable effort that strained his throat, he rasped out enough of a greeting to calm them down. "Hey, don't be ah...f—." He growled in frustration. Bad move. The horses pawed the ground. "Fraid," he said. "I'm Damon Najor, trapped inside this dog. Like you, my mem'ry transfer fay-failed." He huffed. "I'm looking for others."

The horses' heads cocked and they stopped pawing the ground.

Their mouths moved, but Damon wasn't sure if they would be able to speak.

Slowly, through a combination of fragmented English, neighs, whinnies, and snorts, some of which he found tricky to understand, along with scratched words into the dirt, the horses told him their story.

"We are memory transfer failures," said a male, chestnut-colored horse.

"From the same transfer pod two weeks ago," said another who was female, and more of a bay color.

"All of us are Elites," added the chestnut horse.

Not having any experience with horses, Damon used color to distinguish them, although all were different shades of brown.

They started to relax as they conversed. By the time the conversation was done, they were in a looser cluster. The two horses who had been talking had separated a bit from the other three who were smaller and perhaps younger.

The chestnut horse spoke. "I'm an Elite elder, Archibald 'Archie' Blankenship. Damon, I knew your father from serving on the Elite council, but of late I questioned his aggressive leadership style. He often spoke about you."

"Oh, pleased to meet you." Damon felt nervous about meeting another Elite who would know who he was. That he was also quick to criticize his father didn't sit well either. What had his father told his colleagues about him? No doubt his entitled lifestyle was well known to all of them.

"Can I introduce my coyote friends and invite them to join us?" Damon asked.

"Coyotes are predators, like wild dogs. Why should we trust any of you?" said the bay horse.

"We are all Elites with memories transferred into animal hosts," he replied. "We control our animal host, just like you do. The coyotes will not harm you."

With this assurance, the horses agreed to allow the coyotes to approach them.

Damon called out, "Robert, come on over, slowly."

The three coyotes emerged from the shrubs at the other end of the field where they had been camouflaged. Robert led the tight group. Damon remained about ten feet away; the coyotes stopped behind him, now about fifteen feet from the horses.

"I could hear most of what Damon was saying." Robert spoke from the front of the group. "I'm Robert Giovanni; pleased to see you, Archie. It's not been too long since we were sitting around the table in the council room."

Once they got talking, the horses' English language pronunciation improved, and it didn't take long to explain what had been going on. The horses were just as angry as the rest of the animals about what had happened.

"Najor has a 'you are with me or against me' style that several of us disagreed with," Archie said. "There were rumblings about proposing a vote of no confidence. But, like Robert, my body was wearing out with age, and I stepped away from the Council to get my memory transfer procedure taken care of. And look what happened."

"Same for me," added the chestnut horse. "I'm Marta McNeal. I worked in the power plant in the Center and was looking forward to a new body. Since we became horses, the five of us have been feeling more and more that Najor and the memory transfer unit should have seen this problem coming. Where were the safety checks on the process?"

'It's all very well to blame Najor," said Robert, "but he's an administrator. I think more blame should be on his chief scientist Shanya Tourni and her team of memory transfer technicians. She developed the memory transfer process and runs the unit."

"All blame aside, what's been done to help us?" said Archie.

"What can be done? Do they even know what happened and where we are?" asked Robert.

As a first-body youngster, Damon kept quiet during this conversation. The increasing anger among the coyotes and horses was clear. *What could be done?*

"Right now, we are trying to get in contact with as many animals like us as possible so we can work together," said Robert.

"We don't know what plans Najor or the Elites have for us, but we need to be ready," said one of the other coyotes.

Two birds, peregrine falcons, with sleek, bluish-gray plumage, white faces, and fine barring on their undersides, came down, landing on the ground between the coyotes and the horses. Their landing sent up a cloud of dust on the dry soil and everyone stepped back in surprise.

They started scratching messages in the mud.

One of the birds scratched, "I'm human."

The other scratched, "We're Elites."

It took a while to work out an efficient way of communicating. However, before long the birds became proficient at human vocalizations, sounding much like pet parrots.

"I'm Captain Bruce White. The two of us were senior officers in the Elite security force," squawked one of the falcons in an energetic and high-pitched voice. "We suffered serious wounds from an explosion during a training exercise and were leapfrogged to the front of the memory transfer waiting list. They managed to capture our memories before our bodies succumbed to our injuries. To our dismay, the transfer process didn't work out. We both ended up in these falcon bodies."

"And, I'm Captain Helen Chartain. We're upset about how the memory transfer procedure turned out, but we are relieved to contact others like us," explained the other falcon. "We've seen guards killing animals. We didn't realize at first that the animals had the lost memories of Elites until we put two and two together."

"Wow!" Damon said. "Your human speech is excellent. How were you able to learn to speak so fast? It took me several days to learn to say my first word."

Helen looked at Damon as though he was a small mammal she was about to eat. "I used to breed parrots as a hobby. Birds have a specialized vocal organ called a syrinx to produce a wide range of sounds and mimic human speech. Since we became falcons three weeks ago, Bruce and I have been learning to talk together. But this is our first conversation with other animals. I'm pleased we are doing okay."

Fair enough, clever sticks. I got the sense Helen and I weren't going to become besties. I wonder if Helen and Bruce are an item?

"Getting back to the guards killing animals," continued Bruce. "Helen and I had been speaking out to our superior officers and complaining about the new shoot-to-kill policy we had been told to follow."

"Wait. What? A shoot-to-kill policy?" said Robert.

"Yes," continued Bruce. "We had ignored warnings not to question our orders and refused to tell the guards under our command to kill animals. Although many people in the Center had learned about an increase in the number of lost memories, everyone claimed they had no idea why or if lost memories were retrievable. We had been ordered to kill suspicious animals. We think our memories were lost intentionally because we disobeyed. It wasn't until we woke up as birds and talked to each other that we put the pieces together."

Robert agreed, "As you both may know, Isaac Mallory was the senior Elite who used to run the security force. However, all these memory losses and the animals with Elite memories came about after he went on sick leave and needed a memory transfer. He had spoken against Najor's policies, but from his sick bed in the hospital he was ignored by Kalinksi, who took over his job. Isaac is one of the coyotes in our group."

Archie asked, "Does Najor and the Elite Council know that animals like us are from memory transfer losses?"

"They only claimed disease," said Bruce. "But there's too many of us who objected to a political situation for it to just be a coincidence. It does seem they are trying to get rid of people with opposing views through memory transfer failures. But, if we are still alive as animals, then they would view us as a threat."

Everyone nodded in sad agreement.

"This is a very worrying development," said Robert.

Damon slouched to the ground, closing his eyes. *Wake up Robert, this is more than just worrying. I was about to die of a disease but signed up for a memory transfer using an ID from a moderate Elite. Now I'm an animal about to be killed by my father's security forces. Can life get much worse?*

Evelyn Sinclair, one of the other coyotes, asked, "Bruce and Helen, can you help us with aerial reconnaissance and long-distance networking? I was a school biology teacher in the Center. Raptors like you can hover and travel considerable distances without expending much effort."

Bruce and Helen glanced at each other.

"Yes," said Bruce. "I've found that my falcon host can hover in place while hunting for prey. In fact, we were hovering high above you for quite a while before swooping down at high speed. Our abilities would be useful for reconnaissance of guard patrols."

Helen added, "I've found that my host can take advantage of different speeds and directions of wind flows to gain altitude without flapping my wings. It feels amazing to just hover and swoop around. As you suggest, that helps with traveling long distances."

Bruce spread his wings, showing off his forty-inch wingspan. "Flying makes me feel like Icarus before he flew too close to the sun and the wax on his wings melted."

Evelyn wagged her tail excitedly. "That's just as I remember from the textbooks. I don't mean the Greek mythology, but your technique of diving at speeds of up to 200 miles per hour is called a stoop, and staying aloft without flapping your wings is called dynamic soaring. You are like living drones!"

Bruce and Helen glared at Evelyn with their piercing eyes, suggesting they weren't too happy with her choice of analogy.

"Okay, Evelyn," said Robert. "That's quite enough technical detail. I want you two to help us set up an avian network."

Damon wrinkled his nose at Robert's assertiveness. The man—er, coyote—was starting to remind him of his father.

"Err, sure," both birds said at the same time.

Bruce added, "It's good that our falcon hosts have skills we can contribute."

Helen started listing ways to set up the avian network. "We need to enlist a variety of other types of birds with different skills, such as birds of prey, crows, rooks, and migratory swallows. Even house martins can travel between the Centers around the world. They can carry messages between animal groups."

"Can you find all those different types of birds with human memories?" asked Damon.

"I don't see why not," replied Helen. "The main thing will be to find birds that can fly long distances."

"Right," said Bruce. "And, with our security force background, you and I can help anticipate the tactics of the guards. Heck, we know the other captains, and we trained many of the lower ranks."

"Brilliant," said Damon. "We'll have a tremendous advantage in future encounters with the guards."

Damon worried when three coyotes who had been hunting rabbits near the river didn't return to the den.

As the evening drew in, Bruce swooped down to where Damon and several of the animals were resting. The low sun was casting long shadows. Grateful for his enhanced canine vision to see in the gloom, he looked around in the gloom.

"The coyotes had no chance," reported Bruce. "I was hovering overhead and saw the whole episode."

"Why didn't they escape?" asked Damon.

"Not possible. They were in thick brush and didn't see the guards until it was too late. Without warning, they were shot like pigs in a slaughterhouse."

Damon shook his head. "Confirming the shoot-to-kill policy."

Hearing the discussion, Robert wandered over. "From now on, we have to meet guard patrols with deadly force. Bruce, I want you and Helen to organize five-to-six member animal teams, led by experienced natural hunters such as wolves, coyotes, or bobcats. Smaller animals such as skunks and dogs, including you Damon, will be assigned support roles such as scouting and reconnaissance."

"Okay, we can do that," chirped Bruce. "We can organize training sessions where we practice chasing down guards in the forest glades a safe distance from the Center."

These activities gave Damon something positive to focus on since he still struggled in his new life as a dog.

"Our avian network will provide aerial reconnaissance and pass on observations to animal scouts on the ground," said Helen. "We've also learned from our global network of avian partners that similar run-ins with guards have been happening worldwide around the other nine Centers."

"Interesting," replied Robert.

Bruce said, "A few animals were killed in these skirmishes, but in most cases the patrols suffered huge, often total losses. A herd of reindeer that was being tracked by guards across the tundra near the Helsinki Center turned on them, killing them all. Wolves had been training the reindeer, and led them in these retaliatory attacks."

Robert snarled. "Excellent, under my leadership we can do that, too. Can't we, den members?"

Arrogant bastard. Damon widened his eyes, raised his brows, and looked at Danny, wondering if he shared his thoughts about Robert.

———◦———

A couple of days after the slaughter of the three coyotes, Damon was with Robert and two other coyotes, Jerry McPherson, a bobcat, and Merrill Johnson, a skunk. On a routine reconnaissance, they hoped to contact new animals near the Center.

"Okay, we move now," whispered Robert. "Stay inside the edge of the forest using the bushes as cover."

Damon scouted ahead of the team, finding a human patrol. Racing back, he barked the alarm. "Watch out! A patrol of a dozen guards moving up the slope."

The guards were well-armed with weapons drawn. They started firing as they came into view of the animals.

"Back into the forest," yelled Robert. "Circle back and we can come out behind the guards. Then I will lead the attack."

Following Robert's direction, they crept through the brush until they were behind the guards. Robert moved in fast with Jerry close behind. They allowed their coyote and bobcat body hosts free rein in the hunt. Robert covered a lot of ground with his bouncy stride and quickly closed in on the guards. By contrast, Jerry ran at and chased the guards, causing them to stumble as they couldn't get their weapons up and instead turned to run.

Jerry and Robert took down the two lagging guards with swift, lethal bites to the back of the neck. Before the rest knew what was going on, Damon, Merrill, and the other two coyotes followed Jerry and Robert, chasing down the other three guards. Damon ran alongside Jerry and Robert, snarling and growling. He didn't have the natural predatory skills to attack the guards, but barked loud and ferocious enough to scare them. As a sheepdog, he used Shep's herding skills to send them running in the right direction, closer to Jerry and Robert. Natural predators, they dispatched the guards easily.

It was a gruesome sight even though the guards were killed fast, with a minimal loss of blood.

After all the guards were down and dispatched, the animals grasped the bodies between their jaws and dragged them into the forest. Using their paws, they scratched out a shallow mass grave in the soil and buried them, covering the grave with rocks and branches. They had enough control over their animal hosts so they didn't scavenge the bodies. Damon expected any passing coyotes that did not have Elite minds would take advantage of the find.

Trotting back to their den in the forest after the hunt, Robert commented, "We did well today and we had the element of surprise. I'm not keen on killing humans, but it is necessary."

Jerry said, "Killing people is not my thing at all. As a former journalist, I'm more used to fighting my battles with words. I feel quite sick. I'm not sure I can do this again."

"You did great," snarled Robert. "Get used to it. Allowing our host animals to use their natural predator skills worked out well."

"I sensed my host bobcat wanted to eat the dead guards."

"Be strong," said Robert, sounding impatient. "I was able to keep my host coyote from eating the flesh of the dead guards without any problems. Killing them is bad enough, and we can't allow our hosts to scavenge on the bodies."

"I'm glad to hear that, Robert," said Merrill. "As a skunk, I'm omnivorous, but my prey is limited to small animals such as cockroaches, beetles, grasshoppers, and spiders. I would find the consumption of human remains by any of us to be very worrying."

"Don't worry," said Robert. "Eating the guards is off limits, although I am looking forward to feasting on rabbit tonight."

<hr />

Knowledge of the shoot-to-kill policy made Damon worry even more about how his new life was turning out. He had hoped the growing animal community would be left alone by the humans and allowed to develop without interference. It was difficult to comprehend such sickening violence against the animals, especially since the dead coyotes had been Elites, perhaps even colleagues, friends, or family of the guards.

While Robert, Jerry, and some of the others treated Damon like the youngster he was, he became friendly with others. In particular, Danny Ramos, a young wolf. The two of them often hung out together.

Today they were play-fighting outside the den—an activity both them and their animal hosts enjoyed. Damon lunged at Danny and wrestled him to the ground. In response, Danny rolled onto his back before jumping up and batting Damon around the head with his paws, gently nipping an ear. Danny was larger and stronger than Damon, but Damon was faster and able to run circles around the young wolf. He darted in, snapped at Danny's heels, then backed off to relative safety a few yards away.

"Hey, Okay, quit biting my heels," Danny panted.

Both canines fell to the ground facing each other, panting with tongues hanging out and tails wagging furiously.

"You know, being an animal can be fun sometimes," said Danny.

"Yeah, but it's been a difficult adjustment. How did you cope at first?"

"It was hard. I had no idea what was going on. I found myself alone in the forest, in the dark. The whole wolf body thing freaked me out. Co-existing with my wolf host is weird. I tried to get back to the Center, but Romolo found me. He gave me a good talking to. He really helped. Introduced me to Robert, Jerry, and the others."

"Same here. Except I found myself as a working dog with an Underling. My dog-host is really smart and able to herd cattle and sheep. Romolo saved me, too."

Damon rolled onto his back and scratched it against the rocks. "We were about the same age, but following different paths. Even if I hadn't been sick, I was too lazy to work."

"Yeah, I'd heard all about you and your party friends. We were physically about the same age, but I was second-body and from a family that had to work hard to retain Elite status."

"Right, looking back, I'm a bit embarrassed about how I was. What happened to your first body?"

"It got sick, and I would have been dead before I was thirty if not for a memory transfer. But then, my second body was electrocuted one night when I was helping hook up an Underling house outside the Center. I ran cable from the Center along the ground to a house when, whoops!"

"Man! You were helping Underlings? And you still got in line for a memory transfer?"

"Well, yes and no. My family bribed someone to get my burned and barely alive body into the memory transfer unit. I was screaming in pain, but then something happened, my memory was lost—and here I am."

"Hmm, talking of bribing people, did you know Petr Seth?"

"Petr, err, yes. He could get stuff that's hard to find. A friend of yours?"

"Well, I thought so. Not now."

Danny jumped up. "Come with me. I want to show you something."

Damon followed Danny through the forest away from the den. Danny moved at a fast, steady pace, loping along, bounding from one rock to another. His long legs hopped over logs and streams with ease. By contrast, Damon struggled with his shorter legs as he negotiated around obstacles.

Eventually, Danny led them up a rocky slope. He nudged aside some ground covering plants to reveal a stash of looted guns hidden among boulders in a glade.

"These have been collected during our skirmishes with the guards. We need to learn how to use them."

"Wow! Um, I've experience with hunting rifles. I bet we can learn to handle them."

"Yes, the weapons are an opportunity for the den, if we can learn to use them. How can we use our paws and claws to fire the weapons?"

"The lack of an opposable thumb is a problem," said Damon as he tried and failed to use a claw to grasp a rifle. He pushed the rifle away.

Damon kicked a guard's helmet from the pile. It rolled towards Danny's feet. "Another problem is the headset. Can we get our funny-shaped animal heads inside to control a weapon?"

"That's okay. We'll sort it out. I've always enjoyed tackling fiddly problems that required dexterity. My work as an electrician back in the Center often required connecting and welding tiny wires together— like wiring and circuit installation. As I found out, one mistake and bang!"

Danny used a front paw and turned a guard's helmet upside down. "Stick your head into it," he suggested.

Twisting and turning, Damon pushed his snout through the straps and into the front of the helmet. It was a loose fit, but it was on when he lifted his head up. He grinned at Danny. His snout stuck out under the black eye shield and pushed the helmet back on his head.

Damon trotted a few steps while trying to keep his head steady, but the helmet fell off. He gave chase when it rolled down the slope.

Danny yipped loudly at Damon's performance.

Damon caught up with the helmet and pushed it back up the slope with his snout towards Danny. "Stop laughing at me, wolf-breath."

He pushed his head back into the helmet and sat on his haunches doing a better job than before of keeping it on.

"Do you see any mind controls in the helmet?" Danny asked.

"Hang on, give me a second." He had worn a mind-control helmet once before while big-game hunting with his father. It had been tricky at first, but he had learned to control his hunting rifle with thought alone. But, that time the helmet had been fitted to his head and strapped on. He closed his eyes and tried to let his mind relax.

"Yes, I see an orange glow in front of my eyes."

"Can you see any control panels or screens of numbers?"

"Yes, I think so."

Damon was seeing a drop-down control panel with blinking columns of green numbers. The display flashed a command "enter ID."

"We got a problem," said Damon. "I need to enter the guard's ID."

"Okay, let me think. We may have a few guard ID bracelets among the stash of stuff we kept after the last skirmish. Hang tight. I'll be back."

Danny ran off back to the den. Damon sat on his haunches. He felt exposed and vulnerable wearing an ill-fitting guard's helmet out in the open. A few minutes later, though, Danny came trotting back; he had a couple of ID bracelets in his mouth.

The falcon, Helen, followed behind gliding, as though weightless down to where Damon was sitting. He grinned, baring his teeth. She said nothing. He suppressed a sigh. His charm wasn't working on her at all.

She chirped, "Try one of the IDs from the bracelets. Otherwise, we can try my personal guard captain's ID—although that may have been disabled by now. The ID won't be specific for the weapon. It just needs to be a registered user."

Danny dropped the bracelets at Damon's feet. Like bracelets all Elites were required to wear, they were sleek expandable metal bands with embedded electro-chips holding the user's vital information. The silver-gray band showed no information visible to the eye.

"Won't the GPS in the bracelet show the guards where it is once it connects to the rifle?" Danny asked Helen.

"Yes, it will," she replied. "We will need to keep these bracelets hidden away from our den. Once the helmet has authenticated the ID, we can turn off the GPS. Anyone monitoring the ID will be able to see where the ID last pinged its location, but by then we should have moved away."

"Okay, we're in business," said Damon suddenly. "The helmet display connected to the bracelet and authenticated the ID, I've deactivated the GPS."

"We should keep a supply of these ID bracelets as dead guards will have their weapons access deactivated," said Helen. "However, the bureaucracy is slow following the death or termination of a guard."

A signal from the weapon showed up in the headset display identifying it as PsiTech Blaster 6Y. This must have been the model name of the rifle Danny had been fiddling with earlier.

"Yeah, yeah, I see the rifle," Damon said. "Let me see if I can lock onto it."

Damon thought *acquire* and the display flashed the red words, "locked and ready." Focusing his mind on the weapon ID, he thought *fire*. With an ear-splitting blast, the weapon sent a high velocity photon beam from the muzzle. The kickback skittered the gun back at Damon. The beam, however, shattered the rocks in front of it, sending up a cloud of dust. Danny tumbled out of the way. A flurry of feathers followed Helen as she took off out of the way.

"Hey, careful, you idiot!" squawked Helen. "You just about took us out."

"I'll see if I can do better next time." But he laughed, overjoyed by the success.

Standby locked the weapon into safety mode. He shook his head to dislodge the helmet. It rolled down safely onto the rifle.

"You did it!" said Danny. "But you need to improve your handling if you actually want to shoot someone."

"Right. So... next problem. I can hold any of the rifles with my front paws if I'm sitting on my haunches," Damon said. "But, it's sort of balanced on my paws with my claws gripping it. I can then sight down the barrel and point it at a target. Pistols are more of a problem to hold because they are so small. I think we should concentrate on using rifles. I still need a way to hold them steady."

"Okay, but then how can you fire a rifle without the dexterity of fingers?" he asked. "A human hand uses one hand to aim the muzzle and their other hand to hold the grip."

"Look, it's not perfected yet, but if I rest the gun on a rock or on your back or the ground, then I can place the stock against my shoulder and aim."

He tried it with the PsiTech Blaster 6Y, resting the barrel on a rock. After several failed attempts, he managed to clip one of the old rusty cans they had set up as targets twenty-five yards away. His previous experience big game hunting with his Father in Africa wasn't helping as he hoped. Shep's shoulder felt bruised and he had limped away from the last attempt.

Danny put on the helmet, then, to try it out. He yelped as a wild shot went nowhere near the cans.

Danny's second shot was closer to the cans. "This works but is slow. I'm sure accuracy will improve with practice, but keeping the gun steady is a problem. It's better when I rest it on your back."

"We've got plenty of weapons, we'll just have to have them ready to use. We can split our forces into teams of two. A gunner responsible for aligning the gun and shooting, and another who acts as a rest, steadying it. It's kind of like a small version of an old-style field artillery crew. Perhaps we can get 'beaters' to flush out the guards like they were quail." Damon smirked.

"Yeah, and don't forget we only need these rifles for distance as snipers. Once we get in close to the guards, we have the advantage as natural predators. At least we coyotes, wolves, and bobcats do. You might want to stay further back." Danny gave Damon a wry look.

With time, they became proficient in using the captured weapons and carried them on patrols and in encounters with guards. They planned to try the 'British shooting party' approach of shooters and crew during their next run-in with a patrol.

———◆———

A small party of five guards were searching around outside of the Center, presumably looking for animals. Damon and a small group of animals hid among bushes on a hilltop about 150 yards away. The guards gave no indication of being aware of their presence.

Danny organized the attack. "Damon, hang back behind these bushes. Pick off as many guards as you can. The rest of us will then run in to finish anyone you don't take out."

He turned to Merrill, a small skunk. "Hand Damon primed rifles he can rest on your back."

"Sure thing," Merrill said, pushing a rifle over to Damon.

Damon lay down and steadied the barrel of the rifle on Merrill's back. He had a helmet on and got the rifle locked in. He aimed at the closest guard and activated the gun. A sharp crack and flash erupted as the rifle discharged, and it recoiled against his shoulder. His ears rang. The guard he had aimed at went down, though, when the photon beam hit his chest.

Merrill chattered and hissed, and steadied himself. Damon readied a second shot.

By now the guards were in disarray, dragging the slain guard away into the cover of bushes. Damon got off a second shot which struck another guard in the leg. A third blast shot another guard in the shoulder.

The process worked well. He had shot three of the guards and created mayhem. Danny, three other coyotes, and another wolf ran down and closed in for the kill. It wasn't too different from big game hunting he'd done with his father in Africa, which they had always done from a great distance with their magnum hunting rifles. He had bagged Cape buffalo and elephants and made his father proud—a rare accomplishment.

"Well done, everyone," yipped Danny. "Let's collect all the guards' guns, knives, helmets, and anything that looks useful."

Damon felt a bit better now that they could level the playing field in their fight against the guards. How much more of this fighting would they have to do, though? Despite their success, he couldn't shake the guilt that weighed heavier with every shot. The act of shooting people nauseated him. Damon's body convulsed as he threw up a foul-smelling, frothy, yellow-green mess of partially digested rabbit and bile onto the ground.

"Hey, watch out," hissed Merrill.

I'm not up to killing people.

Chapter Eight

CHATURA'S TASKS

After the council meeting, Chatura did little of his epidemiological modeling work, and he even cut back on gaming. Instead, he spent his time investigating the agitated animals. He was sure there was a connection between memory losses, moderate Elites, and agitated animals. Anal retentive by nature, he wrote out a list of three questions or tasks.

First, how often were memory transfers failing and was this happening in a coordinated manner across all ten Centers around the world? Answering this question would be task one.

Second, could he confirm the memory transfer failures were targeting specific Elites, or was it random? At the council meeting, Center leaders sounded like they knew more than they were saying.

Third, if the answer to the second question showed the failures were non-random, who was directing the memory loss failures? Was it just Najor or were other Center leaders involved?

He worried. What would he do with this information? Should he report everything he found to Tourni? How involved was she in the memory losses? Could he trust her?

Chatura could work on the first question using data he already had accessed expanding his initial analysis. He would need help with the second question, and the third would be tricky and dangerous to investigate without arousing suspicions.

Planning these three tasks would take care. If he did indeed find that someone, or several someones, were responsible, they could not know that they were being investigated. Otherwise, he would be strapped onto a gurney and forced to undergo a memory transfer into a cow or a horse. Or worse, nowhere at all.

Tackling the first of his tasks, it didn't take Chatura too long to confirm the memory losses had started about three months ago, but the failures were not synchronized across programs at the ten Centers. Rather, the upward trajectory of memory transfer losses started at different times. It had started at the London Center, but quickly spread to all Centers within two weeks. The spread across all Centers over such a short period suggested several possible scenarios. Either there was a progressive, systematic failure of the memory loss technology or software, or a coordinated attack had compromised the system. He suspected the latter since he found no evidence of corrective action being taken to deal with the problem at any of the Centers. It wasn't until he found the link between the agitated animals and ongoing memory transfer losses that any concern had been raised. Even then, Tourni had changed nothing in her Center's procedures to suggest she was concerned.

Realizing she had possibly dismissed his findings, and by extension him, Chatura worried that she was compromised, either unable or unwilling to act. It seemed unwise to tell her his findings if that was the case.

He turned to the second task and wondered who he could turn to for help. He needed someone with access to the names of Elites who had undergone the memory transfer over the last two years, and what had been the outcomes of their transfers. But this information was highly classified.

Chatura's only friends were other gamers. He had never met any of them in person, or had much of a conversation beyond exchanging of gaming information, tips, and exploits. Who could he trust?

After checking out the gaming profiles of his friends and online searches, Chatura came up with one possibility. Ting Liu. Ting's profile showed she worked at the Shanghai Center in human resources. She should have access to the records he needed. She was at the highest levels of several games he played, including several he didn't. Her photo showed a pretty young woman. He became so distracted looking at her photo he missed important action prompts in the game he was running in the background.

Her current body was the same age as his. Would she be willing to talk with him? Could he trust her?

Besides, he was sure he would like Ting. He had fantasized if he ever were to have a girlfriend, it would be someone who was pretty, but also smart and with the savvy of a good gamer. He didn't have much practical experience in judging beauty, but he liked her dark, almond-shaped Asian eyes, and the way her long dark hair framed the high cheekbones of her face. He'd not seen more than her head and shoulders on his monitor during game meetings but imagined her to be slim and athletic because her shoulders had been narrow and her face thin. Her public hologram confirmed these thoughts.

If Ting accessed records at the Shanghai Center where she worked, then maybe she could access records across all the centers. Relationships between the ten Centers were better than they had ever been between the original host countries. Political differences between countries had been set aside in the face of ecological disaster and declining birth rates. Many tasks were now shared among staff at the ten Centers—including human resources and personal records.

Chatura searched for an innocuous reason to contact Ting. He'd seen reports she was very successful as a player of the Akturi game he had just started. Perhaps he could get onto her team?

The game was complicated, and he did have plenty of questions as a new player. He had credibility as a well-known gamer. Hopefully, she would agree to talk with him and not consider him a rookie trying to suck up to a gaming world star.

He sent her a direct message via Bigo Live, the global gaming platform he and other gamers used, with a few questions about Akturi he hoped wouldn't sound too dumb. To his surprise, she responded right away and agreed to meet him for a live hologram chat the next day.

Most of that night Chatura worried about how he could smoothly bring up the memory transfer issue in a conversation that was supposed to be about gaming. What if she answered his gaming questions, even accepted him onto her Akturi team, and then signed off? How cheesy and clumsy would it be to say something like, 'Hey, have you heard about the agitated animals and memory transfer problems? Is it an issue at the Shanghai Center?' He was well aware he was a poor conversationalist.

He carefully set up the virtual reality holospace they would meet in, choosing a French café setting with smooth jazz background music, the buzz of other holographic customers, low lighting, and a secluded table allowing them sit across from each other. He hoped the café would create the right atmosphere for an intimate, but non-threatening chat.

A good thirty minutes before the time they had agreed to meet, Chatura pulled hologoggles over his head and over his eyes. The goggles were large and 'boxy' affairs and made him, or anyone wearing them, look like they had big bug eyes sticking out from their face. But since everyone was used to wearing hologoggles, their appearance didn't matter. Chatura was embarrassed wearing them even though he was alone in his apartment. He also pulled on a pair of hologloves covered in what looked like big shiny sequins. These gloves allowed his hand to operate the keyboard that would hover in space while he was in the holospace. The gloves also allowed the wearer to grasp things in holospace and manipulate their environment. He pulled on a similarly sequined pair of holosocks that would track his foot movements, allowing him to walk and run around. Of course, he had to run or walk in place on his omni-directional treadmill. Otherwise, he'd run into the walls of his room back in the real world.

Appropriately set up with his hologoggles, gloves, and socks, Chatura entered the French café in holospace and walked over to a table towards the back. The holospace program included other guests in the café and a waiter who came over and asked him if he'd like to order.

"Bonjour monsieur," said the waiter who was dressed in black slacks, a white shirt, and a black apron befitting his role. "Que desirez-vous?"

The waiter's French was instantly translated, "Hello, sir. What would you like?"

"I'd like a coffee, please, and a chocolate croissant," he said. The software translated it to, "Je voudrais un café, s'il vous plaît, et un pain au chocolat."

"Oui, c'est bon," replied the waiter before moving off to the counter to get Chatura's order.

So far, so good, but will Ting turn up?

Ting walked into the holospace café right on time. Tall and slim, she wore an athletic, cream-colored outfit he thought was very fetching. In fact, she looked amazing. Chatura was embarrassed he had never paid much attention to his standard, off-the-rack clothing.

"Hello," she said. Her voice was husky and quiet. "You must be Chatura."

"Um, yes, I am. Ting? Err, sit down, please." *Darn, I sound like an idiot.*

Ting sat down on the other side of the table and asked him if he had ordered yet. When he said he had, she called over the waiter and in fluent French, ordered her coffee and a mille-feuille pastry. Instantaneous translation worked for Ting as well as Chatura. *I bet she speaks French.*

Chatura relaxed. Ting was very easy to talk with. She was interested in his gaming experience and asked which games he excelled at.

During forty-five minutes of gaming questions, Chatura became more at ease than he had ever been talking to anyone else. He blurted, "How do you enjoy working in HR at the Shanghai Center?"

Without batting an eyelid, she replied, "It used to be okay. You know, fairly routine dealing with job applications of Elites and Underlings, transfer and housing requests, that sort of thing."

"What changed?" he asked.

She lowered her voice and leaned forward, as if others might be listening, which was unlikely in their holospace. "Do you know about the memory transfer problems?"

"Yes, a little," he said cautiously. "What are they saying about it in the Shanghai Center?"

"The rumors are that more than the usual number of memory transfers are failing. The Elite mind isn't transferring into the Underling body. The failure rate isn't much more, but some of the sick Elites are having second thoughts about signing up for the program."

Chatura shifted uncertainly in his chair, causing his hologram to bounce around. Should he mention the agitated animals to Ting?

He had to take the chance, otherwise he wouldn't get her help. "There's more to it than just memory transfer failures," he said. "The transfers that fail are working, but the Elite mind is transferring to an animal outside the Center. These animals then seem to have the consciousness of the Elite."

Ting's hologram shifted and pulsated. She was shocked. "But how do you know?"

"I'm in modeling. These 'agitated animals', as they are called, are scratching messages in the ground. It's happening around all the Centers."

"Messages? Really?"

"Asking for help."

Chatura and Ting talked for another twenty minutes as he explained what he knew. Ting was bothered about all of this and explained the recent loss of her father's memories. "Perhaps he's still alive, even if he's now an agitated animal. Can we find him?"

Chatura agreed that communication between Elites and the agitated animals would help find people like her father. "Maybe, but perhaps you and I can help by finding out who and how many Elites have been lost, compared with which Elite memory transfers were successful. It may be non-random."

"The memory transfer records are automatically uploaded into the HR database." Her words confirmed she grasped the significance of what Chatura was suggesting. "I don't have direct access to those records, but I may have a friend who can help. Wait here."

"What?" Ting's hologram disappeared. Chatura was left alone in the café. *Had she been caught, arrested for comments she had made? Was he next?*

Not knowing what to do, he sat still and didn't say anything. He looked surreptitiously around the room. He couldn't tell how many of the people were holograms, or if they were all AI characters.

The waiter came over and pestered him to either leave or order another drink. Frustrated and anxious, Chatura ordered a double espresso.

After a few more minutes, he was just about to leave when, bang, Ting's hologram reappeared. She wasn't alone, the hologram of another girl was with her.

"Sorry about that, Chatura, but I went to get my friend, Min Jiang."

"Oh, hi, Min," said Chatura, unnerved being in the presence of two gorgeous girls.

"Hi, Chatura," Min whispered, though her eyes sparkled with excitement as she greeted him. She was similar in appearance to Ting, but a bit shorter and her hair was even longer, cascading down her back. With her stylish outfit and contagious energy, her hologram pulsated as she lit up the café. How could anyone have so much enthusiasm for life?

"Min works with me in HR and has direct access to memory transfer records from all the Centers. I've explained what we need, but not why."

"Okay, but we mustn't talk to too many people about what we want to do. It would be dangerous to be caught snooping through these records, especially if certain Elites had been targeted for memory transfer loss," he warned.

"I know," she said. "But I trust Min. We've been friends for years."

Turning to Min, Ting continued, "You are still working with the memory transfer records, right?"

"Yes," Min replied. "Although of late there have been quite a few problems and memory transfer failures."

"I wanted to ask you about that. Do you believe it's possible these transfer failures may be related to increased numbers of animals acting strangely outside the Centers? There's a suspicion that the Elite memories are being diverted away from the Underling recipient into wild animals."

"No way," said Min. "How is that even possible?"

Speaking in a whisper, Ting said, "No one knows how it's happening, yet according to Chatura, that is what seems to be going on. Don't say anything about this or we'll get into trouble for spreading rumors. Knowledge of the agitated animals, as they are called, hasn't got out yet."

Min stirred more sugar in the lapsang tea she had ordered. "Unbelievable."

"Chatura and I are looking into the problem and wondering if you could help us get hard data on the Elites who have suffered memory transfer failures. Can you help?"

"Oh, yes, that would be fun. I love the idea of subterfuge. I can access all the memory transfer applications from our Center and can request records from other centers without arousing much suspicion," she whispered.

She looked at Chatura. "Part of my duties are to process payments for memory transfers and debit clients' accounts. The records show who the client is, when and where the memory transfer took place, from start to finish. I can tell how it went because of the post-transfer charges. When a transfer succeeds, there are post-operative recovery charges for the Elite, whereas when it fails, there are only postmortem and crematorium charges."

"Of course!" he exclaimed. "The recovery and postmortem charges will be different, letting us know if a memory transfer succeeded or failed for each Elite."

"Right," said Min. "Another part of my job is to try and chase down payments from the families after a memory transfer fails. They are grieving, and not too happy about paying for something that led to the death of a loved one. Or, so they think. I wonder if they would be happier to learn that the mind of their family member is now running around in a cow or horse!"

"Now, we don't know that's happening for sure."

"Give me a few days, and I'll gather and send you the Shanghai Center records for the last year while waiting for the records from the other nine centers around the world. That's all I can do, I'll let you analyze the records. I don't want to arouse suspicion. This will be fun!" With that, her hologram blinked out and she was gone.

"Are you sure about her?" Chatura asked Ting, worried Min was too ready to help.

"She's fine. That's just how she is. She's a candle that always burns bright."

After sipping her drink, Ting continued, "You know, Chatura, thanks for asking me for help. This is just the sort of project that will make me feel I can make a difference and maybe help find my father."

Chatura blushed and nodded. "Okay, then let's meet again in a week to compare our progress."

He leaned back in his chair and gazed at her. She blinked out and he ended the holospace and returned to work. This was good—he'd made progress on his second task, finding out about memory transfer loss victims, and he was starting to think the super cool and gorgeous Ting might like him.

———◆◇◆———

Two days later, Chatura received the memory transfer records from the Shanghai Center.

"Be careful with these records," Ting said in her note to Chatura. "Let me know what you find, and we can meet again."

Chatura was excited to get the memory transfer records, and even more excited about the prospect of another meeting with Ting. He didn't play a video game for three days solid. Instead, he set running some long epidemiological models that wouldn't require his attention. Then, he asked his Nav for a large box of cream donuts for sustenance and a gallon of Powerade. Sleep and personal hygiene were ignored.

As he started digging into the records, he looked for patterns of memory transfers to help explain what had been going on.

For the last year it seemed, memory transfer successes had been people with personal or political ties to the ruling, right-wing Nationalist One Elite World (NOEW) party. Taurus Najor had mentioned how great they were in speeches and referred to them as "good people, patriots." Their platform had expanded to use any means, including "fake news", subversion, and outright lies to perpetuate their control of Underlings and "liberal-soft" and even middle-of-the-road Elites. Elites were the only ones allowed to vote in local elections, but NOEW wanted to restrict it further to only male party members. They had been implicated in intimidation and violence at polling stations in the Helsinki Center. Was this pattern typical of memory transfer losses at the other centers?

It took Ting a couple of weeks after their first meeting to get the records from the other Centers, and they dribbled in one Center at a time. In a note to Chatura accompanying the records, she asked, "Are the patterns the same across all Centers?"

Examining the records, Chatura wrote extensive computer code to run correlations and regressions between memory losses, the date of memory losses, Center location, the political affiliation of memory transfer patients, and various demographic characteristics, including age and gender. It didn't take him long to see that the memory transfer losses were decidedly non-random and had been increasing over the last month. NOEW members had successful memory transfers; non-NOEW members memories were inevitably lost.

The records confirmed Ting's father was one of the many unfortunate memory loss failures, but just like other failures, the report did not shed any light on what happened or whether he was now an agitated animal.

A few days later, Chatura received a message from Ting asking if he had made any progress with searching through the records. "Can you meet again in a couple of days?"

"Yes, absolutely," he replied, trying not to sound anxious. "How about tomorrow, or the next day, or the day after? I'm free whenever you are. *Damn that was stupid.* Nevertheless, he set about sprucing up his outfit before Ting had even agreed.

When they met in holospace the next day, Chatura's hologram now had personal touches including a neon-colored gaming t-shirt and silver shoes that looked a lot like those of one of the Akturi game characters.

Okay, my outfit is too nerdy. He went online. "Hey Ting, how are you?"

"I'm doing great, let's turn on our cameras to show live headshots on our holograms," she said.

This suggestion sent Chatura into a full-on panic. He quickly dragged a comb through his messy hair and attempted a smiling pose. Of course, Ting looked more gorgeous than ever when she turned on her camera. Her perfect dark hair framed her face and her radiant smile disarmed him.

"Are you okay?" Ting asked, looking at his hair.

"Err, yes," he replied. "I'm a bit tired from working on these records all day long and trying to do my job at the same time."

Ting smiled, "I know what you mean, it's been stressful here too. I couldn't get my hair right today at all. What have you found?"

Chatura reminded Ting of the three tasks he had set himself. "The first task was to see if the memory transfers were coordinated among the Elite centers—my examination of the detailed records you provided suggests that they were coordinated. The first instance of a memory transfer failure involving more than the occasional one or two Elites was five people at the London Center three months ago."

"That's a surprise," Ting jumped in. "I was sure it started with the Boston Center in North America where that dreadful man Najor is in charge with his sidekick bitch Tourni. I don't trust either of them."

"I know what you mean, and this first transfer failure in London doesn't mean they weren't both involved. There are several options. They could be coordinating everything from Boston with collaborators at other Centers, they could be running everything remotely from their Center, or the whole thing could be spearheaded by others elsewhere with Najor and Tourni having secondary roles or even nothing to do with it. Did you hear Najor's own son's memory was lost in a transfer failure? Regardless, after the first set of unusual memory transfer failures in London, additional failures started popping up across all the Centers, jumping quickly to five percent—not enough for the public to notice, but statistically significant. Now there's no geographic pattern other than a consistent pattern of memory transfer failures every time at each Center."

"You're right," Ting said, the brightness of her hologram dimming. "We'll have to think about how to eliminate one or more of these options. They must be coordinated at some level. Otherwise, the technicians in each memory transfer facility in each Center would be asking questions."

"That's true. Either the technicians are involved, or their bosses aren't saying anything about it. And, don't forget that most memory transfer technicians are Underlings who are afraid to question anything suspicious."

"And remember, Najor only brought this up when he lost his son," said Ting, sounding more emotional. "I still think he's involved in some way,"

Chatura, losing focus for a few seconds, couldn't help noticing the cute way her brow furrowed, and her nose crinkled when she got annoyed.

Tearing his thoughts back to the point, he said. "My second task was to see if the memory transfer failures had a pattern."

"Perhaps it's just a glitch in the code controlling the memory transfer process that all of a sudden got worse. I mean, the memory transfer systems are integrated into a single software system that allows each center local control."

"That's possible," he countered. "But that can't be the whole answer. I did quite a bit of digging into the family background of the memory transfer failures and successes. To make it manageable, I took a random sample of ten percent of the cases. It was no surprise to me that most people getting a memory transfer are old Elites, with some young and sick individuals, like Najor's son Damon. It was also clear that the memory transfer failures were all Elites, and their families spoke out against, or didn't support, the NOEW party."

Ting's hologram dimmed again. "So, it is politically motivated. The NOEW party members are extremists and are known for acts of violence. A couple of months ago, they kidnapped the teenage daughter of a moderate Elite leader in Australia and demanded a ransom for her return. They sent three of her fingers to the family until the ransom was paid, and then they killed her anyway."

"Yeah," said Chatura. "Authorities said that they had no leads, and no one was ever arrested."

He dwelled a moment on the ransom victim's sad situation. "My third task," he said, "was to work out who was responsible. We don't know yet. Perhaps Alan Moorehead, the leader of NOEW in London, is involved. I need to start this task next. In addition, we need to contact the agitated animals to find out what's going on with them."

"That will be our fourth task," Ting interrupted.

Excited Ting said "our" fourth task, Chatura agreed, worrying this would become quite involved and more dangerous.

CHAPTER NINE

COORDINATION OF AGITATED ANIMALS

After the first few skirmishes with the guards close to the Center, Damon could see how their policy had shifted from 'peace-keeping' and reconnaissance to trying to eliminate all animals with Elite memories. Whereas the guards had been cautious at first, they were now actively searching for animal groups.

One evening, Romolo paid a rare visit in the den. His coat didn't seem to shine as it had when Damon had first met him.

"The guards brutally killed the horses," he said, his deep baritone carrying across the den. "Archie Blankenship, Marty McNeil, and four others are dead. They were undefended in their pen and didn't have a chance to protect themselves."

"This is awful news," Damon whined. "Archie was a friend of my father and a surrogate uncle to me when I was a young boy. Although the poor man was an elder, senior Elite, he had always been kind to me. Why did his memory transfer fail?"

Romolo looked across at Damon with sad eyes. "I don't know, but he had been critical of your father's policies."

Were those of us who became animals perceived as threats to my father and the Elite council? Was memory transfer failure a way to get rid of dissidents? Was he trying to get rid of the man whose ID I used?

Later on that evening after Romolo had left, the den members gathered outside their cave at the base of the bluff. Damon raised Romolo's concerns with other members of the animal group. Several group members had known Archie well and were upset he had been killed.

"But surely the guards didn't know that Archie was one of the horses," said Danny Ramos. The former member of the Elite inner circle in the Boston Center had been a friend of Archie. He was now a wolf.

Several other den members nodded in agreement.

"It doesn't matter if Archie was there. As we've discussed before, they are out to kill off all the animals," Danny said.

The cruelty of the guards upset the entire den. The animals paced back and forth, growling and bristling, eager to do something, anything.

"I am wondering if extremist NOEW members are behind this," said Jacques Grimball, a former teacher of political science who was now a coyote. "As you have suggested, Damon, perhaps the memory transfer failures that led to all of us becoming animals are deliberate. After all, we are all moderates, not NOEW members."

Jacques's explanation sent a shock wave of uncomfortable realization around the den of animals packed closely together under the shelter of a rocky bluff deep in the forest. Damon was the lone dog, but there was a mix of wild carnivores, as well as two owls and two falcons. Over the last several weeks, they had contacted over a hundred other animals in the surrounding area and many more of them joined the group every day.

The pack was not structured into any form of hierarchy, despite the presence of wolves. Rather, some members were more outspoken than others, reflecting prior seniority among Elites, rather than the trophic level status of their animal hosts. Nevertheless, Robert acted like the pack leader. He led the discussions drawing upon his previous experience as a senior Elite. Damon was reticent to speak up for fear of retribution or suspicion as Najor's son. He was definitely the youngest member, well aware he'd lived a life without any real responsibilities.

The discussion went around and around as the night drew on. The cloudless sky was full of stars shining bright as diamonds through the overhead tree canopy. The night air was cold, and Damon was chilled. Several of the coyotes huddled together, which struck him as a bit odd since they were also former humans.

During a lull in the conversation, he screwed up the courage to ask. "How about a fire to warm us?"

"Good idea. Does anyone know how to make a fire?" asked one of the coyotes.

"And we could also use a fire to cook the rabbits we've caught," said another.

One of the bobcats stood up and stretched. Flexing her sleek muscles, her body arched with grace in the gloom of the night. "Absolutely. Out of necessity, I've allowed my animal host to eat raw flesh, but I crave cooked meat."

"It's not a good idea," said Robert. "Animals have never used fire. We aren't humans anymore."

A dissenting murmur rippled around the pack.

One of the bobcats spoke up. "Well, I think Damon has a good idea, and as someone else said, we can cook meat. I too am tired of raw flesh."

This exchange made Damon uncomfortable as he didn't want to cross Robert. But, sensing he had the backing of the pack, he asked. "How about a few of us go gather dry twigs and branches that we can use as firewood? We can try to make a fire on the flat rocky area over there beneath the bluff."

Robert glared at him, but didn't say anything. Damon worried he had crossed a line.

Jerry McPherson, who had become a bobcat, stuck his face into a sack. "There's a cigarette lighter among the materials we retrieved from guards that we took down during a recent skirmish."

"Good," said Damon. "But do we have the dexterity to get it to work?"

Danny jumped into the conversation. "I figured out how to fire rifles—I bet I can work a lighter."

After a few minutes of fiddling around with the lighter, he said, "Look this isn't too hard. If I hold the lighter down on the ground on top of this kindling with one of my front paws, I can use the claws on the other front paw to get the lighter to strike."

Famous last words.

Danny tried and failed to get a flame five or six times.

The first two or three times, the lighter slipped out from under his paw as he tried to get it lit. What started as a low growl from Danny got louder the longer he struggled. Several pack members crowded around, amused at Danny's efforts. All of a sudden, the kindling caught fire. An orange-red, two-to-three-foot flame flared up.

"Aha, you doubting Thomas," Danny said with a proud look on his wolf face as he moved small twigs into the blaze.

Robert acted anxious around the flames, but pushed a large log onto the growing fire. Despite apparently accepting Damon's idea, he moved to reassert himself as pack leader. "Well done, Danny. Fires like this will keep us warm in the cool evenings. You two bobcats, use your claws and teeth to skin and dress the rabbits, then we can cook them on top of these larger logs and on these flat stones as they heat up. Danny, make sure we've plenty of firewood to keep the fire burning."

"Yes, I'm looking forward to eating cooked meat, even though my bobcat host finds raw rabbit flesh quite palatable. Bobcats also prey on small livestock such as pigs, sheep, goats, and poultry. I will try and find some to vary our diet," said Jerry.

Damon glanced up at Jerry. "That's fine, Jerry, so long as you don't include dogs on your list. Perhaps you should focus on the smaller prey such as birds, reptiles, and rodents while I'm around."

"I'll try to restrain myself!" He grinned.

Damon shook his head and tried not to laugh. Looking around it seemed that a few of the newest pack members, especially the wolverine and the kestrel, were afraid of the fire—probably on account of their animal hosts, but after a few minutes, their now-dominant human mind overrode such fears. Danny cooked the rabbits along with a couple of rats the others had prepared. He passed around pieces as they were ready to eat. A kestrel brought in finches she had hunted that provided meatball-sized nuggets of meat after cooking.

"Here you go." Danny carried a leg of cooked rabbit over to Damon in his jaws and dropped it on the ground. "See what you think of that."

Damon took a few bites, wondering what Shep thought of eating cooked meat for the first time. "Hey, this is good." He savored the gamey, moist flesh and crunched into the bones to get at the marrow. "Where's the wine?"

"Eau-de-stream water," quipped Danny. "Over there in the creek."

The other pack members offered similar compliments, promoting Danny to unofficial head chef.

Damon was comfortable eating rabbits because none he'd encountered acted like they were Elites.

As the evening drew on, fireflies came out adding sparkles to the air. The light from the fire cast shadows of the group against the rock face of the bluff. Damon lay down about ten feet from the fire and its warmth made him sleepy, along with the roast rabbit that filled his belly. Despite being raised as a city boy, he was starting to feel more comfortable in this wild setting. He was enjoying the camaraderie of the other animals. If this was to be his new life, perhaps it wouldn't be too objectionable. It was better than spending time in hospital as he had done lately.

The conversation drifted to what they could do as animals.

"Surely, when the Elites remaining in the Center know of our fate," said Janet Browne a former senior Elite, but now a bobcat, "then they will allow our memories to be transferred out of these animals and into the Underling minds we are supposed to be in."

"Are you forgetting the shoot-to-kill policy?" asked Damon.

"Besides, and with respect, Janet, I don't think so," said Sherill Jones, another bobcat. "I used to work as a supervisor in the memory transfer unit. I don't think it's possible to transfer an Elite memory from an animal into an Underling without transferring the underlying animal memory at the same time."

"Which would mean the Underling would end up with an Elite's memories and animal memories in the same body, like us," said Danny. "What would be the problem with that?"

"It would be different from our situation," said Sherill. "Our memories were transferred into our host animals on top of their memories which were already in place. With your suggestion, it's possible only the animal memories would transfer, with at best, just a portion or none of the Elite memories. If both memories transferred, there would be unforeseen complications as both memories vied for dominance. When I was still working in the memory transfer unit, the technology didn't allow the necessary separation of memories during transfer. In any case, as a supervisor, I wouldn't agree to try it, and I can't imagine that Shanya Tourni would approve either."

"But we need to restore the natural order of human society with Underlings serving the Elites like us," said Isaac Mallory, clearly used to bossing around Underlings. His piercing orange eyes and jet-black fur gave him a threatening appearance. "That won't happen if we don't transfer our memories into suitable Underling host bodies and fix the memory transfer process."

"Wait a minute, Isaac," snarled Danny, jumping up. He had been lying by a bush at the edge of the group. His wolf's eyes burned bright red. "I worked in the power plant as an electrician supervisor. The Underlings working with me were my friends, not slaves."

Isaac was a thirty-pound coyote and no match for a wolf twice his size and weight like Danny, but he persisted. "It's always been clear to me who should be leading and who should be serving. If you can't uphold your role as an Elite, then you will be demoted to Underling status."

"Isaac, you're sounding more like a NOEW member than the rest of us moderate Elites." One of the bobcats from the back of the group stood up. "Perhaps you were behind the memory transfer failures."

Isaac whipped his head around, looking for the source of the comment. "I was never a member of NOEW, but I'm thinking their views made sense."

"Listen to yourself," said Danny, jumping up. "Whatever views we all held before, we are not Elites now. You are not an Elite anymore. We are not Underlings, either. We are sentient animals and we need to focus on our future. We know the Elites are trying to kill us all, and we can't expect any help from the Underlings despite the pro-environmental views that some of them have."

Isaac and Danny circled each other in the gloom, their silhouettes picked out by the light of the fire. Other animals slunk backward, looking nervously from one to another. Isaac's hackles were raised, dark and forbidding, and he bared his teeth trying to menace.

But Danny was having none of it. "Back down, Isaac, if you know what's good for you." He growled and stepped closer, looming over Isaac, his expression dark with menace. His powerful frame exuded dominance.

Swaying on his feet side to side, Isaac looked defiant for several more moments. But then he rolled onto his back and exposed his underbelly in a classic sign of submission.

"Okay, you two. Calm it down."

Robert appeared between them. "We don't need to be fighting among ourselves. I agree with Sherill that we are not going to be able to go back to being a human being with a single set of memories. It's clear to me from the attacks by the guards that the Elites regard us as a threat and are trying to kill us off. We need to focus on staying alive and killing off the Elites. It is kill or be killed. The Underlings will just have to take their chances. As Danny said, we can't expect help from them."

"That's a pretty strong statement," said Merrill Johnson. The skunk moved out of the shadows into the firelight. Flickering firelight cast a warm golden hue on his distinctive black and white fur. His tail was raised and flickered from side to side, as though he might spray. "Do we have the numbers and resources to take on the guards, let alone all the Elites?"

Robert looked around the group, his eyes golden, fierce, and penetrating in the fiery glow. "Yes," he said finally, "we can take them on. All of them. It is us or them. It will take planning. We start now."

Robert howled. The haunting sound resonated with a primal power that chilled Damon's heart. The rest of the animals joined in, their collective sounds filling the forest.

———————•◦•———————

Despite being a part of the animal group living outside the Boston Center, Damon spent a considerable amount of time with his master Giles. Robert and others in the group suggested he could provide useful information by eavesdropping on Giles' conversations with his wife and the Underling abattoir workers.

When he returned one evening from the forest, Giles welcomed him back, declaring he looked healthy enough despite being "lost" for a week.

"You poor thing, you must have got lost in the forest chasing rabbits," he said ruffling the fur between Shep's ears at the back of his head.

Giles' wife Elizabeth threw down some food in front of him as he settled down, warming himself in front of the fire. "More likely he just got cold and hungry and came home. You should tie him up again."

Later that evening Elizabeth bathed him to "wash off the muddy, forest grime."

Shep hated being dunked into soapy hot water, but Damon loved the attention after he got over the awkwardness of her rough, callused hands scrubbing the fur over every part of his body. As a former, horny teenager, he had relished young female hands on any part of his body, on the rare occasions he got lucky, but Elizabeth was old, at least 50 he guessed. Shep was wishing all the attention was coming from a female dog giving him a tongue bath. Although unable to read Shep's mind,

Damon got the strong feeling his limited thoughts revolved around eating, sleeping, chasing squirrels, and looking for female dogs to couple with. Apart from the squirrels, that wasn't too different from Damon's old self when he had been healthy.

Giles didn't seem to know too much about what was going on in the Center, but he and Elizabeth talked a lot about what might be happening. One evening, Giles came in excited about a meeting with other Underlings who worked in the Center.

"They say things are getting bad in there," he told Elizabeth. He paused to light his pipe before adding. "The Elites are running out of fresh food because supplies are no longer coming in from the Underling farms. Our cattle shipments have been disrupted so our abattoir has stopped producing meat for them."

"I'm sure the situation will right itself soon enough. These problems have a way of sorting themselves out," Elizabeth replied, continuing to chop carrots for supper.

"It's worse than I've ever known it," he said. "My Elite supervisor, the head of food supplies, called me this morning. He wanted to know when the abattoir could provide more meat for the Center. He was furious when I told him about the problem with cattle shipments. An Underling who had been in the Center yesterday told me that Elite centers around the world are having trouble communicating with each other. They are pretty much isolated from each other now. Other abattoir managers supplying these Centers have been silent for over a week."

"Well," she said. "You spend too much time chatting online with those folk about cattle prices and the like."

"Be that as it may," he said, stuffing his pipe with tobacco. "It's not just beef supplies to the Centers that are breaking down, but the whole Underling food supply chain. Environmental conditions have deteriorated significantly over the last few months. Underlings are dying in large numbers from the toxic fumes, and diseases caused by pollutants. Desperate to obtain supplies, the Elites have been sending out patrols to steal food from Underling communities. I'm telling you, we had better watch out as we might be a target."

"Now you're getting me worried. I've never trusted those guards when they come snooping around."

"Aye, and it's getting worse. As the Underlings are becoming free from the old shackles of serfdom under the Elites, they are forming into small factional groups under local leaders. These groups, though, are fighting with each other for control of the dwindling resources. The word on the street is former guard member, Garond Winner, has been marshaling Underlings south of here and fighting for food against another group."

He puffed his pipe for a few moments. Damon wrinkled his nose, but stayed close, determined to listen as closely as possible for as long as possible.

"There are food shortages among the Underlings," Giles said. "But I don't think it's so bad for us as for the Elites. At least you and I grow our food in our garden, and I can shoot rabbits if we want to add meat to our diet. We won't starve."

"We already have a good supply of potatoes, carrots, and onions out in the shed," Elizabeth added. "And, we can trade with other Underlings. Maybe the Zimmermans will trade some flour for our potatoes."

Giles and Elizabeth clearly relished the idea of not being beholden to Elites anymore. But Damon worried for their future with the continued breakdown of society. He knew the Elites were under siege in the Centers from animal groups like his. Now, outside, the Underlings were fighting with each other and dying in a poisoned world. How would Giles and Elizabeth survive? Being an animal suddenly felt like the best option.

After a few days with Giles and Elizabeth, he returned to the pack's den.

———◆◇◆———

Early one morning, as the sun was rising, Helen Chartain swooped down through the trees into the den. She was exhausted and didn't land elegantly, stumbling onto a rock and knocking her beak into the ground. Normally a bird with an elegant plumage of muted earth tones and a regal posture, she looked disheveled.

"Okay, nothing to look at. I'm fine," she said in a high-pitched squawk that passed for her voice.

Damon looked up in the early morning gloom wondering what the fuss was about. "Oh, hi Helen. What's up?"

"I've got the latest messages that Bruce White and I have via the avian network from the other Centers around the world. Remember about two weeks ago your group sent out word that we had passed a resolution to kill off the Elites?"

"Yeah, I remember," Damon said, pricking up his ears. "Let me go get Robert and some of the others. They'll want to hear your report."

He bounded off and rounded up a small group of other animals. Even though it was just dawn, and most of them had been asleep, everyone followed him back, anxious to learn the latest news. Although Helen and Bruce had set up an extensive avian network, it took two weeks for messages to come back from around the world. By the time the group was gathered, a weary-looking Bruce had also flown in, his wings drooping and eyes half-closed. How far and for how long had they been flying?

Falcons don't like to spend too much time standing on the ground, so Helen and Bruce perched on the lower limb of a large oak that shaded part of the den. They took turns passing on their news.

"The news from the animals around the other Centers is not good," said Bruce. "Guards have been targeting them, murdering many former Elites."

"Bastards," muttered Antoine, a coyote.

"But, this desperate plan hasn't worked out too well, as most patrols are made up of Underling guards who have been mutinying and killing their Elite commanders," Bruce continued.

"Yay," responded Antoine. "That will teach them."

Bruce squawked, "Shut it, Antoine. Helen and I were guard commanders until our failed memory transfer."

Helen said, "In one case, around the Buenos Aires Center, an animal group was fighting alongside Underling guards to take out the Elite commanders. That was working out well until the fighting got too close to the artillery on top of the walls of the Center. At which point a barrage of photon blasts killed all the animals and the Underling guards. Our avian contact was forced to watch a blood bath from her perch. She was powerless to help. It was very distressing for her."

Antoine said nothing.

"Although there have been a few setbacks like this, the animal groups around the world have come to the same conclusion as us—we need to take down the Centers and all the Elites," Helen said.

A howl of approval arose in the fog around the rising sun. The wolves and coyotes started, and soon the bobcats and the other animals in the group joined in. Collectively, the sound resonated through the forest wilderness as a symphony of unity.

Chapter Ten

MAKING PLANS

The animals were determined to eliminate the Elites and planned to breach the defenses of the Center. Like the other nine Centers around the world, it was surrounded by a large, guarded, gray concrete and steel wall. The several entrances each had a steel-reinforced gate. Guard towers, bristling with weapons, stood along the top of the wall at regular intervals. The similarities with ancient medieval fortresses were unmistakable and not a coincidence. As a nod to modernity, large, rectangular, reinforced glass windows looked out at intervals. From the outside, they could see Elites moving around inside like shadows in the forest.

Damon scouted around the Center with a group of other animals. Fewer guards were patrolling than in the past, and they seemed disconsolate and unhappy. After all, these guards were Underlings, clearly searching for any excuse to desert their post. The animals intended to encourage them to leave. They had no reason to kill the Underlings unless they attacked them.

The animals had captured many weapons, including shoulder-mounted high powered photon torpedoes. It was challenging to use these weapons. Damon had worked with Danny, and once again come up with a scheme to make the operation more manageable. It was clumsy, and not easy, but they were proficient in using all the weapons.

Gathering one evening cooking rabbits and some other small animals on the campfires, Danny explained what he had worked out. "It will take two of us to operate a photon torpedo. One of us, preferably a small bobcat or coyote, will either stand or lie down with the weapon balanced across their back. Then, another one of us operates the controls using the heads-up display in a captured guard's helmet. After firing, the two of you work to prime the next photon torpedo."

"Isn't this all a bit slow?" asked one of the bobcats.

"Yes," he replied. "But it works for photon torpedoes. Janet and I tried it out a couple of days ago and we had great success against an Elite patrol. They didn't know what had hit them! Just like with the sniper rifles, the teams must remember to 'shoot and move' so they don't get targeted. Once the patrol gets hit and starts to panic, that's when we move in close for the kill without the need for weapons."

He paused before going on, "To make this work with the photon torpedoes, we need to train teams of two. Any volunteers?"

Several bobcats and coyotes stepped forward. Their eyes reflected the firelight and shined bright with anticipation.

"Thanks," said Robert, stepping forward. "It looks like we have several volunteers. Danny, choose three teams of two and get them trained and ready. This is good and will help us to take down the Elite patrols."

Damon said. "I've been scouting around and listening in to Giles and Elizabeth talk about morale in the Center. We don't know how many Elites are left in the Center, but our den has a force of seventy-five, and I've estimated that memories had been transferred into at least a hundred cattle that were slaughtered in the abattoir. We have killed over sixty Elite patrol members, and although most of them had been conscripted

Underling guards from the farms, about a dozen had been Elite officers. I reckon there must be over ten thousand Elites left in the Center, of which half are women and a few children, and many of the men are old and few have any weapons training. Nevertheless, there is a fighting group of Elites that numbers more than ten times our numbers. Is our plan good enough?"

"I doubt if your estimates are even close to being correct," Robert said, sounding impatient. "Anyway, we have a good plan to attack the Center."

Isaac, with his knowledge of security, then worked with Robert, Danny, and Antoine on an ambitious plan to get inside the Center.

Late the next evening, Robert gathered everyone and outlined their plan. "The day after tomorrow, we will attack in force just before dawn and overwhelm their defenses by sheer numbers. We will show no mercy and kill every Elite we encounter."

Damon shifted anxiously. That didn't sound safe.

"Danny and his teams will use the photon torpedoes to blast open the gates," Robert said. "A photon torpedo team will first feint an attack on the eastern gates as a distraction before Danny and another team will start the main attack firing their photon torpedoes on the southern gates. Helen and Bruce will provide reconnaissance, hovering overhead and passing information down to us. Isaac and I will then lead a team of thirty to forty of us through the southern gates into the outer compound where we will establish a beachhead to secure the area. Once that area is secured, Danny's teams will again use their photon torpedoes to blast open doors and gates to the inner areas of the Center. Our goal is to reach Taurus Najor's office suite where we will establish our control center in the main conference room."

What will I do face-to-face with my father? Despite their differences and his situation as an animal, Damon didn't think he could kill him. He wasn't sure his father would have the same hesitation killing him, though.

"All guards and Elite council members will be killed without mercy," Antoine added. "Other Elites will be told to leave the Center immediately where they will have to fend for themselves and take their chance among the Underlings outside."

Isaac went on, "Danny will distribute weapons in the morning and we will travel to the Center where we will hide in the forest before taking up attack positions in the evening."

Damon had been listening quietly as Robert outlined the plans. But he was worried.

"Won't this plan lead to too many animal casualties? And, are we sure the photon torpedoes will be effective against the gates?"

"Don't be ridiculous," shouted Robert. "What can you possibly know about such things? You were nothing more than a lazy teenager under your father's protection. Well, Daddy isn't here to look after you now."

Damon was shocked at Robert's venom and retreated behind a tree.

"Everyone," Robert said, his voice void of venom now, and encouraging the rest of the den. "Eat well and get a good rest tonight. The next couple of days are an important chance for us to get the Elites off our backs. Although we are former Elites, we didn't choose to become animals, and we didn't choose this fight."

He went on, sitting proud on his haunches. "You may know the day after tomorrow is October twenty-five, St. Crispin's Day of Old. Centuries ago, King Henry the fifth of England inspired his troops on this day before the Battle of Agincourt with these words: 'he that outlives this day, and comes safe home, will stand a tip-toe when the day is named, and rouse him at the name of Crispin'."

Robert's rallying cry inspired the animals, and as before, a collective howl echoed through the woods. Damon cringed behind the tree, deeply worried.

———◆◇◆———

As planned, the next evening, the animals set up in the forest outside the south gate. Damon was assigned a photon torpedo with Merrill Johnson. As small animals, neither of them would have been much good in a close fight with Elite guards, but after a couple of weeks of training, they had become proficient using photon torpedoes. Damon wore a guard's helmet to establish mind control and fired the torpedo while resting it on Merrill's back. Merrill ensured the readiness of the three photon torpedoes they would be operating. Their position on top of a small hill overlooked the gate. Danny's photon torpedo team was about 500 yards away atop another low hill. Both hills had thick forest, and they hunkered down in the shrubs. A third photon torpedo team of two animals was stationed near the east gate for the diversionary attack. Despite his misgivings, Damon was ready.

Although it was still dark, the gate was well lit. Searchlights shined down from atop the adjoining towers on either side. The yellow beam from the searchlights crawled along the ground in front of the wall shadowing shrubs and rocks, ready to pick out anything that moved.

"I can see a lot of guards moving around on top of the wall and there are fires in the compound behind, suggesting to me that there are more of them inside," said Merrill. "I'm worried that it's more heavily guarded than Isaac expected."

"Don't worry," Damon said. "We have a strong force of wolves, coyotes, and bobcats who will make short work of them once we breech the gates with our photon torpedoes."

"But where are they? I can't see anyone," worried Merrill.

"That's the point," said Damon. "I'm sure they're hidden among the shrubs in the valley between these two hills. Those ramshackle Underling huts provide additional cover. They must be only twenty-five to thirty yards away from the gates. It's a perfect staging point for the attack."

Heavy cloud cover blocked the moon's light. The sun was set to come up around seven, but it wasn't going to show through the thick clouds. At six forty-five, Isaac barked, his haunting yip piercing the night. That was the signal to start the photon torpedo attack.

Merrill and Damon made an efficient team. As Damon fired, Merrill reprimed. Every time Damon fired, the photon torpedo recoiled with a deafening roar that knocked him back in a cloud of acrid smoke, making him cough. Fiery trails streaked the sky followed by a trail of white smoke. His first two shots missed the gate, but one of them hit the wall to the left side with a thundering impact and caused minor damage. Danny's photon torpedo team got their aim in quicker than Damon and the blasts hit the gate. Damon's third shot also hit the gate.

"Watch out!" yelled Merrill when guards fired at their position.

Though Damon had expected this response, he hadn't thought it would be so fast.

"Let's move!" he yelled. "We'll set up again ten yards to our left."

They dodged and rolled, finding cover in a new clump of shrubs. Merrill had difficulty handling the torpedo, though. The three-foot long tube was considerably larger than his body. But finally he rolled it into the new cover, and pushed it into position.

Once they set up in the new location, they fired again. When the guards adjusted their firing, they moved again. This cat-and-mouse game went on until dawn. The sun was supposed to be up although Damon couldn't see it amid the clouds and smoke. It had also started to rain, which provided extra cover.

Danny's and Damon's photon torpedo teams stopped firing. Time for the wolf, coyote, and bobcat main force to swarm through the gates.

"Something has gone wrong!" yelled Merrill. "The gates are still intact."

"Oh no," replied Damon.

Merrill was right. A large number of small craters pock-marked the ground in front of the gates. Huts under the wall had been destroyed. The gates and wall had black scorch marks, but otherwise little to no damage. "The photon torpedoes were not powerful enough to break open the gates. We were too far away to be effective."

"But it's too late to stop the attack," said Merrill, flipping his black tail around with dismay.

Below their protected vantage point on the forested hill-top, the animal force was in disarray. The leading animals had run straight into the gates in a bid to push them open, but the gates hadn't budged. The guards on top of the walls laid down a lethal barrage of photon blasts on the animals. They had no chance. Screams and howls of agony filled the air as the animals were hit.

Someone, presumably Isaac, barked the retreat, a more mournful urgent howl compared with the earlier call to attack. The animals who hadn't been hit turned around and ran back into the forest. In the valley outside the gates at least a dozen animals lay prostrate, killed. Their attempt to get into the Center had failed.

Damon and Merrill ran down from the hill-top and joined the surviving animals at their initial staging post in the valley head. They were hidden from view, safe under thick forest cover.

Robert sat at the base of a tree, gingerly holding an injured front paw off the ground. His fur was a bloody mess. "We've got to retrieve the bodies of the fallen animals outside the gates."

"I agree, but the guards aren't going to allow us to approach the gates during daylight. We should wait," said Isaac.

"No!" Robert barked. He turned to two young foxes that had manned one of the photon torpedoes. "You two, go down to the gates." He used his snout to pull a rag out of a bag of supplies he'd brought with him. "Take this white cloth and wave it as a flag of truce. Start dragging back the dead animals."

Damon and Merrill were off to the side of the main group of animals that were lying in front of Robert. "This won't work," muttered Damon. "They think we are a bunch of mad, wild animals. Do the low-ranking junior guards even know we are former Elites?"

"What?" snarled Robert turning to Damon, his eyes blazing.

"Err. Nothing."

Robert glared at Damon before turning back to the two foxes. "Go, now!"

The larger of the two foxes grabbed the white cloth on the ground by Robert and the two of them trotted out of the forest down the valley toward the gates. Damon and Merrill ran back up the hill-top to watch. The other animals waited at the edge of the forest ready to help drag back the bodies.

The plan failed. From their vantage point on the hill-top, Damon and Merrill could see the foxes approaching the gates. Moving silently, their fiery red coats flickered among the shadows of the tangled underbrush. Their eyes scanned from left to right and their ears twitched as they stepped precisely around rocks and branches on the trail. The large fox held the white cloth in her mouth. She tilted her head back as she walked so the cloth fluttered behind like a flag. The other, smaller fox trotted by her side, slinking low with his tail tucked. Despite their non-threatening, cautious approach, they hadn't even reached the first body when a bright plume streaked towards them, stranded out in the open before the gates. Under a barrage of fire, the two foxes went down.

Immediately, the gates opened. A team of a dozen guards streamed out alongside an armored truck. They quickly threw the bodies of the dead animals, including the two foxes, into the back of the truck and retreated into the Center. The gates slammed behind them.

Merrill's black and white tail swished back and forth. "Shit. They'll incinerate the bodies. There'll be no dignified burial."

"Yep," snarled Damon. "Another one of Robert's bright ideas has worked out well."

The two of them slowly trotted back down the hill, rejoining the rest of the animals. The spent animal group limped back through the forest in the pouring rain to their den under the bluff. No one said anything as they mourned the loss of their animal colleagues.

Antoine had been killed. Damon was devastated by the loss of his friend. His background as a former Elite athlete was quite different from Damon's, but they had both been first-body Elite youths, about the same age, with mutual party friends.

Antoine had teased Damon a few days ago. "Before you got sick, your greatest talent as an Elite was drinking yards of ale. Whereas, my talent was running yards on the track. A lot healthier!"

Life was unfair. As a human, he had become sick and had to watch his young friends enjoy the party life he had loved. Now, he was healthy, but his friends were being killed by people under his father's direction. Was there a third option?

Damon moped around the den, sleeping all day and night alone under the shaded canopy of a large white oak, ignoring the other animals. He went back to Giles' home for a few days and was similarly lethargic, so much so that Elizabeth again dosed him with the cod liver oil. Not knowing quite what to do, he returned to the den where he was greeted by a grinning Jacques.

"There you are! We've missed you."

"Hmph, what's to smile about?"

Jacques gave him a pep talk. "Listen, we're all upset at the loss of the other animals. We have to channel these setbacks into strengthening our resolve to beat the Elites. It's us or them. We have to find a way forward, and we all need your help."

"You're right," replied Damon. "I've been hoping this new life as a dog would be an improvement over my sick life before, but I'm not so sure now."

"I understand. Adjusting to this new life is hard enough without seeing our friends die. But, you know, I believe it will be a good life when we get through this adjustment period and are free of the Elite humans."

"Bloody optimist," muttered Damon.

Their conversation continued through the evening and Damon agreed to "buck up." He was grateful for the friendship and mentorship of Jacques and other animals. He had been lonely in his previous life, he realized. His friends had been superficial friends and he had no family beyond his tyrant for a father.

———◆○◆———

After a few more skirmishes where Damon and the animals tried and failed again to breach the entrances using photon torpedoes, it was clear a better plan was needed. These attacks hadn't penetrated the steel-reinforced doors but, instead the guards swarmed out to attack. Generally, these counter attacks by the guards failed because the animals killed them. But these attacks didn't get them inside the Center. And as Damon had predicted, too many animals were killed.

A stealthy approach to take over the Center was needed, utilizing the unique skills of the different animals in the group. They needed a set of plans of the Center to help them find a way to get inside. Damon knew where to get them.

———◆○◆———

Damon took Sherill Jones, who had been an Elite with coding skills, into Giles' office in the abattoir.

It was well before dawn, about three in the morning. The main building of the abattoir was a large metal shed with different work areas partitioned off inside. He had been inside with Giles a few times, but preferred to stay outside since the smell of the carcasses repulsed him, though not Shep.

They reached a side door Damon knew was kept unlocked. Jumping up, he pulled down on the handle, opening the door with a loud creak. The smell of death wafted out. They crept into the main processing area.

"Oh, God, this place stinks," hissed Sherill.

"Ssh. It's even worse during the day when the animals are being slaughtered. Quick, follow me."

Damon was relieved that the butchered carcasses already had been cleaned and processed. Empty metal hooks hung on chains from the ceiling and the multi-jointed limbs of idle chrome-plated robots hung down over lines of conveyor belts, casting a macabre appearance in the gloom. The blood that pooled on the floor during the day had been washed away by the cleaning bots.

They hastened to the back and Giles' office. Damon tried to make as little noise as possible, but was amazed how soundlessly Sherill moved—with her body crouched low to the ground—like the natural predator she was.

At the door to Giles' office, Damon again jumped up to pull down the handle. How different it was here compared with inside the Center where the electronic doors would only open after a successful ID bracelet or retinal scan.

Giles' old computer sat on the wooden desk. It had a holoscreen-capable monitor, although Damon had no plans to go into the holospace.

He'd been in the office with Giles enough times to know the man kept his password on a scrap of paper taped to the top of the large monitor— 'Lizbet!'—the affectionate name he whispered to his wife Elizabeth during their intimate nocturnal couplings when they assumed Shep wasn't listening or comprehending.

The nail of the middle claw on his front left paw was long enough to type on the keyboard. Hunting and pecking one key at a time with this single nail, he tried to log in, but failed. The holoscreen flashed red.

"What do we do now?" he asked Sherill. "How do we get into the system? We don't have Giles' ID bracelet to scan and our dog and bobcat faces are not going to fool the facial recognition system."

Sherill shook her head, giving him a broad Cheshire cat grin. "No problem mon petit chein. Computer access is my specialty, so to speak."

"Let me see," she said. Springing up into the air, she landed without a sound on the table. Her tufted ears perked up and her amber eyes focused on the glowing screen. Keeping her nails retracted, she used her soft paws to type on the keyboard and swipe through sites. She grinned at the camera a couple of times, but ignored the flashing lights on the ID scanner.

"Good," she purred. "That didn't take long. He had only a low level of anti-hacking software enabled. Now, let's see what I can find."

Damon had only rudimentary computer skills. His ears pricked up as Sherill narrated her navigation of sites with apparent ease.

"Ah, look at this would you? Who is this Underling friend of yours? Dammit, he's coordinating a huge network of Underling activism. If we were still Elites, I'd have him strung up."

"I would have too, but now I appreciate what he's doing. Perhaps we can use his Underling network to help us fight the Elites."

"I agree, but we won't have time to convince a bunch of Underlings that wild animals like us are reformed Elites! Oh, but did you know your man has a stash of weapons close by? We can help ourselves to them, I think. I'll save the coordinates and security information."

"Okay, that will be useful."

"But, we can help him too. Let's see, yep, I've decrypted a bunch of files which will give your man access to more information about the shipments of Elite resources. The more his network of activists can occupy Elite guards, the better for us. I've also scheduled a couple of software updates to help this crappy computer run faster. He can thank me later."

Sherill hacked deeper into the Center computer system from Giles' terminal, pausing every few minutes to read documents that flashed into view. Her eyes blazed. She was having fun.

"What did you used to do as an Elite?" asked Damon.

"Hmm, my day job was as a coder. My hobby was also coding, so to speak."

After a few minutes more of silence as she worked, she said, "Aha. Here we are." A maze of schematics showed on the computer screen. "Looky here, detailed blueprint plans of the Center."

"Err, yes," said Damon, though he had no clue what he was seeing. "Can you make sense of all of that?"

"Of course. Look, here is the memory transfer center. And, here's your apartment! Do you want to talk to your Nav?"

"What? How did you find that? No, no, no."

"Okay, don't panic. Now, we just need to download these plans onto a device we can take back to the den. Does Giles have a memory tablet in this office?"

"Somewhere. I've seen him use one to calculate cattle feed in the pastures."

Damon looked around the office, opening one file drawer after another. Binders, old coffee cups, empty pill bottles, a few tins of tobacco, some old girlie calendars, pens, pencils. Nothing very interesting. At the bottom of an otherwise empty file drawer, he found a scratched up MemorX tablet.

"Here, try this," he said, using both paws to lift the MemorX out from the drawer. There's a charging station here, too."

He put the charging station on the desk next to the computer and placed the MemorX into the recessed charging area. Lights flashed as the tablet established wireless communication with Giles' computer.

"Brilliant," purred Sherill as she accessed the MemorX. "Hmph, this tablet is so archaic. It's about ten upgrades out of date. I'm surprised it works. Anyway, as you said, it looks like he uses it to store data on the cattle being processed. He'll probably wonder where it is after we take it. Ha!"

"Yeah, it looks familiar. Can we use it?"

"Yes, there's enough battery charge to download the Center plans. If we hang around for ten minutes it will be fully charged and we can take it with us. While we wait, tell me, Damon, what was it like to be a first-body, rich, 'son-of-the-Center Leader' kid?"

"Shut up, you annoying prick."

—◦—

Over the next few days, Damon, Robert, Sherill, and a coyote called Kate Dennett who used to work in the power plant, developed a plan to get a team of animals inside the Center. Sherill walked them through the

Center plans on Giles' tablet, complaining all the time about the small 6-inch screen.

Kate's expertise reading plans and knowing the power systems was at the core of the plan. They gathered everyone around the campfires under the bluff.

Robert took the lead. "All Centers generate their electricity with a nuclear power plant. In the Boston Center, the power plant is just inside the north wall. We plan to sneak into the Center through the plant's water cooling pipes."

"Are you kidding? Those cooling pipes contain radioactive water," said Eli Akroyd, a bobcat, ever the skeptic. "How can we get through pipes filled with radioactive water?"

"Yes," said Kate. "The power plant is cooled by water pumped in from the Charles River two miles away. After the river water cools the reactor core, the three-foot diameter concrete pipes reverse flow and the now warmed, and contaminated water is pumped back into the river. This water pollutes the aquatic communities, but that is not a concern of the Elites. Fresh water is then pumped in through the pipe from the river washing out the contamination in the pipe as it enters the power plant. But, there are brief thirty-minute periods every day while the pumps were being reversed that the pipes are clear of water."

Damon said, "Our plan is to sneak into the Center through the water pipe during those thirty minutes when they are dry."

The fastest animals in the group were the coyotes, which could run 35-45 miles per hour. As a border collie, Damon might get Shep to run up to thirty miles per hour on a good day, and the bobcats and wolves were capable of a similar pace. As smaller animals than the wolves, coyotes would also have an easier time squeezing through tight spots in the pipes.

Damon continued. "Kate will lead a team of three coyotes through the pipes on a trial run. She's a former maintenance supervisor of the power plant, and knows her way around it well."

Kate said, "My team can get inside the power plant inside twenty minutes while the pumps are off and water isn't flowing. We will then scout out the power plant and return twenty-four hours later. If that works out, we can send in a larger task force to invade and overwhelm the Center."

Late the next night, Kate and two volunteer coyotes, squeezed through the metal bars at the end of the pipe outflow in the Charles River just as the fresh water stopped flowing.

They carried one of the radios taken from guard patrols. Using radios had taken ingenuity since the animal paws couldn't grasp hold of them. Danny solved this problem by strapping a radio to the back of one of the coyotes. Kate then pressed down the talk button on the radio with one of her paws. Jacques handled transmissions from the riverbank outside the entrance to the pipe with a radio strapped to Damon's back.

At first, everything went well.

Kate reported. "We have exited the pipe and are inside the cooling tower."

"Copy that," said Jacques.

They had made good progress running up inside the damp but empty pipe. They then squeezed through the metal bars at the other end of the intake pipe inside the base of the cooling tower. The cooling tower was separate from the nuclear reactor.

A couple of minutes later, Kate reported, "Out of the cooling tower. Into the power plant."

They'd made it in. Damon smiled. They had probably pushed open the small hatchway at the base of the cooling tower and climbed out into an open area of the nuclear plant beside the cooling tower.

The water started flowing through the pipe back to the river. Jacques reported to Kate. "Kate, the pipe flow has reversed. We aren't sure why, but warm, radioactive water is being pumped down to the river. That should not be a problem now you are out of the pipe. We may have to adjust the timing of your exit, but we will monitor the water flow."

"Copy that," she replied. "We are scouting around the cooling tower looking for an unguarded door through the wall into the main Center building."

At this point, they should be close to other buildings that housed the turbines generating the electricity next to the nuclear reactor itself. The entire area of the power plant was inside the Center wall on one side, with similar concrete walls on the other three sides.

"Having problems finding a way into the Center," reported Kate.

Guards were posted along the walls of the power plant and there were more guards with Alsatian dogs at each door. Motion detectors and floodlights covered the entire area.

"The guards have spotted us. We're taking incoming," said Kate, against the sounds of gunfire in the background.

The small group waiting outside the pipe by the river sat in stunned silence, hoping for another radio transmission, but it never came.

Kate and the other two coyotes had been valued members of the group. Umberto Ramirez had been a well-known athlete, like Antoine, killed during the earlier attack. They had represented the Center in athletic competitions with the other Centers. Damon had also gotten to know Art Warburg, another sick young Elite youth like him. Although they hadn't known each other in the Center, their few conversations as animals had revealed they shared a similar spoiled history.

"We had better get away before the guards track the coyotes back through the pipe and start coming after us," Damon said to the group.

"Damn, they were good friends," said Jacques.

They ran into the nighttime gloom back to the forest to the den, to lick their wounds and discuss what to do next.

It took a few days to come to terms with the loss of the three coyotes killed during the mission. Damon was miserable—just as he got to know an animal, then they were killed. Antoine, Archie, Art, Katie, Marty, Umberto—the list was getting too long.

Damon went back to Giles' house for a few days. As usual, Giles welcomed him back, seemingly unconcerned with his prolonged absences. Elizabeth was not so happy, giving him another soapy bath and recommending again that he got tied up. They seemed to be coping well with the worsening social situation and were not short of food for their table.

Recovering from the loss of his coyote friends was just part of the mental anguish Damon was going through. The camaraderie of his new animal friends and the kindness shown by Giles and Elizabeth elicited new emotions he'd not experienced before.

For the first time in his life, he recognized the benefits of helping others and just being plain nice. Even if it was possible, could he go back to his prior existence? As he lay by the fire at Giles' feet in the evenings, he turned over these thoughts. Gradually, he reached an epiphany.

Any thoughts he had of returning to the Center and seeking a memory transfer into a new Underling body faded. He had to return to the den and help his new animal family.

The other animals were devastated at the loss of their coyote friends. After a few subdued days when even rabbit hunting was of little interest, the den members gathered around the campfire as the sun was setting. In small groups, the discussion centered around what they should do next.

Robert stood up and called everyone's attention. "Den members, we need to discuss our future plans."

"The loss of our friends is on our minds," said Jacques.

"Kate and I worked together in the power plant," said Danny, voice choked up with grief.

"And, I was just getting to know Art and Umberto as guys in my age group," said Damon. *Compared with the rest of you oldies. Yet, again, I'm losing new friends.*

"I'm grieving, too, but this setback can't diminish our resolve to take down the Centers and all the Elites," said Robert. "Damon's plan to get into the Center through the water pipes was a tragic failure and a bad idea."

"What do you mean *my* plan?" he growled.

"Shut it, Damon. We will go back to frontal attacks on the gates."

"The frontal attacks were a bloodbath," growled Danny.

Other animals growled, too.

Damon spoke up. "Although going in through the water pipes didn't work, we now have a better understanding about how the nuclear core is kept cool with river water. That will help us come up with ideas of how to bring down the Centers. We need to work with the other animals with

Elite memories around the other Centers and come up with coordinated plans."

"Listen!" replied Robert. "I am the den leader and will not stand to be questioned like this."

Damon vehemently barked back. "It's not working, Robert. Under your leadership we've had tragic losses of life. Twice. I appreciate your passion, but we need someone else to lead us. Someone with better ideas that are going to succeed."

"What?" snarled Robert. He bared his teeth at Damon, fur bristling, and growling. Spittle drooled out of his mouth.

Damon worried he had overstepped. But, he resolutely stood his ground. This was too important. It was a fight he had to have. A fight he would win.

They were matched in size, but as a coyote, Robert's host had more experience fighting other animals than Damon's sheep dog host, Shep. But, Shep was used to the fast herding of domestic animals. He was quick and agile, and outmaneuvered Robert's host. Robert lunged at Damon, trying to get his jaws onto his throat. By contrast, Damon darted in and out, nipping at the coyote's legs.

The two rivals paused to catch their breath. Stepping back from Robert, Damon studied Robert's coyote and how his sides heaved. More confident, he stood tall, snarling in the face of the threat. Robert lunged again and caught him by the neck with his powerful jaws. Damon scrambled back and the two of them grappled in a violent clash of teeth and claws. Robert's teeth pierced his skin causing a warm flow of blood. Shep yelped and twisted his body. As Robert released his grip, Damon lunged for the coyote's muzzle and tasted blood. His teeth had pierced the soft skin around Robert's eyes.

As quick as it started, it was over. Robert rolled on his back in submission, blood pouring from the bite on his face. His left eye was a bloody, sightless mess. More blood dripped from slash wounds on his neck. Damon stood in silence over his foe for a few seconds, then he stepped away. Robert crawled off into the darkness.

A shocked hush filled the den. Damon looked around anxiously. Would the rest of the den now turn on him? After a few minutes, several animals murmured their approval of Damon. Their silhouettes, illuminated by the den's evening fire, flickered like waltzing shadows.

Group members began to speak.

"We can't afford more losses of life."

"A more decisive plan is needed."

"A den leader with more inspiration and vision is needed."

Jacques said, "I nominate Damon."

Damon gulped. "What?"

"He's been involved in many of our den activities since joining us. He always has good, reasonable ideas, and I've been impressed with his dedication to our well-being," said Jacques.

"I second the nomination," said Danny. "Damon has been an important part of many of our successful activities, and he warned us about the folly of Robert's plans. He helped me learn how to use the guards' weapons. He helped Helen and Bruce set up the avian network. He has knowledge of Underling activity as a sheep dog for the boss of the beef production facility. And, his inside knowledge of Elite leadership as son of Taurus Najor is unparalleled."

A growl of assent swept through the animal group. Robert's remaining good eye blazed with anger from a far corner of the den.

The den had a new leader.

Damon listened in shocked silence. Then he stood tall and faced the den, accepting the leadership position. *This is something I can do. This is my purpose.*

———————◆○◆———————

After becoming den leader, Damon asked Danny and Jacques to be his lieutenants, members of his inner council. He would rely upon their advice in making decisions for the den. Danny's tenacity mastering the use of weapons and fire lighting were evidence of his valuable technical skills. Jacques was a calming figure in the den and a mentor to Damon, sharing wisdom, feedback, and encouragement.

Helen had news via the avian network. Damon brought Danny and Jacques together for a meeting.

He sat on his haunches on a flat rock in the shade of some tall oak trees in a quiet area off to the side of the den. "Helen, repeat to Danny and Jacques the news you have from the Melbourne animal group."

"Sure," she squawked. "The Melbourne animals took out their Elite Center with no loss of animal casualties."

"Really? Oh, that's great, but how on Earth? Tell us how they did it," Jacques said.

"Well," she chirped. "Remember the water inlet pipes your coyotes used to try and enter the nuclear plant?"

"Unfortunately, yes," said Danny. "That effort led to the loss of three friends, and they didn't even get out of the nuclear plant and into the Center. It was a tragedy."

"Right," went on Helen. "But the genius of the Melbourne animals was recognizing that the inflow of cold river water in those pipes was the only thing keeping the nuclear power plant cool. Blow up the pipe, stop the inflow of water, and the core heats up. Then there's a meltdown and a massive nuclear explosion."

"Oh, my God. Is that what they did? And it worked?" Danny jumped up in the air with excitement.

"Exactly," said Helen. The avian cadence of her speech was frenetic. "The Melbourne Center had a massive meltdown, and there was a huge nuclear explosion that demolished the entire Center. It killed all the Elites and everyone else in a fifteen-mile radius. There are no more Melbourne Elites."

Danny, Jacques, and Damon looked at each other in silent amazement. Their eyes as wide as saucers.

"That's wonderful... I mean that's terrible," Damon said, unsure how he should take the news of this massive loss of life.

"It is terrible," said Danny. "But, we have to do the same if it'll get rid of the Elites and free us up for a life without harassment."

"It is a big decision which we can't take lightly," Jacques said. "As a former political scientist, I know the anguished ethical dilemma the leaders of the Allies went through during World War Two when they dropped atom bombs on cities in Japan."

Damon looked at the three of them in turn. "If we and the animal groups around the other Centers decide to do this, then we are taking an irreversible decision. It will lead to unprecedented destruction of the very group of people that we were a part of just a few weeks ago. In addition to the loss of life, there will be a large contaminated and uninhabitable area around each Center. Jacques is right, we have to think carefully of the moral implications of such a decision."

Perched on a low branch above us, Helen added, "I agree, Damon. The Melbourne animals were unanimous in their decision to go ahead, but only after considerable discussion and a period of moral reflection. We will need to have a similar discussion here. The animal groups around the other Centers have also learned what happened in Melbourne and are having their own discussions."

"If we decide to go ahead," said Danny, "we will need to work out the logistics of stopping the water flow. How long do we need to stop the water flow to the reactor core? How long before a meltdown and explosion occurs? From my work in the power plant, I am quite certain the Elites don't have an effective backup in case the inflow of cooling water is disrupted."

"Yes, Danny," said Damon. "These are all important questions, but as Helen said, we need to be sure that this is a road we wish to go down. Danny, get together with Helen or Bruce, and Isaac, and come up with a plan. Your knowledge of the nuclear plant will be essential in choosing where to stop the inflow of cooling water. Isaac's expertise as former head of security will help us plan how to disrupt the water flow, presumably by blowing up the pipe. Helen, either you or Bruce as former captains of the guard, can add similar expertise, but we need one of you to continue coordinating the avian network. Report back to me when you have a plan, then we will it put to everyone in the den for discussion and approval."

Three days later, Danny, Bruce, Jacques, and Isaac met with Damon under the same oak trees.

Sitting with his hindquarters and tail on the ground, with his front legs straight out supporting his upper body, Damon started the discussion. "Bruce what's the plan the Melbourne animals used that caused the nuclear power plant at their Center to explode?"

"Yes." Bruce perched on the branch of a low-growing redbud. "Basically, they simply blew up the water inflow pipeline close to the nuclear core. Within twenty minutes, the core started to melt down and heat up. Even though the power workers inserted hafnium control rods into the reactor core in an attempt to absorb the excess neutrons, it made no difference. Their containment systems failed and the whole thing blew up within three hours. The sabotage team of dingos made it out safely from the pipe before their explosives detonated."

Isaac provided additional details. "We can do the same with a small team of coyotes. This time, the team only needs to get a little way into the water pipe. They will be in no danger from guards in the nuclear plant. They can enter the pipe at the start of the thirty minutes that it is empty of water. The water pipe has a three-foot diameter with six-inch thick concrete walls that will be easy to breach with explosives. The team can haul a forty-two-gallon drum of ammonium nitrate, agricultural fertilizer, a few feet inside the entrance of the pipe and attach a small blasting cap to the outside of the drum. The blasting cap will connect remotely to a hand-held detonator. Once our team has gotten out of the pipe, they will set off the explosion in the pipe before water enters it again from the river by transmitting an electrical signal from the detonator. After the pipe blows, the team will have three hours to get at least twenty miles away from the Center."

"That all sounds fine," said Jacques "But where will we get the supplies?"

"No problem with the ammonium nitrate," Damon said. "I know where drums of it are in a storage shed on a farm by the abattoir. It will be heavy, but we can put a drum onto one of the handcarts in the shed. A wolf can pull the cart to the entrance of the pipeline. That's only a couple of miles away. No one guards the shed and we can move the fertilizer in one night."

"And I know where we can get the blasting cap, fuse wire, and detonator." Bruce added. "There's a guard storage shed at an abandoned outpost just three miles away from the end of the pipeline that has everything we need."

Damon's tail swished with agreement, and his eyes gazed intensely at the others. "Okay, I'll take a small team to get the fertilizer drum, and hide it close to the pipeline by the river. Isaac, pick a partner and get the blasting supplies from the abandoned outpost and store them securely by the pipeline. When all that is done, we will meet with the rest of our group here at the den and let them know of these plans."

The animals started to separate, to handle their assigned tasks.

"One other thing," Danny added. "We will need to leave this den as we will be too close to ground zero. We will need all animals like us to be at least twenty miles away when the blast occurs. And even at that distance, there can be danger from radioactive fallout which can travel hundreds of miles downwind from the blast site. Can we send someone to find us a new den?"

"Good point," said Damon. "Bruce, how about you fly over the area downriver from here, and find us a new den? Have Janet and Jerry follow you out there and check it out on the ground."

That night, Damon went with Alan Terrell and Danny to get the fertilizer. Alan was a large, muscular wolf who had been a moderate Elite overseeing Underling farmers in the region. He had experience handling fertilizers, including ammonium nitrate.

The night sky was moonless and overcast, allowing them to quickly reach the farm where the storage shed was located. Hunkering down in bushes downwind of the shed, they checked no one was around. All was quiet as expected at two in the morning. The farm buildings were upwind about a half mile away across open fields. Damon didn't want their scent to carry down to any farm dogs.

Alan raised his head, his ears pricked, and sniffed the breeze. He snorted. "I don't hear or smell anything to worry about."

"The shed is over there at the bottom of the field," said Damon.

Danny growled in agreement. "Okay, follow me."

They ran around the edge of the field. Alan and Danny's graceful strides barely making a sound, blending with the shadows. They quickly reached the storage shed. Damon panted, having had trouble keeping up with the two wolves.

The shed was old and constructed of weather-beaten planks of river birch. The door was similarly constructed, its grain worn by time. The door was unlocked.

Alan pushed the door open and muttered, "A fertilizer storage facility should always be locked. The farmer will have a lot of explaining to do when he can't account for a drum of ammonium nitrate."

"It looks like there are several drums in here," said Danny as they went inside. "Are all of these ammonium nitrate?"

"Yes," said Alan. "And look, here's the handcart you mentioned, Damon. Loading the barrel on the cart will be tricky, but between Danny and I, we should be able to do it. Sit back on your haunches, Danny, and I'll roll the barrel onto your front legs, then I can help you lift it onto the back of the cart."

"Damn!" growled Danny.

The barrel had rolled back down onto the floor of the shed with a load clatter. They froze at the sound of distant barking.

Damon let out a low growl. "That's the farmer's dog,"

The barking got louder and closer. "Stay quiet, everyone, I'll go out and head her off," said Damon.

Running outside of the shed, he crouched behind a pile of logs and waited for the dog to approach. She came fast, only stopping when she was a few yards from the shed. She looked to the left and right and sniffed the air, clearly trying to locate the source of the earlier sound.

As she came into view, Damon gasped. She was a beautiful young black and white collie. Even in the dark, her coat gleamed. His host, Shep, strained to run over and try to couple with her, and it was all Damon could do to restrain him.

"Over here," growled Damon, hoping she would understand. "Can you understand, if I speak English?

She walked over slowly, panting and suspicious. "Yes," was her breathy and labored reply. "Not spoken to anyone else. Been trying to speak. Hoping to find others."

"Good, I'm Damon. Who are you?"

"Eve."

"You should join our group, but not tonight. We've an important project. In a couple of days, run down into the forest and someone will guide you to our den. For now, please return to the farm as we don't want the farmer to know we are here."

"But..."

"Please, it's important. You need to make the farmer think you were barking at a passing fox."

"Okay, but please find me. I'm very scared about being a dog."

"I know, it's still new for me, too. It gets easier. When you reach our den, I promise I'll help you. I want to help you."

He was anguished, suppressing Shep's physical attraction for her. Yet, he understood and felt the feelings of attraction, just the same as he used to have for good-looking girls his age in his human life. He ached to make a move on her.

Unlike in his previous life, sensibility won out this time. "I've got to go back into the shed now. I'll see you later, okay?"

She nodded, turned around, and started running back to the farm.

Filled with relief and loss, Damon returned to Danny and Alan already laying in the shadows at the back of the shed.

After another attempt, they finally loaded the fertilizer drum onto the handcart. With the rope they had brought with them, they constructed a harness for Alan and Danny's shoulders and chest. Connecting the harness to the sled with additional ropes, they pulled the cart in tandem, much like a traditional dog-sled. Damon ran alongside the cart and called out directions.

They headed out of the shed, moving slowly across the fields and pastures. The two wolves grunted with the effort. The ground was bumpy, and Damon worried the drum would fall off the cart, but Danny had secured it well. He thoroughly enjoyed directing them this way and that.

But they didn't seem to be having as much fun. They growled often, telling him to keep quiet.

After a couple of hours, the three of them reached the outlet of the water pipe by the river. Hiding the drum of fertilizer in nearby bushes, they abandoned the cart a half mile away in a dry stream gully, then hastily ran back to the den.

As they made their way back, Damon thought about Giles and Elizabeth. They had been kind to him, but they would be in the blast zone. Should he warn them?

He asked Danny, "What would you think about warning some of the Underlings, telling them to get away from the area around the Center for a few days?"

"Absolutely not! If we start telling people, then the element of surprise may be lost. People talk. Besides, what would you do? You're a dog. Would you start talking English to them? That would freak them out."

"But, Giles and Elizabeth, the couple that my host dog Shep lived with, were always very kind to me. I hate to think of them suffering."

"Perhaps they were, but they didn't know you were a human. How would they react to that news?"

"Well, I'm sure I can explain everything to them," Damon said, though he felt uncertain.

Danny stopped and stared at Damon, his wolf eyes burning like embers in a fire. "No! That's a stupid idea."

He pushed his muzzle into Damon's haunch, almost knocking him down as he shoved him forward. "Get a move on, we need to get back to the den."

"Screw you."

Damon set off running in what he hoped was the direction of the abattoir and Giles' house. In the dark there were few familiar landmarks.

He didn't get very far. Danny and Alan were large, powerful wolves, and both much faster. He didn't have a chance. They quickly caught up and circled around him like they were hunting prey.

Alan reached him first, grabbing the scruff of his neck with his jaws. Danny wasn't far behind and pushed him down to the ground and put his open jaws into Damon's face. A pungent, gamey odor was on his breath. "No," he said. "You're coming back to the den with us if you know what's good for you."

"You're supposed to be our den leader now. Act like it," snarled Alan.

Damon could do nothing against two 150-pound male wolves. He pulled away from their grasp and rolled over on his back, exposing his underbelly submissively. He avoided Alan and Danny's gazes.

He whined with a high-pitched yelp. "Okay, I get it. I'll return to the den."

They backed off him and let him get up. Danny displayed his dominance as an alpha male, holding his head high. "Come on, then," he growled. "I'll be watching you for the next few days."

By the time they got back to the den, they were exhausted. They crashed out by the smoldering embers of the campfire. Damon lay awake, knowing that Danny had been right—he was happy with his decision to remain with the animals and he had accepted Elite lives would be lost. If he wanted to remain leader of the den, he needed to act like a leader. Besides, he needed to stay in the den, in case Eve turned up. The possibility of seeing her again filled him with erotic excitement, and gave him hope. But he was despondent about the loss of life that they were about to cause, and especially the fate of Giles and Elizabeth.

When the sun came up the next day, after finally getting a good rest, Damon was ready to move forward with their plans. He wasn't happy with what they were planning, but it was what they had to do. Perhaps there was still a way to save Giles and Elizabeth. But he had to act strong as the den leader and set aside his personal feelings.

The next evening, as the usual meal of roast rabbit was being cooked over the fires, Damon called everyone together. "I want to share the plans we have come up with to take down the Center."

Damon outlined the plan, adding it had worked in Melbourne. As he went through the details, a murmuring built up among the den members. Several were growling, whining, and others had questions.

"Was it a nuclear blast that caused the Melbourne Center to blow?" asked one of the bobcats.

"Wasn't there a huge loss of Elite lives?" asked someone else.

"Wouldn't we be killing a lot of our friends and relatives with this plan?"

"And what about the Underlings living around the Center? Won't they become innocent casualties?"

"It's too risky," growled Robert from the back.

Several of the animals hissed at him.

Since being deposed as leader by Damon, Robert had kept to himself. He hadn't caused any trouble, but hadn't been very helpful either, moping around like a child whose favorite toy had been taken away. A couple of other coyotes followed him around, but the rest of the den had turned away from him. Damon kept a wary eye on him, ready to act if he tried to challenge his leadership.

"Yes, there will be a loss of Elite lives, and Underlings caught outside in the blast zone," he said. "But many moderate Elites, especially members of MEE, have been escaping the Center over the last few days. We believe most are now out as animals. Our numbers have been steadily growing."

"This may seem like a radical approach," said Jacques Grimball. "But, back since the early twenty-first century, environmental advocates have argued that sabotage was a necessary tactic for the climate change move-ment. And, look what the radical Underling activists have been doing. I believe a similar radical approach is now needed by us."

Isaac said, "As you know, at first I was against us taking on the Elites, especially given my background as a former Council member. But, we've all seen what Taurus Najor and his acolytes have been doing to anyone who crosses them. That's why I'm here. My memory transfer failed because I spoke up against his policies, and he didn't want me around anymore. We have to kill the Elites before they kill us. I worked on developing this plan with Damon and the others. It's a good plan that won't cost any animal lives."

"Thanks, Issac," said Damon. "Den members, will you support the plan?"

A haunting howl echoed through the forest wilderness, signaling uni-ty, and the primal beauty of their new existence.

CHAPTER ELEVEN

CHATURA AND TING'S 3RD AND 4TH TASKS

Chatura met with Ting at the usual French café holospace they both liked. They now met daily to discuss their next two tasks--finding out who was responsible for the memory transfer failures, and contacting the agitated animals.

Chatura's French was improving, although he was speaking in Hindi and hearing his auto-translated hologram speak French.

"Who should we consider?" Ting asked.

Their primary suspects were Najor and Tourni at the Boston Center, and Sydney Fortesque-Hamilton, leader of the London Center.

"I'd say that any of the Center leaders must be suspects, along with NOEW members such as Alan Moorehead. But, not many of them will have the coding skills needed. They will have used forced or paid help from a computer jock."

"Or a fanatical loner who will be hard to track down," Ting replied.

"Yes, I wouldn't put it past some of our extreme gaming friends to be involved. Remember a few years ago when that Australian gamer Adam Waru hacked into the accounts belonging to leaders of the Oculus Quest game? He wiped out their accounts and sent them plummeting down the leaderboards. It was chaos until he was caught."

"And he was finally caught by other gamers entering the code via the holospace—that's what we are going to have to do," she replied.

"Wait. We can enter the memory transfer code through the holospace?"

"Yeah, there we can watch as the code runs activities coordinated across the globe, such as communications, food supply, military operations, transportation systems, and, of course, the memory transfer facilities. Access is restricted to all but a few with appropriate entry codes, and gamers and computer geeks with hacking skills. I can get us in to parts of the code, but we will have to be careful."

Chatura's hologram flickered as it did whenever he got emotional. "Yes, let's do it. What if it's someone like Waru who's responsible for the memory transfer failure? Is he still active in the dark web?"

"Er, I don't know if he's still around."

"Who else would be leading gamer suspects? We should draw up a list. I'd include that asshole Bjorn Järvinen from Helsinki, Havier Jornadas from Buenos Aires, and Jianguo Wei from your Center in Shanghai. Do you know Wei?" asked Chatura, his hologram glowing bright red as he said 'asshole' and Järvinen's name together.

"Wei? I know him only by reputation, fortunately." Ting's hologram shaded toward a rose in response to Chatura's emotional outburst. "He's bad news, and most of my gaming friends try to avoid him. Not too long ago, he humiliated my friend Chang by hacking her gaming code to make it take self-defeating decisions. He spent a week denigrating her achievements developing the Pegasus and Pyramid games. I wouldn't put it past him to enjoy messing up the memory transfer code just for fun."

Chatura nodded. "Yeah, he's bad news. But the memory transfer failures have been going on for three months now, and the targeting of moderate Elites suggests something more than nefarious fun by a sick mind."

Her gaze locked with Chatura's. "Okay then, let's go into the code. Give me a couple of days. I'll send you entry codes from one of my gaming friends and let you know where we can meet."

⸺◆⸺

"Wow! Look at this place," exclaimed Chatura. He'd met up with Ting in the code holospace. "And listen to it. I expected it to be silent. That whooshing sound, as code routines are running, is like an electronic synthesizer permeating the holospace. It reminds me of the early music of Neon Dream."

"What are you talking about?" hissed Ting.

"Neon Dream? They were a 2100s German band who later scored the soundtrack of the influential InteractaQuest V video game. You must know of them."

"Err, no. Definitely before my time," replied Ting, sounding unconcerned.

Chatura and Ting entered the code via the holospace a couple of days after their last meeting in the French café when they could get away from work unnoticed. They were used to the holospace for meet-ups with friends, and gaming, but exploring code was a new experience for both of them.

It wasn't too different from entering the holospace using a virtual reality headset. One difference was that they were represented in the code by an icon or avatar rather than a dynamic hologram. Not knowing too much about what to expect, they both created nondescript gray avatars and met up near the start of the memory transfer code.

Navigating the code holospace was like walking along a trail in a dark, shady, forest. The code appeared on the ground, the walls, and the roof as a fluorescent, glowing green trail. The memory transfer code was much like other code. It appeared as a long and dimly lit tunnel winding off into the darkness. 'Gates' led off to subroutines, and portals connected to the code of other systems.

Chatura couldn't contain his excitement. "I can't believe this place. With the right access codes, we could travel the virtual world, accessing everything."

Off in the distance down the tunnel, the gray avatars of other people were moving around, working on the code.

"We'd better be careful not to draw attention to ourselves," whispered Ting. "We'll end up in the lithium mines if we are caught."

The closeness of their avatars to each other sent a thrill through Chatura. When his avatar shimmered, Ting gave him a quizzical look.

She whispered, "My access codes allow only limited access to the memory transfer code, but we can follow its main thread down this tunnel."

"Yeah," said Chatura. "I could spend days exploring these other areas. Let's look at some gaming code. What fun!"

Ting moved her avatar closer. "Focus! I wouldn't call this fun. More like creepy."

Although they were in a virtual space with limited tactile sensory input, he got a thrill from the closeness of her avatar. Occasionally, his fingers and hands tingled as his hologloves picked up input from Ting's hologloves. As someone who had never had a physical relationship, these feelings sent cold shivers and unfamiliar, yet excited sensations through his body, particularly in his groin. He scrunched his eyes closed, held his breath, and formed his hands into tight fists to return his focus to exploring the code with Ting.

Ting gave him a questioning look. "Are you okay?"

"Yeah, yeah, I'm just a bit disoriented in this holospace. I'll be fine," he replied and opened his eyes, showing her a firm smile.

Creeping along with Ting through the tunnel, he had hints of the code in other areas. After a while of reading the code that glowed green on the tunnel floor, they reached the area that controlled the memory transfer module.

"Look at this code snippet in Python," exclaimed Chatura. "Memory signals from the Elite are allocated to a temporary source buffer and copied to the Underling destination buffer. It's simple, but brilliant!"

On the floor were lines of code for handling memory management.

```
# Allocate memory for two buffers
buffer_size = 10x10E6
src_buffer = (ctypes.c_int * buffer_size)(*range(buffer_size))
dest_buffer = (ctypes.c_int * buffer_size)()


# Function to transfer memory content
def transfer_memory(src, dest, size):
for i in range(size):
dest[i] = src[i]


# Perform memory transfer
```

```
transfer_memory(src_buffer, dest_buffer, buffer_size)
# Display contents of the destination buffer
print(list(dest_buffer))
```

"And, here's where technicians input code identifying the Center, date, Elite and Underling patient information, and the paired beds in the treatment facility," said Chatura pointing to more lines of code.

"Right, that sets up, authorizes, and documents each memory transfer," Ting added, continuing, "If we can access these records, we will know even more about the history of memory transfers."

"We can see here that this is quite old code written when the memory transfers were first set up," he said. "But here in the brighter color is recent code controlling the memory transfer unit. When a '0' is input, the transfer unit head points directly to the Underling so they can receive the Elite's memories. When a "1" is input, the transfer unit head points a random direction 45 to 315 degrees away from the Underling."

"Damn," he exclaimed. "As soon as that code is input, the Elite's memories are transferred out and away from the Underling recipient. That's how the Elite's memories are lost. Memory losses are controlled by accessing this code, probably by a technician in the memory transfer unit."

"Yes, but how do those diverted memories end up in a semi-sentient animal?"

"There's an ID tag here that shows this piece of code was inserted by someone called Peter King on February twenty-fifth, three months ago. It wasn't too long afterward, in my data, that the agitated animals started to show up. We should talk with him about this."

"Hold on," Ting whispered as her gray avatar faded away.

Chatura's avatar spun around looking for her. "Wait, where are you going?"

Ting had left the holospace. In a panic, Chatura realized he was alone. She'd done it again, disappeared.

Has she gone somewhere, or have they been discovered, and Ting captured or killed? What should I do?

He backed into a corner of the tunnel by one of the portals to adjacent lines of code and tried to shrink his avatar. The eerie sound of Neon Dream's 'Rubycon' was playing in the tunnel creating a lonely, anxious feeling that scared him. Every few minutes, an avatar from a coder whooshed past on their way to part of the code. Fortunately, no one stopped to ask him why he was standing around and not working.

After an eternity, Ting's gray avatar reappeared right by the recent code they had been looking at. At the same time, a bright pink, candle-shaped avatar appeared next to her.

"Here's the code that I wrote," the pink avatar said.

"But why did you write it, what was the purpose? You must have known it would doom the person whose memory was being transferred," Ting replied.

"Hang on, Ting, what's going on? Who is this?" He moved over toward Ting's avatar and the pink candle.

"Oh, sorry, but Peter King's name cropped up as the writer of this recent code. I immediately searched for him in the holospace. I hadn't met Peter before, but knew of him as a code writer for the Elites with, shall we say, moderately progressive views. My search showed he was already in the code. I took a chance and found him quickly. After I explained what was going on, he agreed to come and look at this code with us."

"Actually, I don't make a habit of wandering around the code at the whim of gals I've not met before," said Peter. "But, I've been worried that these bloody lines may be causing problems even before Ting found me. And after she mentioned the agitated animals, well, here I am."

"Why did you write this additional code allowing the memory transfer technician the option to send the Elite's memories away from the recipient Underling?" Chatura asked, trying to ignore Peter's annoying upper-class English accent.

"It came through as a work order from head office. Although somewhat unusual, it wasn't signed. I got on with the job without thinking of its implications. I assumed the technicians needed to point the memory transfer head in different directions, like if the Underling is on the left bed instead of the right bed, or testing. I get a lot of code requests that don't make much sense. I get them done and move on to the next work order. Later, as word of the increasing number of memory losses started circulating among us coders, I wondered if my code had some connection. I asked a few questions but was told by my bosses that that aggravating twit Fortesque-Hamilton had put the word out to keep anything to do with memory losses under our hat, and for coders like me to just get on with my job, and not ask any bloody questions."

Chatura got closer to Peter. "My God, this comes from the top, Fortesque-Hamilton—the London Center leader? And, I'll bet he's acting in cahoots with Taurus Najor who runs the Elite Council."

"I don't know, but that's probably true. And, to my shame, my code killed anyone whose memories were diverted."

"At first, yes," said Chatura. "But it wasn't long before those diverted memories were being picked up by animals."

"How though, would diverted memories, with just enough strength to reach the intended Underling, reach a semi-sentient animal two to three, or even more, miles away?" Ting interjected. "The memory transfer head is designed to point right at the recipient Underling's head with just enough power to deliver the memories. Did you also add boosters?"

"No, I didn't. And you're right, signal boosters have been added. I've no idea by who, though."

"The number of memory losses started increasing after you inserted the new code three months ago, and then two months ago agitated animals started to appear. The two things didn't happen at the same time," said Chatura.

"That means the memory signal boosters were added in response to the uptick in memory transfer losses," said Ting.

"Yes, exactly. Can we find out who added the memory signal boosters from the code? The coder's name must be there as with any other code," Chatura said.

"Absolutely, old chap, I think you're right," said Peter. "But it's not near the rest of the memory transfer code that I've been working on. I'm familiar with that code."

"But we can set traps to intercept memory transfer code activity, and track it back to where it's being boosted. Since we already know where it will be coming from, we can then triangulate to find the boosters," Ting said.

"Yes, great idea. Let me think about it a bit and insert some discrete code in the right places to do exactly that. I'll let you know what I find. Toodle-pip." With that, Peter's pink avatar blinked off.

"Wait!" But Chatura was too late, Peter had gone. "Can we trust him? He was awfully eager to help. And what the heck is 'toodle-pip'? Perhaps he's setting a trap for us, so the authorities can catch us."

"We can trust him," said Ting. "I hadn't met him before today, but he hates the NOEW Elites because of their anti-gay policies."

He shrugged. "Oh, I just hope he can find something out about the boosters. But meanwhile, this whole memory loss problem is much worse than we first suspected."

"Yeah," she said. "If the Center leaders are getting rid of Elites they don't like, then this is the equivalent of a police state. We need to be very careful."

Ting's avatar dimmed as she left the café, but not before her avatar merged seductively into his. "Be careful, Chatura."

A few days later, Chatura was studying new mapping data when his hologoggles chirped. Ting asked him to join her in the code holospace. When he put on the goggles and joined her, he found Ting and Peter's avatars in a place he didn't recognize.

Confused, Chatura looked around. "Where are we? We are a long way from the code for the memory transfer unit."

They were in an area of nondescript-looking gray code. The electronic synthesizer sound that had permeated the areas of highly active code was absent. Instead, the holospace was silent, except for clicking sounds as lines of code were accessed.

"Thanks for joining us, Chatura," said Ting. "Peter has been making progress finding the memory signal boosters. You had better make your avatar gray like ours. We are trying not to be found in this part of the code."

Peter said, "This part of the code is well hidden in the cleanup area where routines are reset after a memory transfer session. Look at these lines of code." He pointed to the ground of the tunnel. "These two thousand lines of code turn on four memory signal boosters that have been installed at each cardinal direction in the air vents of the memory transfer room at each Elite Center. The weak signal misdirected away from the recipient Underling is boosted ten thousand times. That would give it plenty of strength to reach outside the Center and be picked up by a semi-sentient animal."

"But, even with the strong signal," queried Chatura, "how does the diverted and boosted memory signal get picked up by an unprepared semi-sentient animal? I mean, in the memory transfer facility, the recipient Underling has its mind wiped, and wears a special headset with electrodes that picks up the memory signals allowing the Elite memories to take over its mind."

"I agree," said Peter. "It's a mystery to me too how animals pick up the memory signals. Presumably, it's got something to do with the difference between the minds of humans and animals."

"Wow," said Ting. "Regardless of how it works, this means that there has been a coordinated installation of the memory boosters at each Elite Center. Who could have done that?"

"Well, do you know about the underground MEE group? It stands for Moderate Elites for Equality. As you know, the identity of coders shows up in the code anytime new lines are added. Look at these lines of the signal-boosting code here." He pointed to an area of code on the floor. "It is brilliantly written code with an encrypted signature. I couldn't decipher it, but after off-the-record discussions with a few of my moderate coding friends, I learned it was Pierre Fortrand. He's a French-born coder based in the Helsinki Center. He's a member of MEE. He inserted the code and MEE members in each Center installed the actual memory signal boosters."

"Great work," said Chatura. "Now we know NOEW members were responsible for the memory transfer failures to try and kill off moderate Elites, and MEE members have been boosting diverted memories with enough strength to be picked up by a semi-sentient animal. Was that on purpose or a last-ditch attempt to save loved ones?"

"I'm not a member of MEE, but I know Fortrand slightly. I can get in touch with him." Peter's avatar blinked off and he was gone.

Chatura and Ting looked at each other, uncertain of what to do next.

"The NOEW and MEE members are opposing Elite groups. No one told me there were different factions of Elites, let alone that they might be fighting with each other," said Chatura.

"You need to get out more," joked Ting. "But, I didn't know about NOEW and MEE, either. And it seems they don't care that their selfish feud is ultimately reducing the Elite population when we should be working together to increase our numbers."

"Yes, ideally, and we should be careful and keep our heads down as I don't think the NOEW Elites will stand for us poking around in the memory transfer code. So far we've not been caught, thank goodness, and Peter is not a NOEW member."

Just as Chatura stopped talking, the tunnel of code they were in turned red and the wailing sound of sirens filled the air.

"Intruders in the code, stay where you are."

Chatura's avatar spun around—several bright red security avatars raced down the tunnel toward them. "Gotta go! Meet me in the French café."

A large security avatar appeared in front of Chatura. If it merged with his avatar, he would be captured. He twisted away, ducking down to the floor and ran past the avatar. Charging forward, he followed Ting's avatar to an open portal. The portal led to a narrow service tunnel back to the memory transfer unit code. As they dashed through the portal, Ting's avatar turned around and punched some numbers into a keypad on the wall; the portal closed, leaving only a smooth tunnel wall. The chasing gray avatars rushed past Chatura and Ting's location.

"How did you do that?" he screamed.

"One of my friends gave me access codes she said would come in useful in an emergency. Now we can get back to the café without being tracked."

———◆◇◆———

Chatura arrived at the French café two days later to meet Ting, Peter, and Pierre. Although they were in holospace, other people were still in the café. They chose a table towards the back for privacy. It was Chatura's first time meeting Peter in person and he was a bit surprised by the Englishman's bright and flamboyant clothing. Pierre was a new addition to their group. His hologram showed him dressed sensibly in blue jeans and a light brown button-down shirt.

"Thanks for joining us, Pierre," Chatura said after explaining what they knew to him. "We're not sure what to do next. We can't take down the NOEW Elites as they are too powerful."

Pierre sipped his cappuccino and spoke in English auto-translated from his native French. "You are right, and that's why MEE members have been trying to save lost memories by boosting the signal, in the hope they can be picked up by someone else. We had thought that Underlings outside the Centers could absorb their memories, but that wasn't possible since their minds hadn't been wiped. It's only recently with the emergence of the agitated animals that we came to understand where these boosted memories were going."

"Are the animals receiving these memories getting them at random, or are they selected?" asked Chatura. "I mean, if MEE wanted, say, birds of prey to receive a boosted memory signal, could that happen?"

"That's not how it's set up," said Pierre. "I assume the memory signals will go to the first semi-sentient animal that it reaches."

Peter drummed his fingers on the table in front of him. "But perhaps it could be directed toward a particular type of animal. What if the code included functions with 'if-then' statements conditional upon a desired animal? The conditions could include recognition of genetic characteristics of different types of animal."

"C'est stupide," said Pierre.

"Not so, old chap. The memory transfer code already includes the need to recognize, so to speak, electrical signals in the brain based on the DNA of the recipient Underling. That's why the Underling always has a cheek swab and DNA test done before the procedure. Why not just, instead, include a preference for the incoming memory signals to recognize the genetic ID of, say, falcons or foxes? Not a particular falcon, but falcons in general."

"Ah, I see," said Pierre. "We can use the GENBANK database to get DNA IDs of the animals we wish to look for. Formidable!"

Ting frowned. "But what if there weren't any falcons or foxes in the vicinity?"

"No problem," said Peter. "The signal would then default to the first semi-sentient animal it reached as a backup. Let me write new code that might work and see if this can happen."

"But wait," said Ting. "Why would a memory transfer technician choose an option that would allow diverted memories to go into any sort of animal? They are instructed to allow diverted memories to fail, not end up in an animal."

Peter fiddled impatiently with the spoon in his coffee cup. "Right, they wouldn't, but we can set it up as a hidden option that only MEE members can access from within the code, or technicians sympathetic to MEE. This way there will be an option to avoid memories diverting into animals who aren't going to live long, such as the cattle in pens around the Boston Center abattoir."

"Or pigs, lambs, or other domestic livestock about to be slaughtered," said Pierre.

Even though they were all in holospace in the virtual French café, Peter accessed his console back in his London Center office. The keyboard appeared as a ghostly, glowing apparition next to his hologram. His fingers danced across the keys that lit up as he typed. New lines of green code appeared in an image of the floor of the tunnel on the screen like waves breaking onto a sandy beach.

He muttered to himself as he typed. "Hmm, getting GENBANK DNA codes for falcons, foxes, eagles, bobcats, coyotes, wolves. Okay, here's a bit of code to recognize coyotes and bobcats, but excludes cows."

```
# Function to check if input DNA matches coyote or bobcat, but not cow

def recognize_animal(dna_sample):
for animal, dna in animal_dna_sequences.items():
if dna == dna_sample:
if animal == "Cow": return f"This is a {animal}, not a target species."
else: if animal == "Coyote", "Bobcat": return f"Recognized DNA of a {animal}."
```

Pierre looked over Peter's shoulder as he typed. "That's elegant code, Peter. It might just work."

```
# Start memory transfer

def memory_transfer(species):
if species in ["Coyote", "Bobcat"]:
return f"Transferring memory for {species}..."
else: return "Memory transfer not possible for this species."
```

"What else? I know, eagles, falcons, foxes, horses, mountain lions, skunks. Yep, that should do for now."

Chatura leaned back in his chair, watching Peter and Pierre, "I can't imagine choosing what sort of animal I want to become."

"Chatura, don't be such a gloomy Cassandra," said Ting. "The point is to save lives, not to give choices of animals that someone can become. Thanks, Peter, I think that will be useful as we help those ending up with memory transfer failures. Becoming a falcon or a fox would be much better than a cow about to be slaughtered. But still, are we certain the memory transfer failures are as deliberate as they seem?"

"Perhaps we can set up a trap," offered Chatura, trying to recover from the embarrassment of his last remark.

When Peter finished coding, his keyboard and screen disappeared. His eyes lit up as he turned to face Chatura. "Great idea, let's see what happens when the code is accessed during memory transfers."

Ting's job in Human Resources allowed her to see the schedule of memory transfers as soon as they were entered into the system. The London and Helsinki Centers each had twenty memory transfers scheduled in two days.

At the scheduled time, Chatura, Ting, Peter, and Pierre entered the code again from their computer stations, met up, and waited by the segment of memory transfer code. They had each donned opaque gray avatars, and hid in a recess by one of the side channels where ancillary code was stored.

About ten minutes before the scheduled transfers, a shadowy avatar approached. It must have had coding access since it stopped and worked on the code related to the memory transfer unit. Right at the scheduled time, the code pulsated as the avatar accessed it. For a good twenty minutes, the memory transfer code waxed and waned in intensity as the transfers occurred. Although they were some distance away, Chatura saw the code being accessed was the one Peter had written to divert the memories away from the recipient Underling. The gray avatar was monitoring the code. Then, as suddenly as it started, the memory transfers were over and the avatar moved away down the tunnel in the direction it had come from.

Chatura and Pierre followed the avatar to see where it went. They hung back, hugging the sides of the tunnel to avoid being seen. After ten minutes, the gray avatar entered code into a recessed panel, opened a portal, and disappeared through it. They raced to follow, but the portal closed before they reached it. Pierre's avatar crashed into the portal and, in turn, Chatura crashed into him. Back in his basement office, the crashing together of their avatars sent an electrical shock-wave sensation through Chatura causing a buzzing in his ears.

Disoriented for a few seconds, Chatura wondered, *Did the gray avatar turn briefly as they ran down the tunnel? If so, did they recognize their avatars?*

"That was close, no?" said Pierre, who sounded unaffected by his collision with Chatura. "My codes don't give me access through this portal. But, I can read some of the code showing through. There are clear identifiers of the London and Helsinki Centers."

"Of course," said Chatura. "That makes sense since the scheduled memory transfers were from the transfer units in these two Centers."

They raced back to the others where they had left them at the memory transfer unit code.

"We couldn't follow the avatar once it went through its exit portal, but the identifying tags confirmed that it came from the London Center," said Chatura.

"Right," said Peter. "That's the portal I use to get back to the London Center after I've been working on the code. There are several technicians there in the memory transfer unit, but most don't have coding skills. Martin Keyness comes to mind—he's a senior technician, a coder, and he reports directly to Sydney Fortesque-Hamilton. He's talked about Elite superiority, referring to Elites as a Master Race; I've always suspected him of being a member of NOEW. I'll bet that the gray avatar was him."

"Good work," said Chatura. Let's see what we can find out about the memory transfers from London and Helsinki that Keyness was just messing with."

"We can see here in the memory transfer code the details of this recent activity," said Pierre. "There were twenty memory transfers scheduled at each of the London and Helsinki Centers, forty in total."

Pointing at the code, he said, "Here the code shows that, of the forty transfers, most were successful. I recognize the names of five of the successful memory transfers as senior Elites from Helsinki where I work. The ten that were unsuccessful are not familiar to me except one. Mon Dieu! Ailana Leino is a moderate friend of mine. She's only 35, but has been very sick and must have been banking on a memory transfer to keep herself alive. Where have her memories gone?"

"There's no way we can know where her memories have gone or if she's now an agitated animal, perhaps a reindeer or an arctic fox in the tundra around the Helsinki Center," said Ting.

"Right," said Peter. "The animal DNA recognition option won't have been visible to Keyness. As far as he knows, the diverted memories are lost as planned."

"What about the London group, Peter. Do you recognize any of the names?" asked Chatura.

"Yes, some of them," he replied. "Martin Silvertown and Ken Chapman were both Senior Elites known to have strong views aligned with NOEW and their memory transfers were successful. Christopher Franke was an old, moderate Elite who ran a program where left-over food from our restaurants was made available to our Underling service workers. His memories have been lost. There are others, too, that I believe were moderate Elites whose memories have also been lost."

The evidence seemed overwhelming. The moderate Elites were being targeted for memory loss. Who would be next? Would they come after him and his friends?

Back in the French café, Chatura met up with Ting, Peter, and Pierre to discuss their next move.

"We need to get in contact with animals who may have received lost memories," said Chatura, reminding Ting of their fourth task.

They all ordered coffee except Peter, who made a fuss asking for Earl Grey tea with milk.

"Has there been any contact with the agitated animals to confirm that they have absorbed the lost memories?" said Peter.

"No, not yet," said Pierre. "But, the coordinated attacks on people by these animals suggest they are sentient with lost memories."

"And now that the animals are attacking the Centers, it's getting dangerous for everyone," said Chatura.

"Every time a guard patrol goes outside a Center they are wiped out," added Ting, "even though many of the foot soldiers in the patrols are conscripted Underlings."

"I've got an idea. Don't the guards have communicators in their helmets?" said Peter. "The agitated animals have been using them against the patrols. If they've picked up some helmets, then maybe we could broadcast a message to them."

"Most of the fighting has been around the Boston Center," said Chatura, dunking a biscotti into his latte in an attempt to hide his social anxiety. "Can we broadcast a message on the radio frequency that the patrols use? Or, can we hack into the communicators remotely?"

Peter smirked, "I can do that. In fact, I did it for a lark when I was first learning how to code as a teen. I hacked into the code of guard communicators and broadcast fake orders. One time, I ordered a patrol to wade waist-deep across a snake-infested swamp around the Buenos Aires Center. My father was boiling mad when he found out. He said I was endangering the lives of the guards. I was banned from coding for a month." He sniggered.

"Let me see if I can hack the communicators and contact animals around the Boston Center."

Peter brought up his virtual keyboard and screen again in front of his hologram. He typed quickly. The keys blinked on and off as he typed in commands, and lines of code raced across the screen. Occasionally, he paused and studied the holoscreen waiting for responses to his inquiries.

"Here we go," he said after a few minutes. "I've found signals from two helmets that must have been lost by patrols outside the Boston Center. By hacking into the communicators, I can have them broadcast a message. What shall I say?"

"Do we know any Elite memories that were lost from the Boston Center?" said Ting.

"How about Damon Najor, Taurus Najor's son? His name was on one of your lists, Ting," said Chatura.

"But he's a total self-centered jerk," replied Pierre. "As we say in my country, 'Il a un poil dans la main' - literally, *he has a hair in the hand,* or that he is lazy and unwilling to work. And, if his memories were lost, it must have been an accident. As Najor's son, I'm sure they would have wanted his memory transfer to be successful."

"And he was very sick. A new Underling body would have been just the ticket for him," added Peter. "But, if he's an agitated animal, he will know any senior Elites that are similarly affected and may have established good contacts. At the least, he's a known entity, rather than a random Elite who happened to pick up a communicator."

"Is there anyone else we could try to contact?" said Ting.

"Antoine Arnold's name is on the list," said Peter. "He knows a lot of people as a world-famous athlete and is well-connected in moderate Elite circles. I remember him doing some hot moves in a London nightclub a year or so ago. He was super cute. He would be a NOEW target."

Pierre raised his eyebrows. "Hmm, what's cuteness got to do with it? Okay, never mind. Let's try to get hold of Damon Najor and Antoine Arnold. If we get hold of them both, we can assess their differing points of view about how things are for agitated animals."

"But wait," said Chatura. "What's to stop the Elite guards from listening into the broadcast and any conversations we have? We don't want to put Damon or Antoine in any danger."

Peter's hologram glowed with smugness. "Yes, good point, my young friend. But, I have scrambled the message we are sending. It can only be broadcast to the specific communicators. And, I hacked into each of the helmets so they would also broadcast encrypted messages that only my computer can decode and on a frequency not used by these communicators. The encrypted broadcasts will be picked up by local branches of the holospace in the Boston Center, becoming accessible internationally and to me here in London. Clever, huh?"

"Exactly. Just what I would do too," said Chatura.

Peter looked confused, but not Ting. Her hologram glowed with amusement.

"But still, the security guards can use GPS to locate the communicators when they start broadcasting, even if they can't decrypt the messages," said Chatura.

Peter cocked his head. "Correct," he said finally. "Hmm, well, all we can do is warn the animals to move around a lot and watch out for guards. It's a risk they will have to take."

"Okay then," said Peter, and he set up a message for the communicators to broadcast. "Chatura, speak your message now as I record."

"Damon Najor or Antoine Arnold, are you there? We are a group of moderate Elites who want to help. Please talk with us."

"Okay, done."

"I've set the message to repeat every two minutes until someone hears the communicator and replies, or the batteries in the helmet run down," Peter added.

"Now we sit, wait, and hope for a reply. Nice job you two," said Ting.

Chapter Twelve

MAKING CONTACT

D amon was napping under the shelter of a cliff at the den when Jacques bounded over, returning from a skirmish outside of the Center.

"Come with me. I need to show you something important," Jacques said.

He followed Jacques through the forest for about fifteen minutes until they reached a grove of shrubs.

"Listen to this. Someone's asking for you on the communicator in this helmet."

The communicator squawked. *"Damon Najor or Antoine Arnold, are you there? We are a group of moderate Elites who want to help. Please talk with us."*

"Who is it? Do you know?"

"I don't know," replied Jacques. "But he's got an Indian accent and it seems he and his friends want to talk with you or Antoine. The message repeats every two minutes."

"Well, they must know that Antoine and I suffered memory transfer loss, and suspect we are animals. But they don't know Antoine has been killed."

That evening, under the shelter of the rocky bluff where the animals gathered, Damon called a small group together. They were nervous and suspicious of this new development.

"I think it's a trap," he worried. "The guards want to lure us out, so they can slaughter us. They are using GPS in the helmet to locate us."

"That may be true, so I've hidden the helmet with the volume turned down under a rock in a grove of dogwood shrubs a mile away from here. I didn't bring it down here," said Jacques.

"Good thinking," said bobcat Jerry McPherson. "Let's watch the spot and see if the guards come out looking for it. If they do, then we'll know it's a trap."

A couple of days later, after taking turns to watch the thicket of shrubs where the helmet was hidden and not seeing any activity, they retrieved it. As an additional precaution, they took the helmet to a grove of post-oak trees on a bluff two miles from the den and out of sight of the Center. Turning the volume back up, they listened again to the message. It was still being broadcast and hadn't changed.

"Damon Najor or Antoine Arnold, are you there? We are a group of moderate Elites who want to help. Please talk with us."

Damon put on the helmet and activated the communicator using the mind-activated control. "Hello, this is Damon. Who is this?" He hoped his English vocalizations would be clear enough for humans to understand. Three times he repeated his response.

"Damon?" a crackly voice replied. "This is Chatura Singh, a computer modeler in the New Delhi Center. Are you okay? Are you outside the Boston Center?"

"Yes, I'm okay," Damon replied. "But I won't tell you exactly where I am because guard patrols are trying to hunt me and others like me down.

How can you be in the New Delhi Center and talking with me here on a short-range communicator on the other side of the world?"

"I understand your concerns. I am indeed talking to you from the New Delhi Center. My colleagues have written code to patch into the Boston Center via the holospace to interact with the communicator in the helmet you've found."

There was a bit of silence on the line and Damon experienced anxiety. Then the headset crackled to life again.

"Anyway, the important point, Damon, is we now know your memories were lost during your memory transfer despite being the son of Taurus Najor. Are you in a new body? Your voice doesn't sound normal. Are you one of the agitated animals?"

"Agitated animals? Is that what we are called?"

"Sorry. Yeah, animals with human memories."

"Okay, yes. I'm in the body of a dog. Others are coyotes, bobcats, wolves, horses, or birds of prey. Some unfortunate individuals had their memories transferred into cattle that get slaughtered in the abattoir. We have learned to vocalize in English to communicate, which is why my voice sounds a bit strange."

Jerry jumped into the conversation. "Won't these transmissions be picked up by the Elites—I'm Jerry McPherson, by the way. Former journalist, now a bobcat."

"Good to hear from you, Jerry. Being a bobcat sounds cool. Good point, but no problem. It's sorted so all transmissions are encrypted. They may know that something is going on, but won't be able to make sense of the pops and whistles they hear. But, you are right, they can GPS the location of helmets during broadcasts. Watch out."

"Got it, thanks," said Jerry. He looked at Damon, quietly adding, "Be ready to move if any guards appear."

"Have you seen Antoine Arnold?" said Chatura.

"Antoine Arnold's memories were transferred into a coyote, but he was killed by guards. That's all I'll say about our situation, unless you tell me more about who you are and what you want."

"Totally. I'm happy to learn that you and others are okay, although I'm sorry to hear about Antoine's death. He was a well-respected international athlete. I'm part of a small group of moderate Elites who have recently worked out what's been going on with the memory transfer failures. Under your father's direction, senior Elite members of NOEW have been using the memory transfer process to kill off moderate Elites. They didn't expect that in response, diverted memory signals would be boosted by MEE group members and end up in semi-sentient animals. Thankfully, the boosting of diverted memory signals has been successful."

Damon was shocked. He could see Danny and Jerry, who were with him listening in, were also wide-eyed with shock. Damon talked a while longer with Chatura. Without divulging too many details about where they were and how many of them there were, he explained their situation. In return, Chatura told them how he and a few other Elites had worked out what had happened. Although Taurus Najor was Damon's dad, the NOEW and MEE groups were unknown to him. And because of their conflict, he and so many others were caught in the middle. Agitated animals? This was all the same plot? He didn't entirely understand, but then he hadn't known much beyond his life of leisure as a privileged Elite.

"I've got to go. We need to rebury the helmet far from our position to avoid being caught," said Damon.

"Okay," said Chatura. "Can we talk again in a few days?"

"Yeah, that will be fine. I'll discuss this development with my animal group."

"Good. I'll talk with my friends. I'll keep the communicator on and listen for your broadcast. Cheers for now."

"Um, yes, cheers to you too." With that, Damon signed out and turned off the helmet to conserve its battery.

Danny, Damon, and Jerry looked at each other in astonishment.

"Well, I'll be," said Jerry.

"I'm not sure how talking to them will help us, but it's good to learn what's been going on."

"No, it's very useful to talk with Chatura," said Damon. "He can provide us with insights into what's going on inside the Centers, and what the Center leaders, including my father, are planning."

Jerry bared his teeth and snarled. "Those NOEW members are sons of bitches."

Distraught by hearing his own father was part of the plotters, Damon had to agree.

———— ◆○◆ ————

A few days after their first conversation, Chatura and Damon spoke again while Jerry listened in. They were still being cautious and taking measures to avoid traps. They were hidden in a dense grove of trees, some distance away from their den, and had placed the helmet in the shrubs. Helen kept a watchful eye from above to alert them of any approaching guards.

"We've got word that the siege on the Centers around the world is getting more intense," Chatura said. "The Melbourne Center is already destroyed with no known survivors. There was a massive explosion that killed all the Elites in the Center and most of the Underlings in the surrounding area."

Jerry and Damon looked at each other. By silent nods, they agreed not to tell Chatura what they already knew.

Chatura said. "We need to get MEE members out of the other Centers to safety before your agitated animals destroy them. And, NOEW is rounding up MEE members with some getting a lost memory transfer and others simply disappearing. It's become too dangerous for moderate Elites like me to stay inside the Centers, and we can't run outside and try to live with the Underlings. Are you Okay with saving MEE members that become agitated animals?"

Glancing at Jerry, Damon said, "I can't speak for all the agitated animals everywhere and those around your Center, but here, we think that saving MEE members is essential. The problem is how it can be done. The Senior Elites control the memory transfer units. They aren't going to just allow MEE members to get memory transfers into animals. More importantly, every memory transfer involves the sacrifice of an Underling."

"Everything you say is correct, but we've got ideas about how to sort it all out. First, we have coded the memory transfer to ignore the need for an Underling and divert the memories out via signal boosters that we've already set up. Second, we are covertly using memory transfer units during the night when they are not being used by the Elites in charge."

"But, how can memory transfers ignore the need for an Underling? Each memory transfer requires the sacrifice of an Underling, at least their mind, since their body is taken over by the incoming mind," said Damon.

"Normally, that's true, but it can be overridden with new code since the memories don't need to be transferred into an Underling, just diverted elsewhere, and boosted outside. An Underling isn't even needed."

"Interesting. Okay, but where will the memories go? Can animals be ready to receive the diverted memories? Or will it be random in the hope that the diverted memories will find a suitable animal?"

"I'm sorry, we don't have an answer to that problem. We don't think specific animals could be put in place to receive the memory signal without a level of coordination we don't have time for. But, we believe the large number of agitated animals out there already indicates a high level of success for memory signals finding a semi-sentient animal host. We've also added code to allow our memory transfer technicians to choose a particular type of animal such as a dog, a fox, or a wolf, avoiding the risk of becoming an animal about to be slaughtered, such as a cow. There's still a lot of uncertainty, but it's a risk we have to take," said Chatura.

"Okay, hopefully it will work. We'll send out messages via our avian network to alert the animal groups at other Centers around the world to be on the lookout for more animals over the next couple of weeks. But, you know, getting your memory transferred into an animal is just the first step."

"What do you mean?"

Damon took a breath and blew out his cheeks before glancing at Jerry again. "Well, it's no bed of roses becoming an agitated animal," he told Chatura. There's a lot of trauma getting used to sharing a body with a semi-sentient animal host. Some people don't cope well with the transition."

"Transition?"

"Yeah, the transition—physical and psychological challenges. F'rin-stance, I'm now a dog who likes to eat cow shit. My friend Jerry here is a bobcat. Neither of us have hands with fine motor skills anymore. I can't even pick my nose. I've got falcon friends who complain they have to eat raw sparrows constantly to deal with their incredibly high metabolism. I've seen animals change their mind and try to get back into the Center only to get shot by the guards."

The line was silent for a long time; Damon hoped Chatura was only thinking, that he hadn't cut the communication.

"So," he ventured after a moment, "are you planning to have your memories transferred out?"

"Um, yes, soon," Chatura replied, though his voice was quavering. "Then I will be safe. I can then try and get in touch with other animal groups around the New Delhi Center. You know, to help out."

Damon raised his eyebrows while Jerry shrugged silently. "You'll have to get some new skills, my friend. There's no computer modeling or gaming as an agitated animal."

After a few seconds of static, Damon signed off. "Okay then, good luck Chatura—I really mean it, and thanks for your help."

Nevertheless, Damon worried. The Elites running the memory trans-fers might find the new code allowing the diverted memories to be boosted. Can the memory transfer units be taken over in time to allow MEEs to get out before the Centers are destroyed? Perhaps these mem-ory transfers can be run surreptitiously at night as Chatura suggested. How many MEE members needed to be rescued and gotten out? Which Centers were at the most risk? Had he frightened Chatura too much?

Just after Damon finished talking with Chatura, Helen came swoop-ing down. "There's a guard patrol coming in from the north. Get away quickly," she squawked.

"Two of us can't fight a patrol. Scatter, and meet back at the den later," barked Jerry.

Damon ran south, away from the guards. As he bounded out of the grove of trees, the guards crashed in. The blasts from their weapons filled the air with sound and fury. Helen screeched from above to distract the guards.

Jumping, Damon hid behind the broad trunk of a large oak tree. Was Jerry safe? He'd run the wrong way. The guard patrol split up and came into the grove from the north and the east. Jerry had run east, straight into two guard members. He never had a chance. From the safety of his hiding place, Damon witnessed the blasts from their photon guns hitting Jerry squarely in the chest.

After Jerry went down, the guard members circled round the grove of trees, clearly searching for the helmet. They turned over rocks and upended downed tree trunks. But the helmet was strapped to Damon's back and not broadcasting. Knowing there was nothing he could do for Jerry, he ran further south, going downhill and deeper into the forest.

After a couple of miles of running through the forest, skipping from rock to rock, wading across a couple of streams, Damon paused under the shade of a large boulder to catch his breath.

Helen swooped down, perching on a low tree limb. "I think you're safe. The guards have given up the search for the helmet and are heading back to the Center. They've taken Jerry's body with them. He's dead and you have the helmet. There's nothing they can learn from his body."

"Thanks, Helen. Your warning saved me, at least. I'm gutted we've lost Jerry. He was such a good guy."

"I'm sorry I didn't spot the guards sooner. They knew where they were going and what they were looking for. We have to be a lot more careful using these communicators from now on."

"Right. If we use them at all."

Now feeling safe, Damon traipsed back to the den to pass on the sad news about Jerry. This new life was perplexing. Some moments it was so good—like helping the other animals. But he would never get used to witnessing the death of friends.

He was reminded of the savagery implied in a line from an old poem a literature teacher had tried to get him to learn, "Tho' Nature, red in tooth and claw."

<hr />

They decided to blow up the Center in two days' time.

Sitting around the fire that evening, Damon addressed Romolo, "I want you to coordinate members of the den in an all-out effort to find and bring in as many new agitated animals as possible."

Danny, next to Damon, said, "We will need to get all new animals at least twenty miles away from the Center quickly to avoid effects from the explosion scheduled for noon. This den is twenty-five miles from the Center so will be our meet up place for the new animals and for all of us afterwards."

Romolo looked at Damon with his serious dark eyes. "Okay, I'll need fifty animals to establish a perimeter around the Center. New animals will be confused and disoriented but they should be sent downstream into the forest where other den members will meet them to bring them back here."

"We need to be in place before dawn to avoid detection from guards or their drones," Danny said.

"Right," said Romolo. "We leave the den at midnight tomorrow."

Damon sat up tall on his haunches, and addressed the den. "Everyone eat and rest before we leave. This action will change all our lives. Again. But after it is over, we will be a strong group, and we will be free of the Elites."

The next night, Romolo positioned the animals in a large perimeter around the Center. Because of his familiarity with the area, Damon's section included the Beef Processing Center and the cottage where Giles and Elizabeth lived.

Damon had spent much of the previous day with Giles, who sent the last group of cattle through the chutes into the abattoir. None of these cattle appeared disturbed. Perhaps the code Chatura had talked about was working. Giles was getting annoyed with him because he kept rushing off into the forest to check for new animals. But, he worried, was this the last opportunity to warn Giles to get away?

Danny was right. He couldn't stroll into their house and announce in English they needed to leave. He knew them well enough—they wouldn't take kindly to listening to a dog, even Shep, especially if he claimed to have once been an Elite. Especially Damon Najor. He could use a communicator in one of the helmets they had picked up from the guards. But even if he smuggled a helmet into their cottage and broadcast a message to them from another helmet outside, the transmission might be picked up inside the Center and give away their plan. He didn't have time to ask Chatura to hack in and reprogram two communicators—even if he was still in the New Delhi Center. He was probably a fox or badger by now. What if he wrote a letter warning of the impending nuclear explosion? No, his paws didn't make holding a pen or pencil easy, and he didn't have time to learn the dexterity needed to write. Finally, he decided to send Giles a computer message and hope he read it in time. Even that wouldn't be easy.

The evening was overcast and dark. Perfect for his plan. He'd been watching the fields outside the Beef Processing Center for several hours, sending three new and confused animals—two foxes and a skunk—down into the forest. Hoping MEE memory transfers were over for the night, he crept out of the forest, around the edge of a pasture, and to the side of the abattoir.

As before, he entered the abattoir through the unlocked side door and crept over to Giles' office. Once inside, he jumped up onto the desk and logged into the computer. He had persuaded Sherill to tell him how to hack in. It turned out to be easier than he expected. The process involved entering a few key commands to call up dark web protocols. "Not generally known even to most computer jocks," she had told him.

Hunting and pecking one key at a time with the single nail of his middle claw, he logged into Giles' account and accessed his messages.

He quickly composed an audio message. "You and Elizabeth must get twenty miles away from the Center within the next twenty-four hours to avoid the fate of those in the Melbourne Center. Leave in secrecy and haste. Good luck. A friend."

He listened to the message back. What would Giles make of his rough canine voice?

Hoping Giles would check his messages early in the morning, and leave soon, Damon left the office and the abattoir, and rushed back across the pastures to the edge of the forest to resume his watch for new animals. His conscience eased, he was ready to be fully involved in the new animal society without any guilt or longing for his former human life—except for his father.

It still pained him, but there was nothing he could do to help his father. A message from Giles' account was out of the question and would have endangered Giles and Elizabeth. He didn't think it likely his father had any chance of escaping the upcoming nuclear explosion of the Center.

———◦———

Chatura knew he and Ting were in danger in each of their Centers. NOEW members were rounding up suspected MEE members and sending them to the lithium mines. Scared, many Elites were pledging their loyalty to NOEW, even though they held different views in private.

Chatura met Ting in their favorite French café in the holospace. The restaurant was almost deserted since work at the Centers had dwindled. A few people were scattered around the café and there was only a single surly waiter taking orders. Most people were staying home in their apartments, worrying about the future. Elite society was breaking down.

Feeling nervous, they wore subdued outfits to blend in rather than impress. Nevertheless, Ting still looked stylish, wearing a subtle combination of earth tones.

They waited in silence until the waiter brought over their drinks. Chatura's cappuccino had an ugly blob of foam on top instead of the usual latte art. *Things must be getting bad.*

Ting made a face as she sipped her tea. "Ugh, the water isn't even hot. Were you able to contact Damon or Antoine, or any other agitated animals?"

"Yes, I spoke with Damon a couple of times. He is a dog. The animal groups are welcoming MEE members as they get away as agitated animals. The animal groups don't trust Elites, which is why they are blowing up the Centers."

"Can things get any worse?"

Though the question was rhetorical, Chatura's hologram reached out and grasped Ting's hands. "I've been meeting in secret with MEE members here in the New Delhi Center. They've told me there's a mass exodus via memory transfers into animals outside and they are doing it without the sacrifice of an Underling recipient. These MEE members are desperate to get out and are taking a huge chance. Even with the memory signal boosters in place, there is no way of knowing in advance whether their memories will be transferred into a semi-sentient animal or totally lost."

"I don't talk to many people, but the same is going on here at the Shanghai Center," she replied. "There are rumors of massive nuclear explosions at some of the other Centers. According to accounts, everyone is dead at these Centers. Radioactive fallout is killing everyone in the surrounding areas, including the Underlings. We need to get a memory transfer out before the same thing happens at our two Centers."

"But, I worry. What if I agree to it and my memories are lost or transferred into a bug or some horrible animal?"

"That won't happen, Chatura. We know the memory signals are boosted to be strong enough to reach outside the Center, and suitable memory recipients have to be semi-sentient animals. You won't become a bug. With MEE sympathizers running the memory transfers at night, you can ask to become something neat such as a bird of prey."

"Yes, you're right. I'm on the list for a memory transfer during the night in two days. I'm scared I could be discovered," Chatura said as his hologram dimmed and shimmered.

"If you do it, I'll do it. I'll get on our list as soon as I can."

His hologram glowed again. "When we become animals, let's try and find each other. Shanghai is a long way from New Delhi where I am. But at least there's no ocean to cross, just a lot of rivers and mountains. Let's plan to meet halfway, say around the Chagelazi Mountain in the Arunachal Himalayas. I already checked it out, there's no pollution there. It will be the perfect place for us."

"Okay, let's try. I'll ask to become an eagle and cross the mountains to find you at the Chagelazi Mountain. I'll see you soon."

With that, Ting's hologram approached Chatura and kissed him gently, directly on his lips. His hologram blushed profusely.

———◄O►———

Chapter Thirteen

ESCAPE

It was late after another exhausting day and Tourni was in her office catching up on administrative work. How she hated the necessary drudgery of her administrative responsibilities. She much preferred laboratory research. As her career had progressed, increasing seniority had been accompanied by more tedious administration.

At least she had a nice office now. The large, uncluttered corner office on the fifteenth floor had windows looking out across the Center with a view beyond the wall of the Charles River in the distance. She sat with her back to the window, facing her oak desk. Three holoscreens took up most of the space. Anyone coming into her office had to stand or sit to the side.

The stress of the current crisis with the memory transfers was taking its toll. Chatura had stopped sending reports on memory loss and agitated animal numbers, even though she requested them. Kalinsky reported more guard losses in encounters with animals outside the Centers. Now, all contact with the Melbourne Center had been lost. The Buenos Aires Center had gone silent in the last few hours, too. Elite society was falling apart.

"Nav, display my heart rate and blood pressure over the last hour."

A holoscreen appeared in front of her desk, showing the recent track of the two vital signs. Neither were good.

"Nav, play calming soundtrack."

"Certainly, how about a bubbling mountain stream?"

A soothing and tranquil sound filled her office. Water rushed gently over rocks. Birds chirped in the background. A gentle splash signaled a fish rising for an insect.

Tourni sat back in her chair, closed her eyes and breathed calmly through her nose. Meditation had been her savior over the years. A better solution to get through the day than endless cups of coffee.

Five minutes later, Nav reported, "Vital rates decreased to acceptable levels. Shall I continue the soundtrack?"

Before she had a chance to answer, her office door crashed open. Tourni opened her eyes at the interruption as her vital rates shot back up.

Kenton Chambers stumbled in. Kenton was one of her chief coders in the memory transfer unit. As usual, she was unkempt with wild, thick, graying hair pulled this way and that. Her pale blue, button-down blouse was untucked, with a food stain on the front, covering the top of slate-gray camo slacks. Despite ophthalmic advances, she wore a pair of horn-rimmed glasses with thick lenses that magnified her bright-blue eyes, adding to her eccentric look.

Tourni took a deep breath, wondering what this interruption was all about.

"Nav, discontinue soundtrack. Kenton, what do you want? Can't you see I'm meditating?"

She stood against the door jamb, looking nervously around the office space and reluctant to come any further inside. "Um, yes, sorry. I've found something you'll want to see."

"Can it wait? I've got a mountain of paperwork to deal with before going home today."

"Well, maybe, no, I think it's important. You definitely need to see this." Fingers of her left hand were tugging at strands of hair as though she were trying to pull it out.

"Okay, Kenton, calm down. Come in and sit down. Show me what you have."

"Um, I can't show you. You'll have to come with me."

Tourni shook her head and raised her eyebrows. "Where do you want me to go? As I said, I'm very busy."

"Into the holocode."

"I'm not a coder, Kenton," Tourni snapped impatiently. "I've never been into the code. How do I even get access?"

"I'll send you instructions."

Kenton dashed out of the room, seeming relieved to make her escape. Five minutes later, Tourni received a message with a brief set of instructions on how to get into the code via the holospace. "I'll be waiting for you," it ended.

Thankfully, the instructions were clear enough, and it was not much more complicated than entering the holospace the usual way. A gray avatar was specified.

Tourni knew coders worked in the holocode, but she was unprepared for what she experienced. The long dark and twisting tunnel, the blinking green lights, and the rushing, wave-like sound overwhelmed her. But determined not to show Kenton her feelings, she affected a cool "Hi" in response to Kenton's usual nervous greeting: "Ah, yes, err, Dr. Tourni, you're here, good."

"Okay, where are we? And what's so urgent and important that I need to be here?"

"It's the memory transfer code. That's where we are. See those lines of green code? They run the memory transfers and are activated by technicians from their terminals in the memory transfer unit, at any of the Centers around the world. Oftentimes, the technicians come into the holocode as avatars to monitor and run the code."

"Okay, I get it."

"Well... See these lines of code here?" Kenton's avatar pointed to hundreds of green lines on the wall.

Before Tourni could form a question, Kenton explained, "These are the lines of code that allow technicians to divert memories. London's Peter King added them recently, following the policy directive from the Center Council."

"Good, I appreciate seeing this, but I drafted the directive, and this is an operational level of detail I don't need to be familiar with."

Unfazed, Kenton's avatar sped down the tunnel.

Tourni followed quickly through several portals and into a poorly lit area.

"Ah, yes, you kept up with me. Good. Now we're in a sort of backwater area of the code. Look at these next two thousand lines, here."

"I don't read code, you'll have to tell me what it means."

"Oh, really? Well, these lines redirect memories to a series of boosters. I don't know physically where the boosters are. But, the point is the diverted memory signal would normally decay to zero, if its not pointed to the recipient Underling, but after being boosted, it has enough strength to go beyond the Center into the surrounding countryside, like a radio signal."

The implications were immediately clear to Tourni. "And, that's how memories can be picked up by semi-sentient animals?"

"Exactly." Kenton's avatar bounced up and down with excitement.

"Who did this?"

"I don't know. The coder's ID is encrypted. It was someone working out of the Helsinki Center."

"Is there anything else you need to show me?"

"Yeah, there's more."

"Well, what?"

Kenton pointed down to more lines of code. "These most recent lines of code allow a choice of animal to be made— coyotes, eagles, horses, that sort of thing."

"Jeez. Why are you just telling me this now?"

"I only found out a few minutes ago. I came to your office immediately."

"Okay, Okay. It's fine."

"What shall I do about this code? I can disable it."

Tourni took a deep breath. "No, leave it be. Don't tell anyone else. This is between us only for now."

Back in her office, Tourni logged out of the holocode. Closing her eyes, she leaned forward in her chair, placing the palms of her hands on her forehead. She didn't want to think about what her blood pressure was like now. The hacked code Kenton had showed her explained a lot. She should have instructed Kenton to disable the memory-boosting code and gone after the hackers, whoever they were. But with the way things were with Elite society falling apart, it might be an escape route she'd need to use very soon.

The next morning, Tourni received an urgent summons to meet with Najor in his office. He was waiting impatiently when she arrived. His office still retained the opulence from the heyday of Elite power, but the strain from recent events showed on his face. His formerly tanned skin held a gray pallor and his cheeks were deeply lined. What looked to be three-day-old stubble darkened his cheeks and throat. On the other hand, despite her stress, Tourni was well turned out as usual, although her sleek, jet-black hair showed gray streaks she hadn't bothered to conceal.

Najor tapped the fingers of his left hand on his desk. She couldn't help but notice they were unusually long and bony with dark hairs covering the first knuckle. "I've received reports that there's a group of Elites going under the name MEE—Moderate Elites for Equality—who have learned about your program to lose memories."

"My program?" exclaimed Tourni. "I've known about MEE for a while. Remember, you are the one who told me to set up the program with Fortesque-Hamilton's coder."

"You have no evidence to support such a claim. Nothing," he retorted.

"Is that why you brought me in here today? To blame me for the fallout from the memory loss program?"

"Listen carefully, Tourni. You work for me. I'll not have memory losses tarnishing the reputation of this office."

She pulled out her personal Nav and waved it in his face. "How dare you threaten me. I may well work for you, but you'll not threaten me with cleaning up the shit following failure of your policies."

She stood up and prepared to leave his office.

"You don't think I've recorded every 'off the record' conversation we've had? You think I haven't stored security camera footage of you sneaking down to meet the black marketeers and visit the young boys in the Lustra District? I have plenty of evidence of your duplicity and corruption."

He stood up then. Ashen-faced, he looked like any bully unused to someone standing up to them.

"Wait, Shanya," he said, tone conciliatory. "Sit down, please. There's not going to be any investigation into the memory losses. Things are too far gone. There aren't even any courts you could take your recordings to. We need to work together. The Center is in crisis. We have a crisis."

"*We* have a crisis?" she said, but she sat down again and stared at him coldly.

"We need to get out before the Center is overrun, or ends up like Melbourne or Buenos Aires." He sounded worried. "Find a way."

She looked at him with undisguised disgust. To save herself, she would have to help Najor. She'd seen before how he retaliated against his presumed enemies—like a cornered wild animal, kill or be killed. Her eyebrow raised at her own bluntness, but it was the truth.

He'll shut down the memory transfer unit if he suspects I'm plotting against him.

"We can schedule ourselves for a memory transfer," she suggested calmly. "The Elite population at large is still unaware what's behind the memory transfer problems. We are still scheduling transfers, although numbers are dropping fast."

He continued tapping his fingers on his desk. "We would need to make sure that our memories aren't transferred into an Underling, but are instead diverted off-site. You have to guarantee we will end up in an animal and not lost."

"I agree," she said. "I don't see any alternative. There are no guarantees, but it will probably work. We are learning that a high percentage of diverted memories end up in animals. My technicians think that members of MEE are using memory transfer to animals as an escape. They've hacked the code controlling memory transfers to improve the chance of success."

"What sort of animal would we become? I don't want to become a pig or a sheep, or one of the poor cattle heading into the abattoir," he said. "Have you found out what happened to my son Damon? Did he become an animal?"

She didn't think Damon's fate was Najor's primary concern, but she answered anyway. "We think it's likely he became an animal of some sort, especially since he was using the ID of an MEE sympathizer. Perhaps he used the ID of a moderate Elite on purpose."

"Absurd. My son would never be an MEE sympathizer. It was an unfortunate error that the borrowed ID was of an MEE member," he said, sounding like he was losing patience again.

A hologram flashed onto Najor's desk. A tall guard dressed in black with a bright yellow streak on his helmet stood in front of a forest background. He was outside the Center.

"Not now, Kalinski, I'm busy," Najor snapped.

"It's important, sir. It's about Damon."

"What?"

"We've picked up some encrypted communicator chatter. We haven't been able to decipher much of it except an initial message asking to speak with Damon."

"He's alive?"

"We don't know. But whoever sent the message may think so. Later messages may be from him, but we can't decipher them."

"Where are the messages coming from?"

"They were coming from the comm unit in the helmet of a guard killed outside the Center. We think the animals were using it to communicate with MEE members inside one of the Centers. We've located a bobcat that had been using the helmet before we killed it."

"You've shot Damon!"

"We can't confirm that, sir. There was another animal with the bobcat that escaped with the helmet."

"The dead bobcat had better not be Damon," he yelled. "Find him!" He snapped off the hologram.

He shook his head as though all the energy had been drained from his body like a punctured balloon.

He turned back to Tourni. "He may be alive as an animal. I need to become an animal and find him. Set it up for both of us to transfer out. Tomorrow."

She stared at him, about to protest, but finally, she sighed. "Okay, I'll set it up and let you know the time of our transfer."

Shaking her head, she left his office as he buried his head in his hands.

Tourni and Najor went ahead with their memory transfer a few days later. Tourni had arranged a slot the following day as he'd demanded, but at the last minute, Najor had insisted they bring along his wife, Viola, Damon's stepmother. Tourni didn't much like Viola. She knew all too well Viola, the daughter of Sydney Fortesque-Hamilton the London Center leader, had a crabby, 'superior' attitude toward women scientists.

It was clear Viola was fond of Najor, and he of her, although she stated several times she didn't like Damon. Tourni sensed Viola resented

Damon because, like the majority of Elite women, she had never been able to conceive her own child.

Tourni had told her head technician to set up the procedure without Underling recipients and to code in the directive for their memories to be 'lost'. She suspected he was a MEE member, but she trusted him. He had his own memory transfer scheduled for the next day.

When the time came, she lay down on a bed waiting for the memory transfer process to start. She'd undergone previous memory transfers, but this time felt vastly different and she was nervous. What if there were no semi-sentient animals within the boosted signal range? What if she became something awful like a pig or a hamster? Logic told her she need not have these concerns, but still...

Her aging father Constantine rested on a bed to her right. He had a grim look on his face as he glanced over at her. "It will be fine," she mouthed silently. Najor and Viola were on a pair of beds to her left. She ignored them both.

"You've always treated me well," the technician whispered as he strapped her onto the bed, prepping her for the procedure. "It's not generally known, but I can code in the type of animal you will become if your memory transfer is successful."

She gave him a baleful look. "I already know. But, why are you only now telling me that you knew this?"

He shrugged. "You lot aren't in charge anymore."

"I can have you transferred to the mines for this," she said struggling to get off the bed.

"You could, but you won't. You want this memory transfer. I'm help-ing you because we've worked well together in the past despite different political views. For the last time, what sort of animal?"

"Okay, a dog, fox, coyote, or wolf for my father and me."

"What about him over there?" The technician gestured in Najor's direction.

She met the technician's gaze. "Come here."

When he leaned down, she whispered something into his ear.

Najor glared at her. "Hey, what are you two talking about?"

But she had returned to staring up at the ceiling, and the technician had turned and walked to a control console on the other side of the room.

"I'm scared, Taurus," Viola cried.

"Don't worry. It will be fine," Taurus said. "It's all under control. It will be just like previous memory transfers, except we will end up in an animal instead of an Underling."

"What sort of animal and where?"

"I don't know, but I'll be with you."

Despite his assurances, Tourni could tell from Najor's tone he didn't quite believe everything was under control. He was having a last-minute panic.

"You!" he yelled at the technician. "Don't botch the memory transfer, otherwise you'll be in trouble."

Tourni heard soft steps and then a grunt and the rattle of a gurney. The technician had likely just tightened the straps on Najor's gurney.

Tourni was anxious, too. But, what more could they do than divert their memories to be lost? With this final thought in mind, anesthetic dripped into her vein and everything went dark.

When Tourni woke up, she lay on the ground at the base of a tree at the edge of a forest. On the other side of some bushes she could see grazing animals. Woody roots and sharp rocks poked into her belly. Shifting around onto a bed of moss, plants, and leaves made things better, but didn't help with her disorientation. New and unfamiliar scents and sounds assailed her senses. Earthy, damp soil and rotting wood mingled with the freshness of the forest air, and hints of flowers and greenery. A gentle breeze carried rustling leaves, chirping birds, the hum of insects, and the babble of a distant stream. The forest welcomed her into its embrace.

The memory transfer must have worked, but where was she, and *what* was she?

The textures under her fingertips were fur, a beautiful and dense mix of gray, brown, and tawny shades, with a slight hint of speckling. A female coyote.

Looking to one side, she was startled to see a male coyote lying asleep next to her. His coat was a light gray-red and his gray muzzle held red along the sides. Was he her father?

She tried to stay calm and thankful she was alive. She was relieved her mind had transferred into a coyote. The transfer technician had followed her instructions for the memory transfer. She sensed her host's mind, but it didn't seem to be aware of her presence. With a little initial difficulty, she stood, stretching stiff limbs. She could control her host in the same way she had previously controlled her human body.

A rustling sound in the tree drew her attention up. Perched on a branch were a pair of mourning doves. Their pink claws grasped the branch with three toes on the front of the branch and two at the back. The larger of the doves, a male, shrugged his shoulders, stretching a pair of gray-brown wings. The other dove was slightly smaller, a female appearing elegant with rosy hued feathers. The female gazed at the larger male with blue-rimmed, beady black eyes. Shuffling closer to the male, she pecked gently at its feathered, grayish-blue breast coo-coo calling.

The male stretched his wings again as though preparing to fly off. The female responded with a rapid series of coo-coos and he settled down again, cooing in response. At the doves' commotion, Tourni cocked her head skyward, squinting her almond-shaped eyes. She sensed her host's desire to catch them as prey. But, were they Najor and Viola? The once-great Taurus Najor no longer had any power over her.

The fuss of the birds woke up the male coyote sleeping next to her. He casually turned his head toward Tourni. Unsure how to communicate, she used a claw to scratch "I'm Shanya Tourni" in wet mud on the forest floor.

The brown irises of his yellow eyes lit up. He scratched, "I'm Father."

A jolt of relief pulsed through her. The emotional reassurance the memory transfer had worked for her and her father made her want to cry. But, unable to cry as a canine, her coyote host instead trembled and whimpered. Her father rubbed his head against her neck and nuzzled her face. They wagged their tails in unison.

Her host allowed her to bark a few simple emotions. "We safe, we safe."

Her father responded similarly, "Love you, love you."

The two mourning doves flew down to the forest floor. By force of her will, Tourni convinced her coyote host to remain still and not try to eat the two birds. They started scratching out messages with their claws and beaks.

"Me, Najor," scratched the larger, male dove.

"Viola," scratched the smaller female.

After a while, like other agitated animals, the four of them could converse in simple English, the native language of their memories which had transferred into their semi-sentient animal host minds. As birds, Najor and Viola spoke in chirping parrot-like voices. As canines, Tourni and Constantine's English language was rounded with yips, barks, and harsh growls. It didn't take her long to make quiet vocalizations adequate enough to make sense to the two mourning doves.

"Why we mourning doves, you two coyotes?" chirped Najor.

Tourni's dark eyes held Najor in an unblinking stare. "Technician followed instructions."

"Bitch," cooed Najor with a sharp, piercing tone, and flapped his wings furiously.

She said, "Hush or my host will eat you. You two watch from this oak tree. I will scout around. We'll meet back later and plan what to do."

"Yes," said Viola. "But, Taurus, we look for Damon? What sort of animal is he?"

"We don't know. We hope," he snapped, still seething from Tourni's betrayal.

"Stay here, Father," said Tourni. "I'll go find other animals with human memories. We can start an animal society."

The coyote loped off into the forest, disappearing quickly into the undergrowth and out of sight.

<hr/>

Tourni crashed through the undergrowth of the forest for a while. Her host coyote was surefooted, running over rocks and branches, but Tourni was confused in the unfamiliar surroundings. A lifetime as a human spent inside research laboratories wasn't helping her acclimate to this strange new environment. Not knowing where she was going, she ran back to her father and lay down at the edge of the forest facing a muddy pasture. She ignored Najor's still-angry coos above her. Let him be mad; if they tangled, she now had the upper hand as a coyote.

Across the pasture milled a herd of about twenty scrawny-looking cattle. Their coats were dull, they didn't look healthy. Several of them were restless, pawing at the ground. They were being corralled by a team of Underling farmhands along with a black-and-white sheepdog. The dog ran around the back of the herd and nipped at the heels of cows not moving along fast enough.

A middle-aged Underling with a weathered and sun-beaten face smoked a pipe and leaned on the top rail of a wooden, split-rail fence running around the paddock. He was directing the dog with a series of whistles and occasional commands, "To the left. To the right. Wait, Shep."

Tourni turned her head to her father lying next to her. "The man with the pipe is Jacob Giles, the abattoir manager. He visited with Torrance Hanley months ago."

Constantine looked up. "Isn't he an Underling? Could he help us?"

"Yes, he is, but I wouldn't trust him or any Underling to help. He told Hanley he didn't have any knowledge of agitated animals, although Hanley thought he knew more than he was letting on. He was most unhelpful."

Giles removed his briar pipe from his mouth and in a cloud of smoke, coughed and yelled, "Come on, Doug, get those cattle through the chutes. These are the last of the cattle coming through. They didn't fatten up well, but the butchered meat won't be going into the Center."

"Yes, boss," replied Doug as he ran behind the cattle.

"It's steaks for us tonight, boys," said Giles. "Get the animals processed while I check for messages and do some office work."

Giles and the farmhands followed the cattle inside, closing the large wooden doors behind them. The dog didn't follow them into the abattoir. Instead, turning around, he ran off into the forest, passing directly below the tree where Najor and Viola were perched.

"Those cattle seem bothered, pawing at the ground like that, but Giles didn't seem to care," said Constantine.

Tourni turned to her father. "If he had any sympathy with Elites who might have become agitated animals, he wouldn't have sent those cattle into the abattoir for slaughter. He said they were keeping the meat from the cattle. That tells us all we need to know about whether or not he would help us. If I wasn't a damn coyote, I'd report him for stealing," she said, in as angry a voice as she could manage.

A calm descended on the pasture after the cattle had all been ushered into the abattoir.

In a rush of beating wings, dense flocks of birds flew overhead, heading west across the forest.

"Father, let's try again to find other Elites. Come on, follow the birds."

Tourni and Constantine bounded off into the forest.

CHAPTER FOURTEEN

ENDGAME?

Damon didn't return to Giles and Elizabeth's house that night. Several new and confused animals with Elite memories appeared. After calming them down he sent them off down into the forest to be ushered to safety by his animal friends.

The next morning, when the rain had stopped, a blanket of low clouds covered the sky. All was quiet, and neither Giles nor his farmhands came out to walk around the pastures. Had Giles got his message and left the area? He hoped so.

He was distracted, thinking about beautiful Eve. When would he see her again? Would she escape the farm she lived on and join the other animals? Would she like him as much as he liked her?

Damon moved toward the edge of the forest, taking care to remain hidden among the shrubs. He checked one last time for new animals. A continuous stream of birds were flying overhead. Where were they going, and why?

A large female coyote crashed through the undergrowth, slamming into him. He lowered his head and flattened himself in the undergrowth in a position of submission. This coyote must be an agitated animal—she wasn't reacting as a coyote would after encountering a dog, so much smaller by comparison. She should have assumed a display of dominance; head high, ears erect, tail raised, growling and snarling. Instead, she whined in surprise.

Damon asked, "Who are you?"

She whined in the typical mix of English and animal noises, "Shanya Tourni."

He recognized the name. Shocked that a senior Elite like her would now be an agitated animal, he didn't mention his own name. He'd met her before, but she was the medical director in the memory transfer center who worked for his father. Even though he had been the worst of the entitled Elite youths, he hadn't liked how she always sucked up to his father. He straightened slowly, thinking quickly. Chatura had said MEE sympathizers were redirecting memories into animals. Was it possible?

A second, male coyote walked up slowly and stood by Tourni. "My father, Constantine Tourni," she whined. "You're the sheep dog."

This was no time for niceties.

"Follow me," he barked, and ran off into the forest. Not worrying about their struggles to keep up, he ran deeper and deeper into the dark forest. After a couple of hours, the trees became larger, and older, and cast a thicker canopy. Post oaks, chestnut oaks, and elms gave way to swamp white oaks, red gums, and eventually Atlantic white cedars, tupelos, and red maples. The waterway they followed changed, turning from an immature, rushing stream crashing over rocks, to a slow-moving, muddy river. The soil underfoot changed from dry and stony, to moist and silty, slowing their progress.

The noon sun was high in the sky, although obscured by clouds. But Damon wasn't paying attention to the sky as he rushed through the forest.

Boom!

A powerful shock wave followed the deafening roar. Trees toppled around them and they all stumbled as branches, leaves, and whole trees crashed down. Constantine fell to the ground, stunned by a branch falling onto his back.

Heat singed the fur on Damon's back. As he stood back up, he turned to see a towering, brownish-white mushroom cloud rising above the treetops backlit with a blinding light. The mushroom cloud must have come from an explosion in the nuclear plant at the Elite Center. They were now two hours or only about fifteen miles away—he hoped that was far enough. He hoped that his coyote friends got away safely from the Center after blowing up the water pipeline and setting the meltdown into motion.

His ears rang from the pressure. They had to leave.

"What happened?" yelped Tourni as she struggled to stand. "Was there an explosion in the Center?"

"Hurry!" he barked. "We've no time to lose." He didn't want to talk with Tourni about what just happened. He was not certain what she might do if she found out about the nuclear blast. While he had been experiencing his new life for a couple of months, and was better off for it, on balance she had only been a coyote for a few hours and would still have strong emotional ties to Elite society. He didn't trust her.

As they raced through the forest, the sky was obscured by flocks of scared birds flying overhead away from the Center. They covered the sky and squawked a distressed cacophony of frantic and urgent high-pitched chirps.

After three more hours of running, the wide river they were following meandered in wide loops across a half-mile-wide floodplain. Underfoot was swampy with large expanses where the ground was impossible to run across without swimming. They skirted the edges of the floodplain and followed the base of a large system of limestone bluffs.

As dusk approached, the bluffs became taller. The evening shadows lengthened as the bluff and trees cast a deep shade. Damon and the new human-animals had been running all day. They'd also been joined by two other new coyotes, a bobcat, and a fox. They had been running scared from the explosion. Only he knew where they were going.

They reached an area weathered by acidic waters. A warren of deep caves had been carved into the limestone bluffs. A small pack of wolves, with their hackles raised, growled and bared their teeth, challenging them. Damon moved to the front of the group and they recognized him, letting them pass into an open area at the entrance to one of the caves. The light from a smoky fire built on the rocks silhouetted a small group of coyotes, wolves, bobcats, wolverines, and even a skunk and a horse that were gathered around.

Damon was nervous. Not only had he betrayed his new friends by warning Giles, but he was bringing his hated father's sidekick, Shanya Tourni, into the den. But, Damon was leader of the den and needed to act with confidence.

He whispered to Tourni, "Just so you know, I'm Damon Najor, your boss's son."

"My God," she replied, turning her head to look him directly in the eyes.

"Opa!" said Constantine, using a common Greek expression of joy. "Now we are saved!"

Tourni opened her muzzle, as though she wanted to say something else, but they were ushered closer to the fire where the other animals were gathered. The others looked at her with undisguised suspicion.

Hackles and tails were raised, eyes narrowed, and ears pricked with a latent menace.

Several of them murmured, "Good to see you, Damon."

"Who's that female coyote with you?" said Merrill Johnson, the skunk.

Damon took a deep breath then said, "This is Shanya Tourni, just arrived, so to speak. And her father Constantine."

A collective gasp filled the den. The coyotes and wolves growled, the birds screeched, and other animals made their own sounds of displeasure. Most of them had been liberal-leaning moderate Elites, the group whose memories had been deliberately diverted and assumed lost in accordance with Taurus Najor's policy. They knew Tourni ran the memory transfer program, and that she had a hand in coordinating the memory losses. They all hated her.

Damon didn't like her either, but feared things would turn ugly if he didn't say something. Then Isaac, formally an Elite council member who was held in a lot of respect by everyone, and now a coyote, stepped forward.

"Greetings, Tourni. I'm Issac Mallory. Perhaps you should explain your presence here."

"She can't talk well yet," Damon interjected. "But she can write in the sand."

"Okay, Tourni, we are waiting," Isaac said.

Although initially shaking, Tourni slowly scratched out simple sentences in the river sand at the base of the bluff. She gained confidence as she softly vocalized more words and phrases.

"My father and I were some of the last to get out. I guessed something bad was about to happen to the Center. MEE members had sent many at night. I don't know where they ended up. NOEW members were unable to escape. A few senior Elites, including Damon's father and his wife Viola, made it out with my father and I. They became mourning doves. Taurus and Viola may be among the flocks of birds soaring overhead as we ran here."

"What?" Damon was shocked; his father may be alive. He had to try find him in the morning.

She turned and faced Damon, "I can help everyone survive this new world. I know what you've been doing with the dumb Underling. Yesterday, you helped him herd cattle into the abattoir."

"Dumb Underling? What are you saying?"

"Never mind. I will lead this animal group."

"You're kidding, right?" He growled, determined to focus on den issues rather than his father. "There's no way we can trust you, let alone accept you as our leader."

She stepped forward and thrust her muzzle into Damon's face. "Now I'm here, I'm the obvious leader of this den. I'm a senior Elite, not just a drunk son. I was on the Elite Council and worked closely with the Elite leaders. I know more about organizing and running a team than any of you."

Sensing his chance at redemption, Robert walked forward and stood by Tourni. Pus was seeping out of his injured eye, giving his face a menacing appearance. "Good to see you, Tourni, I'm Robert Giovanni. As former leader of this den, and an Elite elder, I support you. Damon, stand down."

The two of them advanced on Damon. Their threat was clear.

Damon shifted his gaze between Tourni and Robert, locking eyes with each of them in turn. Hackles raised, he was not going to back off. A sheep dog against a coyote and a wolf was not an even match, but he was prepared to fight them both. He lunged at Tourni's throat, which caught her by surprise. Tasting blood, he pierced the skin around her neck. Shaking his head from side to side, he tried to force her to the ground. She yelped in surprise, broke the grip of his teeth, and dragged herself away. Dark blood was pouring down one side of her neck from a deep wound.

Damon's peripheral vision caught Robert moving in fast from his right just as Tourni resumed her attack from the front. He would be in serious trouble if they attacked him together. But, before they had a chance to move, Danny and Isaac stepped into position on either side, protecting his flanks. Other den members crowded around behind them. It was now the two of them against the entire den. Robert backed down. Still bleeding, Tourni crouched in a submissive stance.

The fight was over, along with Tourni's short-lived bid to be the den leader.

"The two of you back off before someone gets hurt," growled Damon.

The other animals closed in around Tourni, pushing Robert off to the side.

"We don't want your help," one said.

"Burn her," barked another.

"Cast her out," growled yet another.

"She'll say anything to save herself."

"Send her back to the Center to fend for herself."

Ever the voice of calm reason, Isaac said, "I agree, we can't trust you, Tourni, at least not now. But, there's few enough of us, although our numbers have been growing in the last few days with former MEE members. We don't have any Elite or Underling human friends who can help us. We need to help each other. If you can prove your value to us, then I say we should give you a chance. I'm not for killing anymore—we've killed enough Elite guards. The explosion at the Center was our doing and killed hundreds or thousands of people, both Elites and Under-lings."

With renewed confidence, Damon stepped in as den leader. "Running the memory transfer program as you did, including setting the memory loss protocol to cast the memories of moderate Elites into the unknown, was despicable and unforgivable. And then you had the gall to escape as you did, leaving other Elites to perish. You will live in exile, outside our group for a year, after which time we will decide whether you can join us. Your father can go with you or stay with us as he pleases. Robert, you will go with them." He looked around at the other members of the den. "Does anyone object?"

The others respected him and murmured agreement.

"Constantine, you were always a reasonable man. Good luck," some-one said.

"We will be watching you," said Isaac.

"One step out of line and I'll not hesitate to eat you," said Danny Ramos, a large wolf at Damon's right side.

Tourni turned away and slunk off with her tail between her legs into the gloom of the forest. Her father and Robert followed closely. Damon was relieved, but like the leader of any animal pack, he would never be able relax while his adversaries were around.

Giles poured himself a cup of lukewarm, stale coffee into the old chipped mug he kept in his office. It was getting late in the day and he was feeling exhausted after spending the entire day moving cattle around the pastures. He took solace in knowing the last group of cattle had been taken to the abattoir where Doug and the other hands would process them.

Before he got the chance to access his computer, Doug came into his office.

"Hey, knock, won't you, before barging in?"

"Sorry, boss, but I've got these for you," said Doug. "The skinny cattle had more meat on their bones than expected. Here's a couple of nice rib-eye steaks for you and the missus."

"Thanks, Doug. No, I'm the one that's sorry. I shouldn't have snapped at you when you came in. It's been a long, tiring day. I'm nervous about us keeping the meat for ourselves, but the way things are with the Center, we can't even send them the processed meat."

Giles unwrapped the steaks. "Would you look at that! Excellent, rich marbling throughout. When grilled it will melt in the mouth. I don't remember the last time the missus and I had steak. These will be a treat. I hope that you and the others enjoy your cuts too."

"Will do, Boss. We'll freeze the rest of the meat and send it to the Center if things improve. Catch you later, then."

Alone in the office again, Giles checked his messages. Most were from other meat processors and cattle farms. All were asking what they should be doing since the two North American Centers had gone into lockdown. Nothing was coming in or going out in the crisis.

By contrast, the environmental groups were celebrating. He opened a text chat to his contacts.

"The authoritarian regime of the Elites is breaking down!" reported Mariah of the Peoria environmental group.

"Not so fast," Giles typed quickly. "Keep your heads down in case this is part of a nefarious Elite plan to flush us out."

Chat closed, Giles went to finish his messages, perplexed to see one he had apparently sent to himself... In the middle of the night?

Reading the message, Giles was even more surprised by its content. "You and Elizabeth must get twenty miles away from the Center in the next twenty-four hours to avoid the fate of those in the Melbourne Center. Leave in secrecy and haste. Good luck. A friend."

Who had hacked into his account? He looked around for signs of a break-in. Could they have even broken into his office and sent the message from his computer? Swearing under his breath, *Dear God,* Giles scanned the room again. Was anything was out of place? There did seem to be more than the usual amount of black and white dog hair on the table and his computer keyboard. And Shep was usually in the office with him, shedding hair everywhere.

That damn dog has been missing more than he's been around recently. Perhaps I should tie him up as Elizabeth is always suggesting.

He transferred the message to his personal tablet to play for Elizabeth later—his cattle feed tablet was strangely missing. As he transferred the message to the tablet, he started to worry. The fate of the Melbourne Center was all over social media. Several thousand Elites had perished in a nuclear explosion along with even more Underlings in the surrounding area. No word about it had been mentioned in any communications he had received from his Elite bosses, but his Underling friends, especially the environmental activists, had viewed it as a victory against their oppressor. No one appeared to know what caused the nuclear power plant at the Melbourne Center to meltdown and blow up, or if it was accidental or deliberate.

He went home to talk with Elizabeth, hurrying along the muddy path through the late afternoon drizzle.

A homely aroma of roasting potatoes greeted him as he walked into the cottage. Removing his green waxed-cotton jacket, he shook off the rain and hung it up on a brass hook inside the door.

"You're back home early. What's wrong?" Elizabeth looked concerned, probably mirroring the expression on his own face.

He straightened. "Yeah. The cattle in the abattoir have been processed but I got a strange message at work we need to talk about."

Elizabeth raised her eyebrows, and stopped chopping the carrots.

Giles busied himself with his pipe for a minute to collect his thoughts. Coughing through the smoke, he said, "The message in my account—apparently from me—says we should leave immediately and get at least twenty miles away from the Center."

"Somebody got into your account and sent you a message? Who?"

"I've no idea. Perhaps they broke into my office, or perhaps someone miles away accessed my account. It doesn't matter. It sounds serious. Listen, I'll play it to you. There's no video, it's only audio."

The cottage chilled as Elizabeth listened to the message. Putting down her chopping knife, she came over and listened to it a second time over Giles' shoulder.

"Is it a joke? Can we believe it?" said Elizabeth. "The voice is strange, too—rough and husky—almost as though he has a sore throat. What should we do?"

Giles shook his head. "I don't recognize the speaker. Perhaps his voice is disguised using a modulator. But we know what happened to the Melbourne Center a few days ago. It sounds like the same thing is going to happen here. I don't know who the 'friend' is who signed the message, but he's warning us to get away. I have many friends who are eco-activists; it's probably one of them. If there's to be a nuclear explosion at our

Center, then we definitely need to be at least twenty miles away. Probably more to avoid radiation sickness from the fall out."

Elizabeth wiped her hands on her apron. "We could go to my sister Joan's for a few days. Her cottage is about twenty miles west of here on the sheep farm that she runs with her husband."

"Hmm, that would work. If the Center blows up, we should be safe there, and if nothing happens, then we just come back here in a few days. Okay, let's pack a few things into the truck and leave first thing in the morning. We'll travel on back roads to avoid guard patrols. We should get to her house by noon."

Giles gave Elizabeth a soft smile. Walking back towards the door, he removed the wrapped steak from the game pocket at the back of his jacket. He pulled the paper wrapping back from one corner and showed it to Elizabeth. "Joseph and your sister will appreciate our vegetables, and will love it if we share this steak with them."

Elizabeth's eyes widened. "Oh, Giles, that will be delicious. But, seriously, should we warn Doug and your farm hands? And where is Shep?"

Giles sighed. Looking down at his feet, he muttered, "We have to just leave. There's no time to tell others. We'd risk causing widespread panic. As for that damn dog, I don't know where he is, again. Pack a change of clothes for us both and we'll leave first thing in the morning. I'll go out to the shed and get a few boxes of vegetables for Joan."

⸺⸺◦❖◦⸺⸺

Giles rushed to put back on his jacket and boots. He headed out to the shed behind their cottage. Like their cottage, it was old, with weathered planks clinging to a rustic frame. A purple-flowered clematis vine trailed over the door. Though it was not very large, Giles used the shed to store his tools and the boxes of vegetables they had grown in their garden. Despite the cold air whispering around and the frosted glass windows, he unlatched the door and entered the shed, carrying only an oil lantern for light.

He selected four boxes of vegetables for his sister-in-law's family, including two of purple-top white globe turnips and two of bronze d'amposta onions. Their garden had been more successful than usual this year; a mild summer had yielded a bumper crop. Their heirloom varieties of turnips and onions had done particularly well. The onions had a honey-sweet taste that were delicious fresh or fried, and the turnips were crisp and fine-grained with a mild, sweet flavor he loved in the casseroles Elizabeth cooked.

Cursing his perpetual cough, Giles hefted the boxes one at a time over to his EV-truck parked outside the cottage. By the time he had the last box in the bed of the truck, Elizabeth had come out with two small suitcases of clothes. She put both in the bed of the truck alongside the boxes of vegetables.

"There you are," she said. "We'll be ready to leave first thing tomorrow. Are you feeling alright? You look like you need to sit down for a while."

"Well, you try carrying full boxes of vegetables from the shed to the truck," Giles replied, coughing some more. "Okay, let's get some sleep. Hopefully, this scare will amount to nothing, and we can return in a couple of days."

At the crack of dawn, Giles steered his old truck out onto the gravel road outside the cottage. Gravel roads like this didn't have mag lines to guide and power the vehicles. Nevertheless, his truck was fully charged and should be able to run for a couple of days.

He turned left and headed downhill, passing the once busy cattle pastures as the road wound into the forest. Elizabeth sat beside him in silence as he drove through the morning gloom. It had stopped raining, but a mist of low, dense clouds shrouded the road. Giles' knuckles were white as he gripped the steering wheel, navigating the shadowed road unfolding through the tall pine trees.

After several miles, the glow of lights broke through the mist. "Damn. It looks like a checkpoint," he muttered. "Grab our travel papers out of the glove box, would you, love?"

The forest was dark and dense on both sides of the road. As the checkpoint came into view, Giles saw two vehicles blocking the road, each facing a different direction. The headlights of the vehicle facing Giles' truck blinded him as they approached slowly. A guard dressed in a long, gray greatcoat waved them to stop. Two more guards, similarly dressed, each held an automatic rifle and stood off to the side.

He stopped the truck and lowered his window. "Good morning, officer," he said as the guard came alongside the truck.

The guard held out a hand. "Travel papers."

Passing over the papers, Giles said, "We're traveling to visit Joan and Joseph Langdale, my sister-in-law's family. We bringing them vegetables."

Under the light of his flashlight, the guard examined the travel papers with a frown. Looking back at Giles, he stared into the truck. "Just you and your wife, is it, then?"

"Yes, just the two of us. Our clothes are in the suitcases in the bed of the truck along with our boxes of vegetables."

The guard gestured for one of the other guards to go around to the back of the truck. "Check it out, Private." Waving his flashlight around the inside of the cab, he stared at Giles with an icy gaze, then leered at Elizabeth. "Mrs. Giles, what are those scabs on your arms? Are you diseased? Sick Underlings are not allowed to travel."

"Oh, that's nothing, Officer," she said, pulling down the sleeves of her dress to cover her forearms. "I burned myself with hot water from the stove a few days ago. It's healing up fast."

The private rattled around in the bed of the truck. Giles glanced in the rearview mirror but couldn't see exactly what the man was doing.

"Everything looks fine here, Sergeant." Giles wanted to exhale in relief, but he'd have to wait until he and Elizabeth were alone. The private's report was a step in the right direction.

The sergeant stared at Giles again as though he was looking for an excuse to arrest them. "Private, take a box of vegetables as tax." He gave back their travel papers, "Okay, you can go. Drive around."

Giles pulled the truck off the gravel road and onto the muddy verge as he drove around the vehicles. In a relieved silence, he drove on.

By late morning, they reached Joan's house. The rain had started up again, and Giles had slowed down to drive the truck with more care. As he drove up, a flock of bedraggled sheep huddled together in a pen under the trees near the farmhouse. A dog on the porch jumped up at the sound of their truck.

Stepping out, Giles patted the dog on its head as he looked around. "Where is everyone? It's very quiet. There are no lights on in the farmhouse."

Elizabeth stepped up to the porch, covering her head from the rain with a scarf. Cupping her hands around her eyes, she peered through a window. "Joan! Joseph! Is anyone at home?"

After a few minutes of calling and walking around the house, it became apparent to Giles and Elizabeth no one was around. Giles climbed up the steps to the porch and tried the front door. Finding it unlocked, he went inside. Elizabeth nervously stayed on the porch.

The farmhouse was a small one-bedroom structure, much like Giles and Elizabeth's cottage. He stepped inside— the place had been trashed. The chairs and a table were upended. Books had been pulled off shelves, kitchen pots and pans were on the floor, along with smashed crockery. Through the open door, he could see clothes scattered around the floor in the bedroom.

"Elizabeth!"

Elizabeth came in and covered her mouth with one of her hands. "What's happened? Who did this? Where are Joan and Joseph?"

She sobbed, as tears rolling down her cheeks.

"I don't know, love," he said, stepping around the mess on the floor. "We might never know, but we can't stay here tonight. Whoever did this might come back. I hope Joan and Joseph got away before this happened."

"Was it the guards who did this? I didn't like the look of that sergeant back at the checkpoint."

"Maybe. People are saying the guards are lashing out because of their conflict with the agitated animals. I wouldn't be surprised if they started taking it out on Underlings like us, too. Let's get back in the truck. We can go on another twenty miles to your cousin Diknu and his family, at least for the night."

Leaving the trashed farmhouse as they had found it, they stepped outside and walked back over to their truck. Just then, a flash in the sky showed through a gap in the trees. A searing pulse of light caused them to cover their eyes with their hands and turn away. The skin on their hands and arms blistered and burned. Elizabeth staggered back against the railing of the steps to the porch. Giles went down on one knee with a fit of coughing.

Three minutes later, as both Elizabeth and Giles were struggling back to their feet, a thunderous roar and a shockwave knocked them down again. The pressure on their eardrums deafened them both and caused intense pain. Trees came crashing down, one narrowly missing them, but smashing onto the roof of the farmhouse.

After a few minutes, the pressure from the shock-wave dissipated to a low rumble. Elizabeth slowly got up, threw up, and staggered over to Giles. He was having trouble breathing. Pushing up from the ground with his hands, he coughed blood and phlegm onto the ground.

"I'll be Okay lass," he said, trying to stand up.

"Here, let me help you." She took him by one arm and guided him over to their truck. "Can you drive?"

"Yes, I'll be fine."

He got into the truck, placing his blistered hands on the steering wheel. "Come on, let's get out of here and drive farther west. We can't go home now after that explosion. The air around the Center, including here, will be contaminated with radioactive fallout. We need to get as far away as possible, quickly. Let's hope we don't run into any more guards and the wind doesn't blow more of the fallout our way. Let's go."

Giles and Elizabeth drove away. As they followed the road west through the forest, the wind picked up, and trees weakened by the shockwave continued to fall. The road became impassable. A tree smashed down onto the hood of their truck, causing it to veer into a ditch and shudder to a halt. Nauseous and weak, Giles couldn't continue. Ashen-faced, he turned to Elizabeth. Her eyes were bleeding. She leaned over close, putting her blistered arms around him.

"We've got a problem, old girl," he wheezed, wiping blood from his mouth onto the sleeve of his jacket as they slumped down in their seats together.

Chatura, like most Elites, had undergone memory transfers a few times as he grew older. His most recent transfer was into a young Indian Underling. Now, he considered the morality of the process. It was a routine practice, and he had always been grateful for each new, healthy body. However, this time felt different.

His appointment at the memory transfer unit in the New Delhi Center was scheduled for two-thirty in the morning. Before leaving his apartment, he checked one last time for messages from Ting. She had left a life-size and glorious 3D hologram message. He felt as though she was in the room with him, although it wasn't possible for him to converse with her prerecorded message.

"I'm just about to leave for my memory transfer appointment," she said. Her voice was quiet and silky with a nervous edge. "I hope both of our memories transfer successfully and we each become an animal. More than anything, I want to meet you in person. Whatever animal I become, I'll be looking for you. I'll try to get to the Chagelazi mountain in the Arunachal Himalayas as we agreed. I've already scoped out the route."

Her head whipped around to one side as though she had been disturbed. "I've got to go. My friend Min is here. We are going to the memory transfer unit together. Goodbye. I love you Chatura."

She blew him a kiss as a tear rolled down her face and her hologram disappeared.

Chatura teared up watching the hologram message a second time. *Pull yourself together.*

He had been told by the MEE contact, who didn't reveal their identity, to make sure he was not seen when he snuck up from his basement apartment to the third floor of the hospital unit in the Center. He crept through empty corridors lit by dim security lights. Unease filled him. He had become more comfortable traveling as an avatar in the code holospace than in the real world.

After a few wrong turns, though, he reached the entrance to the memory transfer suite. The door was ajar. He gently pushed it open just enough to slip inside. He had barely stepped through the door when someone materialized out of the shadows.

"Who are you, and what do you want? Show me your ID." His unknown assailant hissed. Their face remained shrouded in shadows.

"I'm Chatura Singh and have a two-thirty memory transfer appointment," he replied, showing his ID bracelet on his right wrist.

A light scanned his ID and then lit up his face, blinding him. "Okay, your face matches the ID. Go through the door over there, and don't say another word."

Following instructions, Chatura went through the door into the memory transfer room. Inside were six pairs of beds. One bed in each of the five of the pairs was already occupied by people he didn't recognize. No one was speaking. He climbed onto one of the beds in the open pair and laid down. The empty second beds where Underlings would lay unsettled him. This transfer would be different. The mapped memories would be transmitted away from the memory transfer facility and then boosted to find a recipient semi-sentient animal outside. At least, that's how he hoped it would work.

After a few minutes, a technician came in. The technician wore a scarf around their head, hiding their face.

"Stay quiet," they whispered to Chatura. "We are doing the memory transfer process a lot quicker than usual, but everything will be fine, don't worry."

Chatura nodded without saying anything and tried not to worry too much. The technician inserted an IV and hooked up a saline drip. He grimaced when they shaved his head to place the electrodes and cap on his head.

"There are no guarantees, but what sort of animal would you like your memories to transfer into?"

"A bird of prey, perhaps an eagle. Is that possible?" said Chatura.

"Perhaps. Choosing your animal is a new preference I can enter in the code along with the memory diversion. We don't know for sure if it works, but it's better than not trying."

He silently thanked Peter King for his coding skills and closed his eyes in hope.

A cerebral mapper hung off the top of a metal stand by each bed and the technician adjusted it to point toward the mesh cap on Chatura's head. As the cerebral mapper powered up, the electrodes on his skull vibrated and buzzed gently. Anesthetic was introduced into the IV and everything went dark.

———◆———

Chatura woke up slowly, as though from a deep sleep with no sense of how much time had passed. A bright blue lake stretched out in front of him. Was he by one of the lakes in the large Mangar Bani Forest just outside of New Delhi? Was he awake or dreaming?

He took in his surroundings. The memory transfer to a semi-sentient animal must have worked. He flexed and stretched the strong muscles of his new body. Instead of arms, he had wings. Instead of feet, he had sharp and powerful talons clasping a thick lichen-encrusted branch high up in a tall mahua tree. Instead of dark brown skin and hair, he had raven-black plumage with striking glossy feathers.

I am an Indian Black Eagle! —His voice came out in a beautiful eagle's call.

His vision was keener than ever before. The lake's shimmering surface reflected the world in intricate detail. Fish swam lazily beneath the surface, scales glowing with iridescent silver, green, and blue hues. He turned his head to look at the shore—a brown-banded snake slithered across a flat, gray rock. Looking down, he picked out a small black-eyed vole scurrying through the grasses and sedges of the undergrowth. These small animals were potential prey.

That he was now an eagle made Chatura gloriously happy. Both he and Ting had hoped their memory transfer would allow them to become eagles, or big birds, so they could cross the distance that separated them. He had no time to spare. Immediately, he flew aloft, testing his wings on the thermals and air currents, for his long journey to their proposed meeting place in the Arunachal Himalayas.

At first, flying was clumsy and awkward as he fought with his host. He soon allowed his host eagle to control flying, only retaining control over where they would go. He had never flown before, even in an aircraft. The whole experience was novel and frightening. Looking down, he marveled at the contours of the earth below and its patchwork of forests, fields, streams, rivers, and rocky mountains. Flying as an eagle was exhilarating and effortless. His broad wings picked up rising thermals, allowing him to soar through the boundless skies. His view was limited by nothing but the horizon.

He had studied the route to Chagelazi mountain before the memory transfer. Now, he followed the Yamuna River downstream and southeast out of New Delhi where it drained into the sacred Ganges River at Patna on the Indo-Gangetic Plain.

Along the journey, his host eagle took charge of hunting. Eating raw bird eggs plundered from nests, bats, squirrels, and other small mammals was strange at first, but he soon got used to it. His sense of smell and taste was poor, which he considered fortunate as his host eagle ate scavenged dead animals and rotting fish. His host was skilled at swooping down onto nests to pick up eggs, young birds, or even entire nests in its curved claws. Other times, he swooped down and captured mice or voles scurrying through the grass. With a wingspan of nearly six feet and modest weight of about three pounds, he stayed aloft for long periods with minimal effort.

After another 100 miles following the wide and slow-moving Ganges, he set out directly east until he had crossed into the watershed of the Brahamaputra River. He then followed it upstream to the rushing Lohit River reaching its source high in the Mishmi Hills near the Underling town of Tezu.

No humans were visible when he swooped down low over the town. Leaving the Mishmi Hills, the terrain became more rugged and remote as he skirted around the snow-capped mountains of the Arunachal Himalayas. By this point, the air was crystal clear with none of the pollution and smog he was used to around New Delhi.

His journey was not without incident. Flying during storms was a problem as his feathers became too wet to fly. Thunderstorms and lightning were frightening and forced him to shelter in trees or under rocks. Worst of all, he was often mobbed by songbirds trying to protect their nests.

They squawked at him, "No, no, no," "Leave us alone," "Nasty monster," and other choice phrases.

When he passed through the territory of other eagles, he flew as fast as possible at a high altitude to avoid a dangerous confrontation. An angry male and female pair chased him at one point, taking turns swooping in and pecking at him.

"Get away, get away," they screeched.

They plucked out some of his wing and tail feathers as he was flying away. After making his escape, he rested in a tree for several hours to calm down.

After several long and hard months, he reached the foothills of what must be the 20,164-foot-tall Chagelazi mountain.

Perched on a branch high in a tall dead mahogany tree toward the top of a hilly slope, he took stock of his surroundings. From this vantage point, he had a good view of the mountain in front. The foothills of the mountain supported lush subtropical forest crisscrossed by a network of rivers and lakes. Natural resources were abundant for the wildlife here, including giant pandas, snow leopards, and apex predators like himself.

Was Ting here?

For two months, he flew around the mountain, searching each valley and gorge. He ascended high into the cold mountain meadows above the treeline where snowbanks persisted in shaded areas despite it being late spring. He flew down into the warm, humid forest searching among the lianas and tallest trees. He found no sign of any eagles or any other agitated animals.

Then one day, resting in a tree top and beginning to despair, he heard a sudden loud squawk, followed by a series of high-pitched whistles and chirps. High above him, its wings outstretched, circling lazily as though searching, was another eagle, an adult female Golden Eagle. Against the boundless blue expanse of the sky, her dark plumage exuded freedom and mastery of the heavens.

Was it Ting?

Damon and Jacques took a stroll around the area and introduced themselves to the new animals gathered in the group's new den. As expected, there was a variety of animals. Damon was desperately hoping to find his father, but he didn't see any mourning doves.

They spoke to the new animals in English, which they understood, but didn't speak well. They were just learning to speak through their host animals. Most caught on fast, though. They listened to Damon and Jacques describe how to move their lips, tongue, and larynx, and how to control their breathing. As a coyote, Jacques was able to speak with the coyotes through his host—although these conversations were quite limited.

"I assume most of these new animals are former MEE Elites who managed to get out before the Center exploded," said Damon.

"Yes, I think so," said Jacques, stepping around a group of coyotes sleeping together at the base of a tree. "We now have too many of us for one den," he went on.

Scores of animals huddled together in groups, bobcats with other bobcats, coyotes with coyotes, skunks with skunks.

Damon agreed. "We won't be able to hunt enough rabbits and other small prey to feed us all."

"Right. As it is, we've been forced to send our hunting parties out further just to get enough food to feed our group. We need to establish a couple of new dens in areas far enough away to avoid an overlap in hunting territories."

Damon admittedly hadn't learned much in college, but he did recall the principle of animal home territories. Groups of animals, especially social animals occupy an area—or territory—they use and defend against other groups.

He said, "I agree. We need to avoid fighting for food between members of different dens. Avoidance will be better than confrontation."

As they wandered around, Damon was surprised to see a female black and white border collie—it was Eve. She lay alone under a fragrant sumac bush apart from the other new animals. Her ears were drooped, her paws curled, and she conveyed a poignant image of isolation and longing. But to Damon's eyes, her black and white fur contrasted beautifully with the autumnal red and orange foliage of the shrub. He was smitten. He had to concentrate to control his host dog from bounding over and trying to couple with her. Instead, he drooled and tried to play it cool. He sauntered over.

"Hi, Eve, how are you? Remember me? I'm Damon."

She lifted her head in surprise, and her lips curled into a smile. Her English language vocalization was still rough, but she barked out, "Yes,

I remember you from the other night. My full name is Eve Meyer. You said your name is Damon? Would that be Damon Najor, Taurus Najor's son?"

Oh shit. This isn't a good start. I should have stuck with 'Do you come here often?'

"Um, yes," he said. "Did we know each other before becoming animals?" This would be awkward, especially if she was a former party hookup.

"No, I don't recall meeting you before, but a few of my friends had mentioned you as a party animal able to down one yard of ale after another. You had quite a reputation as the son of the Center leader."

This conversation is getting worse. "Well, that was me before I got sick, and before I became a dog. A while ago. I like to think I've changed for the better since then. I've been a dog for a while and have been helping get this den established." He tried to turn the conversation to be more about her. "What about you?"

Jacques joined them and looked on with growing amusement. He growled and quietly interjected, "Hi Eve, I'm Jacques. I also help organize things around here. But, I'll, err, leave you in Damon's capable hands to get familiar with our den."

Jacques moved on to another group of new animals, leaving Eve and Damon alone.

"Good to meet you, Jacques," said Eve, as he wandered away. Her dark eyes traced back to Damon though, her gaze lingering longer than he expected. "I was a nurse in the Center hospital. Although my parents had strong Elite views, I was more moderate and had been part of MEE for a while. The senior hospital staff were making it difficult for suspected MEE members, and after the Melbourne Center exploded, I got out as soon as possible. As planned, my memories were diverted outside the Memory Transfer Unit, and into a farm dog outside the Center."

"Yes, and thanks for helping us the other day. How were your Underling masters on the farm?"

"They were great, although the farmer got in trouble for losing a drum of fertilizer."

Thinking it might impress her, he fessed up. "Ah, yes, I may have had something to do with the theft of a drum of fertilizer that night. And that may have had something to do with blowing up the Center."

"No way. That's cool!"

Deciding the conversation with Eve was turning out to be a success after all, he told her he would be back and loped off to catch up with Jacques.

"Ah, Romeo," Jacques said. "While you've been chatting up that young dog, I've found out from some of the others that they think the birds that flew on past us were planning to form their own colony in the High Peaks Wilderness area about 250 miles northwest of here. It's a very rugged and remote area with an abundance of natural resources perfect for wildlife and an animal colony."

The two of them lay down side-by-side on a large flat rock and looked across at the new den members.

"Is my father with the birds in the Wilderness?" said Damon.

"No one knows who is there. But if he is a mourning dove, he'll get eaten by a raptor. Even if he's not eaten, your father wouldn't be well received in an animal colony, considering his background. Remember how we exiled Shanya Tourni when you brought her here?"

"You're right, but I have to try and find him, even if he is sent into exile." Damon made a snap decision. "I will take a group of these new animals to this wilderness area and help establish a new colony. It will reduce overcrowding here and I can search for my father at the same time."

Jacques gave him an intense look, locking his amber eyes with Damon's. "I thought you might want to do that. It's a good idea."

"I'll take some of our more experienced den members with me and a couple dozen of these new animals. We'll set off in the next few days."

"Keep away from any Underlings you come across. It will be a dangerous journey."

Damon turned his head and looked at Jacques with anxious eyes. "Hmm, you're right. There will be guards roaming around too. They'll be confused and unpredictable without direction from the Center."

"Yeah, we all need to watch out," said Jacques. "Underling factions will be fighting each other for control. Who knows what any guards you encounter will do. You don't want to get caught in the cross-fire between different groups."

Damon's muscles tensed, his paws trembled as he scratched into the soil, digging a small hole—a habit Shep often did when anxious. Seizing control, Damon jumped up and started pacing.

"Anyway, I'll get organized. If we can cover twelve to fifteen miles per day, it shouldn't take us more than a couple of weeks unless we run into trouble." *But when has anything ever gone perfectly since I became an animal?*

The next day, in a flurry of activity, Damon rounded up thirty-five animals to come with him to find the bird colony and establish a new den in the High Peaks Wilderness area. Given her initial coldness toward him, Damon was surprised Helen agreed to come with them to provide aerial reconnaissance. Damon had become good friends with Danny, Merrill, and Sherill, and he was pleased when they also joined the group.

Under a clear sky and a pale autumnal sun, the group was ready to set out the day after. The rest of the den gathered together to see them off. By acclamation, Jacques was selected den leader in Damon's absence.

"Let's go, everyone." Damon took the lead as they left the den. "Merrill, where are you?"

"Back here. I'll bring up the rear."

"Wait," Danny pulled Damon to one side, whispering. "I found fresh guard bootprints a mile south. They're tracking something. Or someone."

"Thanks," said Damon quietly, his heart racing. "Say nothing to the others. We'll be heading northwest. We should be fine." *Shit.*

He jumped up onto a rock and turned to face the group.

"Okay, everyone stay between Merrill and me, and make sure you can see us at all times. If you look up, you'll see Helen. Ah, she's coming down. What's the route ahead look like?"

"It's clear," she chirped from the branch where she alighted. "You'll travel under the forest canopy. There are abandoned farm fields and pastures I'll help you skirt around. I'll let you know if you get close to Underling communities you'll need to avoid."

They traveled light, with weapons in case they were attacked. With no comms, they would be depending on Helen for communication with Jacques and the animals in the den. Damon worried what the other animals in the group would do if they found his father, but he was excited to begin this new adventure. He knew the stakes were high. If they didn't establish a new colony, both groups would starve before winter's end.

Eve had accepted his invitation and was at his side as they left.

THE END

THERE'S MORE TO COME!

If you enjoyed this novel, be on the lookout for the prequel (*Shanya's Saga*), the first book in the Memory Transfer series. A sequel (*Damon's Journey*) is in the works. *Shanya's Saga* is a novella following the early life and times of Shanya Tourni, the duplicitous medical director and sidekick to Taurus Najor. How did she become an Elite and how did she develop the memory transfer protocols? It wasn't a smooth ride! *Damon's Journey* will be a full-length novel in which we follow the dangerous trek that Damon and his group of animals take as they travel to the High Peaks Wilderness. Will they encounter desperate Underlings and confused guards? Will Damon find his father? What other surprises will they encounter along the way? Can they establish a new den and avoid starvation during the upcoming winter?

ACKNOWLEDGEMENTS

The inspiration to write this novel came from Liam Heneghan's suggestion on 'X' (formerly Twitter) to write a January Short story—that is write a short story in one month. I started my short story in January 2022. After one month I was nowhere near finished, barely started, but kept it going as it got longer and longer. I realized after a few months that the tale I wanted to tell was more than a short story. So, here it is as a novel. If you enjoyed this novel, be on the lookout for a prequel (*Shanya's Saga*) and a sequel (*Damon's Journey*) that are in the works.

The idea of animals "taking charge" is epitomized in George Orwell's *Animal Farm* (1945). The focus on memory (or mind) transfers from humans into animals is a popular theme in the science fiction genre, but I hope that this twist is novel and interesting. If you want to read some of the classics involving human-dog mind transfers, I recommend Horace Gold's *A Matter of Form* (1938), Poul Anderson's *The Star Beast* (1950), James Hurbert's *Fluke* (1977), and more recently, Kathleen Ann Goonan's novelette *Memory Dog* (2008). Perhaps you know some others. To date, we don't have the technology to do any of this.

This novel could not have been written without the gracious help of Dan, Stan, and Trish Smith – fellow authors and bibliophiles who provided technical and inspirational motivation reading early drafts, beta reader Adam Rhodes, developmental editor C.B. Moore, copy editor Lara Zielinsky, the wonderful artists at GetCovers.com, and my team of

ARC reviewers. Everyone provided incredible advice and insight to help me make sense and improve the story I wanted to tell. After retiring from a career in academia, I've spent more time at home than ever before — thank you, Lisa, for putting up with me.

ABOUT THE AUTHOR

David J. Gibson was born in Cuckfield, West Sussex, England where he worked as a teenager delivering newspapers, caddying golf, working in a sports shop, and serving drinks in local pubs. He attended Warden Park School and Haywards Heath 6th Form College before going to the University of Reading to study botany. Crossing the Atlantic, he studied for his Masters in botany at the University of Oklahoma before coming back to the UK for his PhD at the then University College of North Wales (now Bangor University) - if you remember him, please get in touch. After post-docs at Rutgers University and Kansas State University, and an Assistant Professor position at the University of West Florida, he settled in 1984 at Southern Illinois University Carbondale where he became a Professor of Plant Biology and University Distinguished Scholar before retirement. Married with two grown-up children, and two grandchildren, he's finally given up dreaming of being a professional football (soccer) player. He remains a fan of Brighton and Hove Albion football club in the English Premier League. His books include textbooks, a popular book on forensic botany, and now this first novel.

David's Website: davidjgibson.com

ALSO BY DAVID J. GIBSON

Fiction: Memory Transfer Series
Shanya's Saga (2025)
Elite Memories (2025)
Non-Fiction
Routledge Handbook of Grasslands (2026, co-edited with Heather Hager
and Jonathan Newman)
Juice of Cursed Hebenon (2022)
Planting Clues: How Plants Solve Crimes (2022)
Grasslands and Climate Change (co-edited with Jonathan Newman)
(2019)
Grasses and Grassland Ecology (2009)
Methods in Comparative Plant Population Ecology (2002, 2015)

www.ingramcontent.com/pod-product-compliance
Lightning Source LLC
Chambersburg PA
CBHW071548110726

47908CB00007B/2037